Chinatown

Yilin Zhong

ATLAS

Chinatown

Copyright

Published by Atlas Books in 2025
ISBN 978-1-300-20371-1

First released in Chinese in Harvest Literary Magazine in 2011. First published in Chinese by Jiangsu Phoenix Literature and Art Publishing House.

Chinatown

Chinatown was first published in the special novel issue of Harvest, and the Kindle version became #1 on the Amazon Paid Kindle Bestseller list within a week. Paperback edition was published with the author's writing notes and postscripts. This English edition included three extra literary reviews and two book interviews.

[About the Book]

They are people who "do not exist" in mainstream society : illegal immigrants, refugee couples, children of high-ranking officials, rich second-generation dropouts, drug dealers, porters, human traffickers and prostitutes... Chinatown is like an oasis in the desert, providing them with mirage-like comfort in their overseas home where they have no relatives. Only in this small world, in the China of their imagination, can they find the final refuge for their wandering souls.

The novel "Chinatown" tells the story of a group of Chinese people living on the fringes of London. They are called illegal immigrants, just a speck of dust in the huge scroll of history. However, their smiles, words and deeds are so tenacious and vivid. The author uses a seemingly relaxed style to outline the heavy image of the Chinese people living on an isolated island overseas, and meticulously depicts their inner and daily lives, as well as their deepest souls.

Harvest Literary Magazine Cover

Chinatown

[Editor's recommendation]

Chinatown is a life story and spiritual history of overseas Chinese who have lived in Chinatown for generations but have been forgotten by literature and history. The heavy and difficult subject of illegal immigrants, their true faces and living conditions, has never appeared in any contemporary literary works due to the absence of overseas Chinese writers, and even formed a shocking blank in the history of contemporary Chinese literature. Yilin Zhong's Chinatown fills this gap for the first time.

[Media Recommendation]

One of the great significances of the novel "Chinatown" is that it has changed our understanding of the world. If there is no such literary work "Chinatown", our understanding of the world might be particularly narrow. However, with this literary work, our understanding of the world becomes different.

—— Dialogue: The Value of Contemporary Literature from the Perspective of the Diverse Lives in "Chinatown", Harvest

Chinatown exists in alleys occupied by Chinese people in various countries. There are music halls, restaurants, Xinhua Bookstores, massage parlors, gangs, prostitutes, stowaways, migrant workers, all kinds of people. Everyone has their own story, whether happy or sad, love or hate. Everything has its roots, and every root is closely related to Chinatown . They live at the bottom, the bottom of society, and they have moved from China to London, Britain. They can and can only live in the same houses as in China, eat the same food, and make friends with the same people. They are still living in the old times, while London has entered the postmodern era.

——China Writers Network

Although the author touches on all aspects of London's black and white society as well as the gray area in the novel, what "Chinatown" shows us is not just a hunt and adventure, but the various characters and their different values in this different world: a vivid and colorful Ukiyo-e of the lives of contemporary overseas Chinese illegal immigrants.

—— China Publishing and Media Business Daily

Yilin Zhong's Chinatown reminds people of Lao She's Teahouse or Xia Yan's Shanghai Eaves. The difference is that this novel tells the story of overseas Chinese happening in the present, in the 21st century.

——Swedish Taiwanese writer: Wenfen Chen-Malmqvist

Chinatown sketches the "non-existent" people: illegal immigrants, prostitutes, Chinese restaurant chefs, food delivery workers, lesbians, pirated CD sellers, refugee couples, vegetable market vendors, restaurant waiters who dropped out of school, uneducated children of high-ranking officials, drug dealers, illegal immigrant pimps, supermarket porters, snakeheads, prostitutes, underworld gangs... They have nothing, no identity, no passport, no job, and can't even speak the most basic English. They are all " black " people, in official terms, illegal residents or illegal immigrants. Not only in the boundaries of history and law, but also because overseas Chinese writers have lost their voice in this field and subject matter, these illegal immigrants who have no voice, called Subaltern , have never appeared in any contemporary literary work. Their true faces and their current living conditions have also become a veritable blank. Chinatown is about such a "non-existent " group.

——Sina Books

They are people who "do not exist" in the mainstream society: illegal immigrants, refugee couples, children of high-ranking officials, rich second-generation dropouts, drug dealers, porters, human traffickers and prostitutes ... "Chinatown" is a life story and spiritual history of overseas Chinese who have truly lived in Chinatown for generations but have been forgotten by literature and history. The heavy and difficult topic of illegal immigration has left a shocking gap in the history of contemporary Chinese literature due to the absence of overseas Chinese writers. Yilin Zhong's "Chinatown" fills this gap for the first time.

——Amazon Editor's Choice

A lifetime of drama on a street;
Life, death, separation and reunion are all essays.

——Jiangsu Literature and Art Publishing House

Chinatown

[Public readers' review]

By chance, I, a student studying in the UK, moved in London's "Chinatown", and came into live with those marginalized illegal immigrants who came to the UK from China to seek their fortune. They did not know English, did illegal business, and could never go back after they got out of China. There was chef who made money and sent it back to support his wife and child, refugee couple who sold pirated CDs, rich student who became prostitute, and children of high-ranking officials who lived a life of drunkenness and debauchery. Most of them did not have legal status, but they lived a colorful and enjoyable life.

It is a set of gouache paintings and landscapes.

——Mandolin

The scenery is beautiful yet cruel.

——See the crazy scenes

[About the Author]

Yilin Zhong is a British writer born in China, an award-winning journalist and a #3 Amazon bestselling novelist. She began to publish poems at age seven; at sixteen, she published her debut novel and was interviewed by China's National TV station, which won her a national reputation. Before she was twenty-five, she had published five books including three novels, known as one of the leading women writers of the post-Maoist Generation.

At twenty-five, Zhong came to study at the University of Warwick and gained her MA degree. Then she immigrated to the UK and has been living in London anonymously. Her autobiographical novel *London Love Story* peaked at #3 on the Amazon Bestselling Fiction list, while *London Single Diary* peaked at #50. *Chinatown* peaked at #1 on the Amazon Paid Kindle Bestselling Fiction list. Both her *novels Personal Statement* and *In London* were highly recommended by Swedish Taiwanese writer Wenfen Chen-Malmqvist, the late sinologist Göran Malmqvist's wife, who wrote a foreword for *In London* but it was not published in China.

After taking a trip to New York, Zhong wrote *Dear New York,* (Book 1-4), her first novel written in English. By 2025, Zhong had written eighteen novels and had published ten books including eight novels, all of which became bestsellers and were sold out. She lives in London.

Chinatown

Table of contents

Chinatown

[Writing Postscript]

People with Stories

[Appendix]

Writing Notes
List of candidate characters
Deleted Paragraphs

[Publishing Postscript]

Chinatown, an Imagined Community

Chinatown

English Edition Extra Appendix

[Interview 1] Dialogue |

The value of contemporary literature from the perspective of the various lives in "Chinatown"

[Book Review 1]

The Day does not Understand the Darkness of the Night
/ Dang Xiaoyu

[Book Review 2]

Oversea Chinese Living in the Post-industrial Imagination
/ Yao Peipei

[Book Review 3]

Chinatown: The Other in the Postcolonial Context
/ Li Jiaoyang

[Interview 2] The Paper Interview |

The Current Situation of Illegal Chinese Immigrants Overseas from the Perspective of "Chinatown" (Part 1, 2, 3)

Chinatown

Yilin Zhong

The new tenant

I met Lv Ping when I was cooking in the kitchen for the first time. She was not a very pretty girl, about 21 or 22 years old, and because of her long face, she wore a pair of round glasses. Her most typical feature was that when she smiled, two small canine teeth would appear at the corners of her mouth, which was very cute.

" Are you the new one who moved upstairs? " She asked me, peeling a scallion skillfully.

" Oh, yes, " I said, " which room do you live in? "

The room I was talking about was the room in the house. In this two-story house with four bedrooms and one living room , the landlord divided the original living room into two more bedrooms, so about twelve or thirteen Chinese people lived in this six-bedroom house. I don't know which room the girl lived in.

" I live downstairs. " The girl said, " What do you want to do? Do you need a pot? " She saw me standing in the kitchen hesitantly, thinking that I had just moved in and couldn't find anything to cook. In fact, I was worried about how such a small kitchen could accommodate the dozen Chinese people in this building to cook three meals a day. When I rushed back to London from other places to see this house a week ago, the whole house was still empty. Zhang Lai had just rented this house from an Indian. As the second landlord, he told me that he was planning to divide this big house into individual rooms and rent them out to the Chinese nearby. " There are many Chinese in this area, " he told me, " All the people living nearby are Chinese, especially this street. Almost half of the street is rented by Chinese people, so everyone calls this area 'Chinatown'." He said jokingly.

But when I was looking at the house, I didn't listen to what he said. I was only concerned about the quality of the house. Because that morning, I had taken a bus for nearly two hours to see a house in South London. The area was good, in London's Zone 2 (London's urban area starts from Zone 1 in the city center and ends at Zone 6 in the farthest suburbs), with convenient transportation, and it was a row of villas on the hillside. " The surrounding environment here is so good, " said the Chinese who introduced me to the rental house, " Look, everyone who lives here drives a good car. This is a rich area. " Later I learned that it was a famous black area, and the crime rate was famous in London, but I couldn't know it at the time, so it didn't matter. The key point is that when he enthusiastically led me into the rental house, after visiting the kitchen and bathroom, which were pretty good and probably had just been cleaned, he opened the door of the small room I was going to live in for me. It was a double door, and he opened it with a "whoosh" and said:

" Look, what a broad view! "

It was indeed a wide view, but unfortunately it was the smallest room I had ever seen. The entire room was less than four square meters. The double door we entered was one wall, and the other wall was two windows. Under the windows was a small single bed that was just big enough for one person. Then there was a small cabinet next to the bed (probably used to store clothes), and there was no more space. Even after I walked in, the landlord himself couldn't walk in. So he stood at the door and said to me:

" Go to bed and look out the window. Our house is halfway up the mountain, so you can overlook most of London. Look, what a beautiful city it is, especially under the summer sun. "

Looking out the window as he spoke, I thought that this sub-landlord should become a poet.

Fortunately, I was not deceived by his beautiful words like a romantic poet. Standing on the edge of the room that could only accommodate one person, I immediately determined that this room was actually a balcony on the second floor.

He saw that I was slow to express my opinion and did not respond to his poetic praise, so he immediately added: " If you live here, I can provide you with a small sofa. Here, I'll put it right here, " he pointed to where I was standing, " so you can read. The sunlight here is very good, and you don't need to turn on the lights when you sit here and read during the day, " he said.

I think he was trying to describe to me a woman's room as described by Virginia Woolf. According to his description, living in this room is simply a supreme enjoyment. Just imagine, living in a villa in the " rich area " halfway up the mountain, in a room with a wide view, or in other words, in a room with a view, sitting on a soft single sofa, the bright and sunny summer sunshine drifting in from the windows on one wall, spreading on the warm single bed and the pages of my open book, bathing in the warm sunshine of downtown London, no need to turn on the lights, sitting on the sofa reading a book, and a fresh and soft breeze blowing gently... oh, this is such a wonderful life like a queen.

I took a deep breath of the fresh air blowing in from the window and said, " Let's go." Then I turned and followed the landlord into the darkness outside the room.

The landlord locked the two doors behind me, which could only be closed by locking them, and then walked with me through the dim corridor, down the stairs so narrow that we had to use handrails, to the first floor, and then through the door to the lawn outside.

" Are you a student too? " He asked me at this moment.

I nodded and said, " Yes. "

" Which school do you go to? Are you studying languages or preparatory courses? " He asked this, probably because he saw that I looked young.

" I'm studying for a master's degree, " I said.

" Oh, " he looked at me with some surprise, then took out a cigarette from his trouser pocket, lit it on the lawn, and threw the matchstick into the lawn.

" Where is your university? " he asked. "Is it far from here? Let me tell you, this is the most convenient transportation hub in London. It's convenient to go anywhere."

I finally understood that he asked me about my studies was just to sell his house from another angle, and I almost thought he was trying to help me because we were both strangers in a foreign land .

" My university is not in London, " I answered frankly.

" Oh? " This time he was a little surprised. He took another puff of his cigarette and looked around at the quiet streets and houses with an aimless look. Because it was morning, everyone was out at work. There were few people in the residential area.

" Why do you live in London, then? " He asked.

" I've finished my course, " I said, " and I'm only back in London to write my dissertation here. "

" Oh, " he understood immediately, " then this house is suitable for you. You just need a place to write your paper quietly. Look how good the environment is here. It's so quiet. There are almost no people here during the day. The people who live with you are also students, but they go out to attend classes during the day, and some have to work at night. There are usually no one in the house except you, so you can read and write quietly. "

Now he is no longer a poet, but a salesman.

" This place is pretty good, " I said, " but I have to go see another house this afternoon, so I can't decide yet. I'll call you tomorrow. "

He immediately became alert: " Where is that house? "

I said the name of the place.

"Oh my God, you shouldn't go there at all!" He said enthusiastically, " It's full of Indians and Pakistanis, it's a mess. I'm telling you, I've been in London for three or four years, I know it better than you do. Anyway, you'll know if you go there, the environment there is terrible, just like a small county town in China. "

" Really? " I had no passion to respond to his words. I took a train to London to look at houses early in the morning, and then took a two-hour bus ride. I was so tired that I felt dizzy and dizzy. Thinking that I had to force myself to look at another house in the afternoon, still in such a bad Indian and Pakistani area, I almost wanted to agree to settle down and live in his house.

Obviously he saw this, and he thought the time was right, so he said, " How about this, I see you're a student too, and it's not easy for you. We're all Chinese, right? If you decide on this house now, I'll give you 5 pounds less per month, how about that? That way your water and electricity bills will be almost paid. "

When he said that, I suddenly realized that I had forgotten to ask an important question - or maybe I didn't want to live here at all, so I didn't ask in detail: " What? You mean, the rent you mentioned doesn't include water and electricity bills? "

" Of course, " he grinned, " the rent is already cheap enough, how could it include water and electricity? Let me tell you, you can ask around, the house I'm giving you is definitely the cheapest single room in London. "

I was completely exhausted, and I said, " Okay, thank you, I'll go think about it and call you tomorrow. "

"OK , " he said nothing more.

About four hours later, I followed the map all the way from the bus station to the address of another house, and after confirming the house number, I called the landlord outside the door. This second landlord was also Chinese, but because a friend introduced him, I knew his name was Zhang Lai.

" Zhang Lai, I'm already at the door. "

" Really? Okay, wait for me, I'll be there in about ten minutes, but you can go in first, the landlord is inside now. " Zhang said on the phone.

I knocked on the door as I was told. After two knocks, no one came to open the door, and it opened automatically. It was pitch black inside.

I asked in English: " Is there anyone inside? "

An old man's voice said, " Come in. "

Then I went in. Carefully bypassing the paint cans, waste newspapers, and painting tools on the floor, I found the landlord who was scraping the tile wall in the kitchen. He was an Indian man in his sixties. It seemed that he was going to peel off all the shabby wallpaper on the kitchen tile wall to make this small and dirty old kitchen look brand new so that Zhang Lai could rent it out at a good price after taking over the house. When I went there, he was working very hard.

" Zhang Lai asked me to wait for him here for a while. " I explained to him.

" Okay. " He didn't seem to be very talkative.

After staying for a while, he was doing his work and I was a little bored in the kitchen.

" Can I see the room? " I asked him.

" Go ahead, " he said, still concentrating on scraping the tiles on the wall.

You can see he really likes doing this.

I like to live in the second floor, so I went upstairs first. This is a very large house, twice as big as the other houses I looked at. Everything is twice as big, including the stairs. I thought that such a wide staircase would be enough for me and another person to haul my huge suitcase upstairs.

I wanted to rent a single room, so I looked at the small rooms in the building. But after looking around, I found that even the smallest room in this house was as big as the large double rooms elsewhere, probably about 16 or 17 square meters. I began to worry about the price Zhang Lai might offer me. If we put aside the price, this house was far better than the one I saw in the morning in every aspect. I was very tired, and it was already 4 o'clock in the afternoon. At 7 o'clock, I had to catch a train around 8 o'clock to return to school in outer London. I was just looking at houses that day, and I would move from school to London a week later.

Zhang came. He excitedly showed me around the rooms. It seemed like he was a sub-landlord for the first time, and I was the first tenant he had received to see the house.

" Your houses are all big, " I said truthfully, " just give me the cheapest one. "

He thought about it, said yes, and then took me to the room on the second floor that I had just seen. This room was also very large and could fit two double beds. The only drawback was that it was probably a study room. The window in the house was very small and there was only one. In addition, the original owner built a whole wall of multifunctional cabinets in this room, probably for storage. However, because these cabinets were built 20 or 30 years ago and were made in a very rustic way, they made the whole room look ugly.

" I'll give you the cheapest price for this one, mainly because these cabinets are too much of a nuisance, " he said.

" It's okay, " I consoled him with a smile, " I can buy a piece of cloth and you can help me hang a curtain to cover them all. I don't need these cabinets anyway. "

We made the deal. A week later, I moved from my university dormitory to this house in north London and started to prepare to write my thesis. But after I moved in, I realized that I had overlooked one thing when I was looking at the house: the whole house had not been rented out at that time. I was the first tenant to rent the house, so I had no idea what kind of people would live in the other rooms in the future. A week later, when I moved in from outer London, I found that all the rooms had been rented out. The house was full of Chinese people coming and going, speaking dialects that people from all over the world could understand or not. And in the whole building, except for me, who had a single room, all the others lived in double or triple rooms.

I was completely stunned by what I saw. I felt like I had entered a Chinatown. On the one hand, it was because the sub-landlord Zhang Lai was capable and was able to find so many Chinese tenants eager to rent a house in a week. On the other hand, it was because this place was originally a Chinese settlement, as he said, and half of the street was full of Chinese people. So when the Chinese who wanted to rent a house came and saw it, they were willing to live here and even paid a higher price than other places. There was only one reason, that is, because none of them could speak English, but they had to live in Britain where English was spoken everywhere, so they felt extremely comfortable and safe only in such a neighborhood where all Chinese people lived and lived. This was also the only small world where they could live freely.

Aguang

One night we played cards together in Lao Zhu's room. I brought two decks of cards from China. It was the first time in a long time that I found so many people willing to play cards. We played the game of upgrade. The score was calculated, and whoever lost had to cook us dinner.

I usually played pairing with Chunsheng, while Aguang played pairing with Xiao D (young bro). Aguang was always very lucky, and every time he punished Chunsheng and me to cook for them. Chunsheng never complained about me, and never asked me to work. He went downstairs and brought up a pot of cooked seafood noodles in a short while.

" Oh my god, this is all you give us to eat? " Aguang asked.

Chunsheng rolled his eyes and said, " If you don't want to eat, go down and cook it yourself. "

Aguang couldn't beat him, so he sighed and picked up the noodles with chopsticks, saying: "Chunsheng, when are you able to win to taste dishes I cook? But you always lose and can never beat us. " Thinking of this, he smiled proudly again. He took the bowl of noodles, sat on the carpet by the window and started to eat noodles with satisfaction.

I was full after eating half a bowl, so I put down my bowl and chopsticks and said, " Let's play again now. I don't believe I can't eat the food that Aguang cooks. "

Xiao D slurped noodles from his bowl and said, " Sis, if you were in Chinatown ten years ago, you would have to queue up and spend dozens of pounds if you wanted to eat Uncle Guang's cooking . "

" Really? " I said, turning to look at Aguang, " Are you really such a famous master chef? "

Aguang had already finished his noodles. He lay on the carpet with his legs crossed, with his head resting on his hands, smiling gently, without saying a word.

Legendary martial arts masters are all like this.

I couldn't help but want to eat the food that Aguang cooked even further. I encouraged Aguang and said, " God knows, Xiao D is the best at flattering people. I don't believe his words. "

Aguang smiled but still said nothing. After he had eaten his fill, he lay on the carpet in front of the window and dangled his legs leisurely.

Xiao D said: " Don't worry, you live here, and one day you will get to taste Uncle Guang's cooking. "

I suddenly remembered: " Get up, get up! Aguang, let's continue playing cards. If you lose, you'll have to make dinner. "

Aguang said: " I haven't finished eating yet, let's take a break. "

By the time Xiao D slowly finished eating the noodles, Aguang had already laid on the carpet, sleeping comfortably with his mouth open.

* * *

Unexpectedly, we soon had the meal cooked by Aguang. One night, we sat together to play cards again. Before we even started to draw the cards, Aguang said happily:

" Little sister (except Xiao D who was the youngest in the house, they all called me 'little sister'), you can eat the meal cooked by me today. "

I touched the cards and looked at them. I had no hope at all: " Guang, if you want to cook, just cook. No one is stopping you. Why are you saying such sarcastic words? "

Aguang laughed dryly twice, hesitated for a second, and shook his head and said: " Well , I will lose today anyway. "

I still didn't understand what he meant. After playing two games, I found that his luck wasn't as good as before. I got anxious and said with a bitter face: " No way, Uncle Guang? "

Aguang finally said proudly: " What do you know, little guy? Do you know that success in gambling means failure in gambling? "

Chunsheng suddenly smiled.

I said, " Haha! Aguang, did you go to a prostitute today? "

Aguang smiled sheepishly, but with a hint of pride: " Oh my, it's not good at all. It cost me eighty fucking bucks. "

" How could that be? " I played a Jack of Hearts . " Isn't it fifty pounds? "

This is the market price. Abao downstairs told me.

" Yeah, " Aguang saw that I had opened the topic, then he also began to chat without any taboos, " I did it twice. Damn, eighty yuan was gone in a few strokes! " He seemed to be a little distressed with pleasure.

I laughed out, " Aguang, why are you so fierce? You even did it twice at once? Did you find a Chinese woman or a foreign woman? "

Chunsheng and Xiao D didn't say anything. They just listened to us and continued playing cards.

Aguang said: " Of course it's a foreign woman! Hey, to spend so much money, why not find a foreign woman to try? I went in first to have sex with her, but who knows that I came after just a few strokes. Well, I haven't touched a woman for a long time, so I cum right away. Then I made the second time. "

Aguang has been in the UK for eleven years and has never been back home. It's not that he didn't want to go back, nor that he didn't have money to buy a plane ticket, but he spent 200,000 yuan to sneak here, and once he went back China, he couldn't come back. What could he do? He just had to stay here illegally all the time, and he hasn't been home for eleven years.

" What about your wife? " I asked him.

27

" What about her? She just stays at home to take care of our kid. " Saying so, Aguang was lucky. Before he smuggled out, he had already married and had a son in China. He was 25 years old at that time, and his wife had just given birth to a big fat boy. His mother was so happy that she couldn't stop smiling everywhere in the village. Then the whole family borrowed money from relatives and neighbors in the village, raised 200,000 yuan, and paid the snakehead to bring Aguang out of China.

" I flew to Malaysia first, then to Europe, to Hungary, then to France, and finally to England from France." Aguang boasted about his history back then, as if he had traveled to so many countries.

In fact, he was terrified all the way, hiding in the airport toilet to avoid border police patrols. If he was caught, not only would he be sent back to China to jail, but the 200,000 yuan his family had borrowed from loan sharks would also be gone. During the smuggling process, he once squatted on the toilet (because if he stood on the ground, his feet would be seen) and locked himself in for the night. It was not until the next day when the situation was not so serious that the smuggler sent someone to pick him up.

" Hey, back then you little brats didn't even know where you were. " Aguang said proudly while looking at Xiao D and Chun Sheng. Chun Sheng never paid much attention to him, but Xiao D always called everyone "big brother or big sister", so Aguang liked him the most.

" Your wife has been a widow for you for more than ten years in China, don't you miss her? " I asked heartlessly. At that time, I was just sympathizing with the widowed woman.

He was stunned for a moment and said, " Hey, who cares about her? I send her all the money I earn every year, and she is still not happy? What else do you want? "

I looked at him and said, " Really? "

" Ah, " Aguang said with his neck straight, " In the past ten years since I came abroad, the money I sent her, apart from paying off the debts I borrowed when I came out, is still more than one million yuan! Is it enough for her to spend? Which man in the village can give her one million? "

This number really shocked me. I said, " One million? What are you going to do with that money? "

" What to do? To raise my son, " Aguang scratched his head, thought for a moment and said, " Hey, what do you think my one million is? Some people in the neighboring village who come out like me can send back more than three million in a year! They built such a big building in the village, which is many times bigger than the houses here in the UK. "

" That won't cost a million, " I said. " Even if you build a villa three times bigger than this one, in your village ..."

" Oh my god, you are such a young girl, you don't understand. It doesn't cost that much to just build a house. Don't you want to decorate it? Don't you want to buy furniture? And there's also a big color TV. Nowadays, large-screen ion TVs are popular in China, and you don't even know that! Just that TV costs 100,000 yuan! "

I was completely shocked by the grand blueprint he described. I didn't expect that farmers in China live such a luxurious life.

" So, " Aguang sighed thoughtfully, " what's the point of earning one million? It's not even enough to dig a puddle (swimming pool). I have to continue to make money. I have to work for another ten years at least. When I earn two or three million, I can go back to repair the house, right? "

I had nothing to say.

* * *

One time, Aguang asked me to make a phone call for him. This was the only time he asked me for help.

" Little sister, are you free now? " Aguang poked his head out of the door of my room and asked me.

I was reading a book, and when I saw him looking for me, I ran to their room and asked, " What's the matter? "

Aguang took Chunsheng's mobile phone and gave it to me: " Sis, please make a call for me. "

" Okay, " I've gotten used to it. I often help them make various phone calls. Whenever they need to speak English, they will come to me. " What do you want to say? "

This question stumped Aguang. He stood there, thinking for a long time before hesitating and saying: " Just say ... just say..."

" OK, tell me what's going on first. Who are you going to call? "

He said: " The boss I worked for a few months ago was a foreign woman, and she still owes me wages. "

" Oh? Why don't you work there anymore? " I asked. Generally speaking, the treatment in British restaurants is much better than that in Chinese restaurants, at least you won't have to work overtime, like seven days a week.

" I couldn't stand her anger! " Aguang shook his head. Obviously, he didn't intend to tell me how that " ghost woman " made him angry. " I worked for her for a week and then quit. Now I want to ask her for the wages for that week. "

" That's fine, " I said, and was about to dial the number, " but why didn't you ask her for it earlier? "

" Hey, " Aguang glared at me, " I didn't know you at that time, where could I find someone who could speak English? "

It suddenly dawned on me that he hadn't asked for the money because he couldn't find anyone to ask for it.

I became more confident: " Just tell me what to say. "

He thought for a moment and said, " Okay, tell him that my name is Aguang and that he still owes me a week's wages. Ask him to give it to me. "

" Okay. " I said, and dialed the number he wrote on the note.

The phone was connected. The ringing continued.

Aguang looked at me nervously, holding his breath. Not only him, but Chunsheng and Xiaodi in the room were the same. Chunsheng lowered his head and said nothing, while Xiaodi sat on the floor, pretending to look at the cover of a disc.

After waiting for a while, the call was disconnected.

" No one answered the phone. " I had to say to Aguang while holding the disconnected call, although I was afraid to see his disappointed expression.

But he was not disappointed at all. It was as if he had expected this to happen.

" Send her a text message. " Said Aguang.

" Ok, " I also thought it was a good idea, and quickly entered the phone number and prepared to start writing an English message, " Go ahead, what should I write? "

Aguang thought for a moment and said, " Tell her that I am Aguang who worked for her before. She knows me. Tell her to give me the money right away. If she doesn't, I will send her to the court! "

I excitedly spelled out his words into English short messages, and then asked: " That's all? "

" That's all, " he said. " You can send it now. "

I sent it.

This trick really worked. A minute later, Chunsheng's mobile phone rang. Chunsheng glanced at the number in my hand, then turned his head away without saying a word.

I answered the phone: " Hello? "

There was a loud Englishwoman on the other end: " Hello, who are you? "

" Hello, I'm Aguang's friend. He said you owe him wages. " I said it all in one breath, afraid that she would hang up.

" Oh, who is that? " The voice on her end was extremely noisy. I guess she was in the kitchen of a restaurant cooking. Or maybe she was outside in a windy place.

" Aguang, the Chinese Aguang, he used to be your chef, making Chinese food. " I tried my best to explain, trying my best to evoke her little memory of Aguang. After all, according to Aguang, he only worked for her for a week, and it had been several months.

" Ah, light? " She seemed to remember something.

I quickly grabbed her and said, " Yes, yes! It's him, Aguang! He worked as your chef for a week, and you haven't paid him yet! "

" Oh, yes, " said the English restaurant manager, " that is true. "

I felt relieved: " Can you give him the wages now? He is by my side now. "

The English woman suddenly started talking nonstop on the phone, almost like she was reciting lines: " Tell him that tomorrow afternoon at 3 o'clock, there will be a red Peugeot car outside the red factory building next to the restaurant. Tell him to find the person driving it. He will give him all the wages. "

I began to write down the words with one hand, saying: " Oh, OK, tomorrow ... at 3 pm ... the logo car ..."

I hadn't finished writing it down yet, and Aguang kept waving his hands at me hurriedly. I quickly said " please wait a moment " on the phone and asked him what was wrong.

" I don't have time to go tomorrow. Tell her to give the money to a friend of mine named A-Ming. "

My God, this is getting more and more complicated. I doubt whether the English female boss can understand such a complicated transaction. But I still bite the bullet and expressed Aguang's intention to her.

" Oh, what friend of his? How do I know him? " Said the English woman.

I felt the same way, but I still translated the English woman's words to Aguang.

" No, no, I can't go there tomorrow anyway. I don't have time. Tell her to give the money to A Ming. I'll ask him to go on time. " Aguang said, shaking his head like a rattle.

I had no choice but to convey it again.

" Well, " the English woman said, "it's three o'clock tomorrow afternoon anyway. If he doesn't come to get it, it's gone. "

I told Aguang what the British woman meant.

" Okay, no problem. " Aguang said, " I'll tell A-Ming to go there at three o'clock. "

Thank goodness, I finally completed this arduous call.

* * *

That night we won the card game. It was a complete victory. It was the first and last time that Aguang lost miserably. He hummed a little tune with satisfaction and went downstairs to cook for us.

When he went to cook, I asked Chunsheng: " Why is Aguang different today? " I meant why he was willing to spend so much money to go to the brothel to find prostitutes. Normally, he would not even buy a pair of socks worth one pound, let alone eighty yuan. When we usually played cards, we sat cross-legged on the carpet, but the socks on his feet were full of holes.

Chunsheng said gloomily: " He is leaving. "

I was shocked: " What? He's leaving? Where to? "

" He found a job at a (Chinese) takeaway restaurant in Scotland and will take the train to work tomorrow, " said Xiao D.

" What? Isn't he doing well here? " Aguang worked as a chef in a takeaway restaurant not far from where we lived. He had one day off a week and worked from 11 a.m. to 11 p.m. every day.

Xiao D said anxiously: " Sister, what do you know? The takeaway shops in London have been inspected too much recently. He is worried. It is better to go to Scotland, which is a little further away. It is in a very small and remote town . It should be safer. "

I know what he means. Now the UK is cracking down on illegal workers and illegal immigrants. Once an illegal worker is found working in a Chinese restaurant, not only will the worker be in trouble, but the restaurant may also have to close down, and the owner may be caught, fined and imprisoned. Therefore, many Chinese restaurant owners dare not use illegal immigrants without identity documents, or have fired chefs who were doing very well. Aguang was an illegal immigrant. He used to be the top chef in a high-end Chinese restaurant in Chinatown. In order to avoid police raids, he had to resign and work in this small takeaway shop in London's third district. This was already a waste of talent, but I didn't expect that he would even leave London to go to Scotland.

After a while, Aguang came up with a tray full of steaming dishes, red, green, and fragrant, all over the floor. Because there was no table in the room, Chunsheng spread a few newspapers on the floor and placed the bowls of various sizes on them. Xiao D went downstairs and brought up the whole rice cooker, and took bowls to serve rice to everyone.

" Come, come, come, eat, eat, eat! " Aguang proudly sat down cross-legged in front of his masterpiece, holding the rice bowl and calling us, " Eat it while it's hot! Sis, haven't you wanted to taste my cooking for a long time? "

Holding the steaming bowl of rice and looking at Aguang's happy smiling face, I ate the first meal that Aguang made for us.

Apple and her friends

When I first met Lv Ping in the kitchen, she told me her English name was Apple , which means " Ping " in her name . For her, she seemed to be more accustomed to me calling her by her English name rather than her Chinese name. This may be the case for all students who are studying, because in class the teacher always uses their English name.

Although her name is Apple , she does not have a round face like an apple. Her face is long and thin, with single eyelids, and she wears glasses. But because she is young, there is still a beautiful look between her eyebrows.

When we first met, Apple asked me, " Are you a student too? " Because she was the only student living in the building, the others were refugees, illegal immigrants, prostitutes, or like her boyfriend, who came here on a student visa, but didn't go to school for a day and went to work in a Chinese restaurant to earn money. Apple lived in a double room with her boyfriend, but for some reason, Apple and her boyfriend only planned to stay here for two or three weeks.

" Why only stay so short? " I asked curiously. I thought, moving house must be very troublesome.

She blinked, because it was our first meeting and she was not sure what the relationship between Zhang Lai and I was, so she decided not to say anything in that split second: " No, it's just that my boyfriend and I want to find another place to live - the people living here are so messy. "

But I still believed that this was not the reason they wanted to move away. But I did not ask any more questions. When she asked me if I was a student, I simply answered her: " Yes. "

She smiled immediately, revealing two small fangs, as if after hearing that I was also a student she found a potential sense of security in this building, or that she had finally found someone like me.

" Where are you studying now? " She began to chat with me in a relaxed and natural way, and she talked more. " How is your school? Are the teachers British? Our school is, but the teacher is not good at all. He speaks English very fast and we can't understand a word. I just want to find a language school with Chinese teachers. "

I said a little apologetically: " I am no longer attending classes. I am writing my graduation thesis now. "

" Graduation thesis? " She was obviously shocked. " What are you graduating from? "

" Well, if this thesis is passed, I should be awarded a master's degree. " I said awkwardly, as if I had stolen this diploma. I couldn't explain why I felt so awkward and uneasy in front of her, as if I had lied to her.

Her eyes widened behind her glasses and she stopped peeling green onions: " Ah? Master's degree? So you have completed language, foundation and undergraduate studies? How many years have you been in the UK? "

For students like her who were arranged by an agency to study abroad after graduating from high school, the study route usually arranged by the agency is: 1-3 years of language + 1-2 years of preparatory courses + 3 years of undergraduate + 1 year of master's degree. In other words, in her imagination, it should be at least six to ten years before she can reach my current stage, and that is only if she passes all the exams smoothly.

" One year, " I answered. At this moment, I suddenly felt deeply uneasy, as if I was sorry for the girl who was still studying language by completing my master's degree in just one year.

She was so frightened that she was stunned. She was too scared to even speak to me. She quickly lowered her head to peel the onions, then took a pot of boiling water and fled back to her room. It occurred to me that she might have boiled water and peeled onions to cook noodles, but because I was here, she took the boiling water back to her room to make instant noodles.

I also began to feel a strong sense of uneasiness involuntarily. I stood in the kitchen for a while, at a loss, and couldn't think of what to eat. Finally, I decided to give up the long process of cooking and took a piece of bread bought from the supermarket from the refrigerator and went upstairs.

* * *

Apple and her boyfriend lived in a room on the first floor. Her boyfriend was a deliveryman for a Chinese takeaway restaurant.

He rode a worn-out motorcycle to work every night, from the afternoon to 10 p.m. He usually came home at 11:30. I lived upstairs and could clearly hear the sound of a motorcycle driving in and stopping on the small piece of grass outside the door. Then, the key gently jingled and opened the door.

But there are also things about his job that are worthy of envy, such as he always brings back a box of Yangzhou fried rice or black pepper beef tenderloin from the restaurant. Since A Guang left, no one in the building works in a Chinese restaurant except him, so every time he brings back these boxes of lunch and puts them on the kitchen chopping board or in the refrigerator, I always look at him with envy.

Because he goes out early and comes back late, I rarely run into him in the building. Even if I occasionally run into him in the kitchen, he always chats with Apple , and I hardly ever talk to him. He is a taciturn man, about 24 or 25 years old, looks very honest, and doesn't like to talk much, but he is very considerate to Apple . Apple told me that he has been in the UK for three years. He also came here with a student visa, but he only attended a few days of classes and knew that he would never learn English in his life. Instead of wasting time and expensive tuition fees in a language school, it is better to come out and earn money early, so he started working from the first month in the UK. He first worked as a dishwasher in a restaurant, and later asked a friend to get a shabby second-hand motorcycle and a driver's license. He used his savings to buy the car and the license, and since then he began his career as a deliveryman in a takeaway shop.

" This job is much better than before, " Apple said. " At least it's not tiring, and I have a car, which saves me transportation costs. " The gasoline for the motorcycle is reimbursed by the takeaway restaurant.

" Then how did you two get together? " I said, " I can see that he treats you very well. "

Apple smiled slightly, and it was obvious that she was very happy. " Well, it can be said that it was very good. At first, we had to rent a house and live in the same building. At that time, Mingming and I lived together (in one room), and he lived with another boy. Later, we became together and moved out to live together. "

Then I understood, that's why they were staying here temporarily for two or three weeks.

" We'll move out as soon as we find a better place. " Apple said, " As a girl, don't you think it's messy to live here? "

I smiled: " I'm fine. They are all very nice to me. "

* * *

About two weeks later, one night, landlord Zhang came to collect the rent. It was not yet my turn to pay the rent, but he suddenly knocked on my door. I saw it was him, so I quickly asked him to come in and sit down.

He looked at my room and said: " You have cleaned it up quite well. "

I started to complain, saying, " Zhang Lai, when are you going to fix the light in my room? Look, I've been living here for a few weeks, and I'm still using the bedside lamp. It only has a 40-watt bulb in the middle of the night, which is not enough - you should find someone to fix my light as soon as possible. I know you're a very busy person and it's hard to find you, but since you're here today, you might as well take a look here. "

Zhang Lai looked up at the hanging lamp on the ceiling that didn't light up even after the bulb was replaced, nodded and said, " Okay, I'll ask someone to come over and check - when will you be there? "

I said, " Call me first when the time comes. Usually I'll be at home. "

He nodded again, and sat for a while before getting to the point: " It's like this, I have a friend, also a girl, who used to live in another house I rented. Now the landlord doesn't want to rent that house anymore and wants to vacate it. I have another house that needs a room vacated soon, but there's a two-week gap between them. As you know, yours is the only single room in this building, so I wanted to discuss with you whether we can let her come in temporarily and live here for two weeks, and then move out once my house is vacant? "

I have absolute respect and sympathy for this powerful sub-landlord in Chinatown: " No problem , just let her live here. It's only for two weeks anyway. It's just this bed ... "

He immediately waved his hand: " Don't worry about this. I'll ask someone to move another single bed in tomorrow. Your room is big anyway, so you can decide where to put it when the time comes. "

I said, " That's fine. Otherwise, I would feel a little uncomfortable with two girls sleeping in the same bed. "

After hearing this, Zhang Lai smiled. It seemed that he wanted to say something, but then he changed his mind and gave up.

" Also, how do you calculate the rent for these two weeks? " I couldn't help but ask.

He stood up and prepared to leave: " Don't worry about this. Since you have helped me so much, I won't charge you rent for these two weeks. You can just stay here for free. "

I immediately agreed with satisfaction. I had no more questions.

The girl moved in on the third day. When she moved in, it was Alang who carried all her luggage on his motorcycle. Only then did I know that she was Mingming.

Apple and Alang came in to help her pack. " You don't need to help, " Mingming said to them. " I'm only staying here for two weeks. I don't need to unpack anything, and there's nothing to pack. "

It seemed that the affection between Apple and her is a hundred times more intimate than that between her and Alang.

" Dear, " she said, " we are just downstairs. If you need anything, just come down to our room anytime. "

Mingming said: " No problem. "

* * *

I asked Apple : " Why are you so close to Mingming? Is she from the same hometown as you? "

Apple said: " No, that's not what you're talking about. She was the one we lived in the same room with. "

I said, " Oh , I think you two are really close. I envy you so much. "

Apple said proudly: " Of course, she is my best friend in the UK. If it weren't for Alang, I would still like to live in the same room with her. "

* * *

Mingming and I were chatting in the room that day. Mingming was studying for a part-time accounting certificate here. Because her English was good, she also worked part-time in a clothing store . Mingming was a tall and strong girl, about 28 or 29 years old. You could tell from her figure that she was from the north. She told me that she was from Shenyang.

We talked about love that day. She asked me if I had a boyfriend in the UK. I said yes, but we broke up now. She asked if he was Chinese or British? I said he was British and showed her the photos on my computer. She looked at them and said, your boyfriend is so handsome, why did you break up? I said, he is not loyal.

" Yes, all men are not good. " She said, " My ex-boyfriend was the same. He said he loved me, but he slept with my best girlfriend behind my back. "

I was stunned and didn't know what she meant. So I didn't say anything.

She probably felt that I shared the same feelings as her about men and love, so her conversation with me went a step further.

" Did you sleep with him? " She asked. " The English guy. " I smiled: " Of course. "

She said, " How is it? "

As soon as she asked the question, she realized that she had asked a question that I had no answer to, so she suddenly changed the subject: " By the way, I've always wanted to know - do you know what snog (an English kiss) is? "

I was stunned when I heard this. Although I knew what a snog was , I was wondering how I could tell her what a snog was?

This is such an indescribable thing. I mean, if I use words.

I found it difficult to answer, and at the same time, strangely, a wonderful emotion suddenly arose in my heart. A very subtle feeling. Even, a kind of sexiness.

I was suddenly shocked by my own thoughts.

Seeing that I hadn't answered and was hesitating, she suddenly leaned over (I was leaning against the head of the bed and she was sitting on her bed next to me), and with her hand, seemingly caressing my bare calf (I was wearing a skirt at the time), she gently and quickly stroked it, and said:

" Wow, your skin is so smooth. "

As if I had received an electric shock, I immediately tightened my legs and crossed them to hide them. But I had nowhere to hide, and the quilt was spread flat on the bed, pressing down on me.

I suddenly realized what kind of person she was. I heard that many Chinese lesbians in the UK are from the Northeast China. At this moment, thinking that I would have to live with this woman for two weeks, I suddenly felt dumbfounded and shuddered.

Fortunately, maybe because she saw that I didn't react, or maybe I was subconsciously suppressing my strange desires, she didn't take any further actions towards me.

After that, I would go to bed every night with my back to her, wrapped tightly in the quilt, and sleep in fear. However, maybe it was all my imagination, and nothing happened in the end.

* * *

Mingming moved out before Apple and her boyfriend did. She said that she had found a house with an elderly lady living alone in the UK with the help of a colleague from the store. Although the rent was a little expensive, the house was in good condition, so she quickly notified Zhang Lai and said that she would move in next week.

I thought to myself, God bless me, I can finally regain my peace of mind.

Apple was obviously reluctant to leave when we moved . During the time Mingming lived here, I never saw her again after that chat. She stayed in Apple 's room downstairs every night until Alang came back at 11pm, then she went upstairs to sleep.

" Please come back and see us often, " Apple said. " And remember us. "

Mingming said: " You can come to my house if you want. The conditions there are much better than here. "

Alang said: " We have found a house, but we haven't finalized it yet. We may have to move out in a week or two. "

This time, because the place was too far, Alang did not drive her there on his motorcycle, but after the taxi arrived, he helped her move all the luggage down from upstairs and into the car.

Mingming hugged Apple before getting on the car . Apple's small size just reached her shoulders in her arms.

" Goodbye. " Mingming said, " Take care of yourself. "

" Goodbye. " Apple snuggled up to Alang and looked at her sadly.

Mingming got in the taxi and it sped away. Apple and Alang turned around and went back to their room.

A week later, Apple and Alang also moved out.

Chinatown

* * *

About a year and a half later, one day I was taking a bus in East London. When I got on the bus, I suddenly noticed a girl dressed very sporty smiling at me.

" Oh, it's you, Apple . " I exclaimed in surprise. It had been almost a year since I moved out of China town .

" Yeah, " she said, smiling slightly, " are you okay? "

" Okay, " I said, " how about you and your boyfriend? "

" We broke up a long time ago. "

" What? What's the matter? Isn't he fine? "

" Well, there are many things that cannot be said, " she said. Although we all spoke Chinese, no one on the bus should understand us, but there was no guarantee that there would be another Chinese person sitting somewhere.

" He was so good to you, " I said with some regret, " that young man looked like an honest man. "

" Yes, " she said, " but in the end we both got tired of each other, you know, we just couldn't stay together for long. " She ended the story lightly. Although I knew that was not the real reason for their breakup. Even so, that guy could not break up with her easily, he would be very sad and painful. I know he would, Alang.

" So where do you live now? " I asked.

" It's right here. " She said, " I left there too. You know, there are too many Chinese people there. It's even more chaotic than Chinatown. Now I live with Mingming. We live in a double room. "

In the UK, it is very common for two Chinese girls to share a room. Except for the British who may make a fuss about it and suspect that they are lesbians, no Chinese would suspect that there is anything wrong with two girls sharing a room to save money.

" Really? Is she okay? " I asked casually, " Wasn't she living well at that old British lady's house? Why did she move out again? "

" Don't mention that old English lady any more, " she said. " She's a pervert. I can't stand anything. She moved out a long time ago. She's only been there for a month or two. Then she moved in with someone else somewhere else. "

" Oh. " I said.

Suddenly she said: " Oh, I'm almost at the station. What a coincidence it is today. London is so big, and I still run into you. "

I quickly said, "Sure. Say hello to Mingming too. See you around. "

The car arrived at the station, the door opened, and Apple jumped down gently. On the autumn streets of London, the bright sunlight shone on the pearl earrings jumping and flashing under her earlobes, a very fresh and bright picture. After that, I never saw her again.

Chunsheng

Xiao D knocked on my door: "Brother Chunsheng is calling you. "

I answered in the room: " Okay, tell him I'll be there in a minute. "

I was in my room with the door closed, watching a Category III movie I had borrowed from Chunsheng and his friends next door. They specialized in pirated discs, and I could find all the blockbuster movies that were still being advertised in British cinemas from their boxes in the next room. Of course, this Category III movie was not a popular movie currently being shown in the cinema, but an old movie that I had found after a lot of searching through their boxes.

" Ha! So you still sell this! " I said with a big laugh.

" We're not selling this. We got it from our eldest brother a while ago just to play with it. " Chunsheng said.

The big brother he was talking about was Lao Zhu. He was also the tenant of the largest room in the entire building (about

30 square meters). After Lao Zhu rented this room, it became the base for his group of brothers, all of whom followed him to make pirated CDs. Chunsheng was one of his key men, and Xiao D was just a relative of his friend who asked him to take care of him, so he took him along.

" Anyway, let me see it first. " I took it out with a smile, and on the cover was a SM blonde girl with a slim figure and big whip-shaped breasts .

" Sis, you're still looking at this? " Xiao D shouted first, and came over with a smile to grab it.

" Go away, go away. How old are you? You're not even 21 years old, the upper limit for watching Category III films. I'm your sister, of course I can watch it. " I took advantage of my age.

" Haha, " Xiao D smiled and said nothing. I know he was thinking that from now on he would change his opinion of this older sister.

" Chunsheng, let me borrow these today, " I counted the discs in my hand and shook them in front of him, " The Matrix, Gangs of New York, and this pornographic film, three in total, okay? "

Chunsheng nodded without saying a word. He didn't care at all what I said.

Xiao D said: " Sis, do you want me to watch it with you? "

I spat at him: " Go to hell, you little brat, you have been thinking about women all day, I don't think you will ever achieve anything. "

Xiao D smiled awkwardly and watched me go out.

* * *

I opened my laptop to watch those DVDs , because I wanted to save the good movies for the evening. It was noon, so I picked the third-level movie that I could interrupt at any time. When I opened it, I found that the preview clips were all about sexual sadomasochism games, three-way battles, and even multi-person orgy. I really had no interest in these. Western third-level movies are too exaggerated, and have become mechanical movements. Instead, they are boring. I still like to watch Asian third-level movies, one-on-one, the kind that are filmed with emotion and style.

Who knew that I had just picked a group of two women and one man and had only been watching for a few minutes when Xiao D banged on the door. I knew he was just trying to cause trouble.

" Okay, okay, here I come! " I said impatiently, while pressing " pause " on the computer player .

When I opened the door, Xiao D was gone. I walked to their room next door and saw Chunsheng sitting on the sofa, smoking and playing games on his mobile phone.

I opened my mouth and cursed: " Xiao D, you are a dead man, how dare you lie to your sister? "

Xiao D said aggrievedly: " No, it was really Chunsheng who asked you to come, you can ask him. "

" Then why doesn't your brother Chunsheng speak? "

" Sis, you know him very well. He is the worst at talking, especially when he sees you ..."

" Do you want to die... !? " Although I knew he was joking, I still got angry. " Huh? You dare to make fun of your brother Chunsheng? "

Xiao D chuckled and stopped talking.

Chunsheng still sat there looking at his phone without saying a word.

I left alone out of boredom. I returned to my room, not in the mood to watch porn movies, so I turned off my computer and prepared to go downstairs to cook.

Just as I was about to go downstairs, I suddenly heard Chunsheng from next door calling me when he saw me passing by his door: " Hey, come here for a moment. "

I was stunned and realized that Xiao D did not lie to me and it was he who wanted to find me.

I immediately went over and said, " Why didn't you say anything just now? "

He didn't explain, but took out a piece of paper with English written on it and asked me, " Can you help me figure out what this means? "

Oh, I see. This is a common occurrence. Living here, since Mingming and Apple moved out, I am the only one in the building who knows English. Everyone treats me as an all-round translator, and they come to me for anything related to English. For example, if a British person knocks on the door, or the postman asks them to sign something to pick up a letter, they will all come up to call me.

I translated it for him, and the general idea was to ask him to deliver something to a certain address, and then the address was at the end. I told him this, but I didn't understand what the note was about at all.

" Oh. " He listened and said nothing. He just took the note back calmly, folded it up and put it aside.

" Where's Lao Zhu? " I asked casually, " Where has he gone? Why can't I see him all day long? "

Before Chunsheng could say anything, Xiao D interrupted: " Ha, do you miss Lao Zhu? I'll tell him when he comes back. "

I don't mind him making fun of me and Lao Zhu: " Haha, I'll be surprised if he doesn't beat you up. "

Chunsheng said: " He went out to pick up the goods early in the morning. "

I said, " Oh. "

Then he said, " Okay, let's play cards when he comes back. "

Since Aguang left, we always need one person to play cards, and Lao Zhu is not often at home. I stayed alone in the room to write my thesis, which was really boring. I wanted to join them for a card game to change my mind.

I accidentally saw the mobile phone in Chunsheng's hand: " Wow, your mobile phone is the latest model, very expensive. "

He flipped the phone over in his hand: " Yes, it was just released this month. "

I took it and looked at it: " How did you buy it? It's very expensive if you don't pay the monthly fee. " In the UK, you can get a free mobile phone if you pay a monthly fee, but because they all came here illegally, they have no identity or documents, so they can't buy a mobile phone with a monthly fee. They can only buy recharge card type mobile phones that do not require registration of identity documents, so the mobile phones can only be purchased separately.

Chunsheng smoked a cigarette and said, " It's nothing, just three hundred pounds. "

I was shocked: " You guys are really rich, three hundred pounds is enough for me to pay one month's rent. And more. "

" Is the house Zhang Lai gave you so cheap? " Chunsheng asked, " But it's true, yours is a single room. "

" How much did Zhang Lai give you for this room? "

Chunsheng gestured a number with his hand, which scared me.

" With that much money, you can rent a separate unit outside, " I said.

" Can you rent it for us? " he asked.

I then remembered that they didn't speak English and couldn't deal with British landlords. They were also illegal immigrants with no identity or documents, so no British people would be willing to rent a house to them. No wonder Zhang Lai dared to ask them for such a high price.

One time, Lao Zhu took them and me to Chinatown for afternoon tea. On the way to the subway, he suddenly remembered to do some calculations, and was shocked. He first explained it to them in Fujian dialect, and then explained it to me in Mandarin:

" I just calculated that from March to now, we have spent more than 10,000 yuan (equivalent to about 160,000 yuan) in half a year, excluding rent. "

I said, " How could so much be used? "

" Hey, " said Lao Zhu, " money is needed everywhere. "

Only then did I realize the meaning of what he said, especially for those who came here illegally to make a living.

But for them, this kind of life is already a good one. Although they are doing illegal business and are always in danger of being caught, it is better than working in a restaurant from dawn to dusk, working six days a week, working fourteen hours a day, and earning less than 10,000 yuan a year.

I asked Chunsheng: " You are so young, why don't you go back to find a job, make money and marry a wife in your hometown? There are many ways to make money in China, no less than here. "

Chunsheng didn't even look at me. He just lay on the sofa, looked up at the ceiling and said, " I spent more than 200,000 yuan to escape, is this the only way to go back? "

" Then what are you doing for? "

He was silent for a moment, then said, " You don't know. "

After a while, he said: " How do you know what it means to come to England in our hometown? Coming to England is my whole ideal, all my dreams are here. "

This is the most truthful sentence Chunsheng has ever said to me about himself. He usually doesn't talk much, and he talked even less at this time. He never talked to me about similar topics again.

* * *

Sometimes when Lao Zhu was happy, he would take his brothers out to have fun . If they did not plan to go to a brothel that night but just wanted to have some fun, they would happily call me to go along as well.

" Come on, come on! Let's play together! " They usually invite me like this. I am flattered and quickly ask them for ten minutes to wash and dress up, then I hurriedly spend five minutes putting on makeup, and five minutes changing into the most beautiful dress and high heels.

" Let's go! " Xiao D knocked on my door. They lived next door to me, so my door was right outside, which was very convenient for them to knock on.

" Coming, coming! " I answered while tying my shoelaces in the house.

Then we all ran downstairs happily. Sometimes we went to the subway station together. They didn't even know how to buy tickets at the window. They always paid for tickets by inserting coins at the ticket machine. If I was with them, I would go to the window to buy tickets for everyone.

Sometimes when Lao Zhu has friends over, we would go out together in his friend's car. Although the back seat is a bit crowded, fortunately we are all thin, so it's no problem to squeeze three or four people.

Among this group of people, Chunsheng is always the one who likes to talk the least. No matter what the situation is, you will rarely hear him say anything. Even Xiao Ds will say something when they are happy, or pat someone's horse casually, but Chunsheng says nothing, whether he is happy or unhappy.

Maybe I have never seen him truly happy. Or maybe I just don't know what he looks like when he is happy. Only once did I know that he was truly happy and completely free. He said a lot that day, although it was all nonsense, but it was also the first time I saw him talk so much.

That was also when we went out with Lao Zhu. It was already past three in the morning, and Lao Zhu didn't want to go home, so he took two of his friends' cars and went to his friend's house in another district.

I was hungry and all the restaurants outside were closed, so I ran to the kitchen to make myself some instant noodles. When I came out, I was holding a big steaming bowl of noodles and was going to walk through the corridor to the living room to eat noodles. Lao Zhu and his friends were all there.

Unexpectedly, I ran into Chunsheng in the corridor. He was the only one in the corridor, and there seemed to be something wrong with his eyes. I held the bowl of noodles and shouted at him:

" Hey, what are you standing here for? Let me pass. "

But he didn't seem to hear me. He turned his head and looked at me vaguely, but it seemed that he didn't see me at all. Then he leaned against the wall, lowered his head, and took another puff of the half-smoked cigarette in his hand.

Only then did I notice that his cigarette looked like a cigar, very thick and dark brown.

I was about to pass by him when one of Lao Zhu's friend's men came out of the living room, probably having heard me talking.

" Chunsheng, why are you here? " he said, patting his shoulder. " Come on, go in. They are all inside. "

Chunsheng seemed to be dragged away by him. I followed him and planned to go over as well. Unexpectedly, Chunsheng suddenly noticed me. He turned around from the arm of the subordinate, raised the cigarette in his hand and said incoherently:

" Do you want it? Here you go. "

I finally realized that he was completely out of his mind. At that moment, I finally felt that he really liked me. Only at that moment, he didn't know what to do with such a good feeling, how to make me feel it too. He wanted me to share it with him. Because it was his best thing, the highest level of enjoyment he could feel.

I was so flustered that I could hardly hold the hot bowl of noodles. I looked at him and shook my head, but I didn't know what to say: " No, I don't want it. "

His confused eyes glanced at me indifferently, and then he leaned against the wall again. He said, "Awei, I'll go in later."

Awei looked at me, let him go, and laughed: " Can you do it, Chunsheng? Don't scare this little sister. "

Chunsheng said: " You go. "

Awei and I looked at each other, and we didn't know whether he was talking to himself or to me.

Then he took another puff.

I smiled at Awei and said, " He's already high . "

After hearing this, Awei looked at me and smiled. This was the first time he met me: " So you knew. "

Chunsheng said: " Don't pay attention to him, go eat your noodles. "

I finally realized he was talking to me.

Awei said: " We have everything you want here. You can ask for whatever you want. Don't worry, they are all good stuff - that's what our boss does. "

I said, " No, I'm just hungry and want to eat a bowl of noodles. "

Awei smiled at Chun Sheng and said, " You are a very good little sister. "

Chunsheng said: " Stop bothering me here, take her to eat noodles. "

Then he suddenly remembered something and looked into my bowl like a drunk: " You cooked some mess. "

Seeing that he had really fainted, Awei hugged him again, winked at me and said, " Go over quickly, I'll stay with him. "

" Oh. " I said.

" Get the hell out of here! " Chunsheng suddenly yelled at Awei. It was the first time I saw him so fierce, and for no apparent reason.

" Get out. " Suddenly he returned to his normal calm tone, but his eyes were still confused and blurred, as if he was looking for something but couldn't find it.

" You guys take your time chatting, I'm going in. " Then I walked around him with the bowl of noodles.

I don't know what Awei whispered to Chunsheng, but he suddenly became quiet again.

Maybe he never realized what he just said.

He was completely free.

* * *

" Why don't you find a girlfriend? " I said. I knew Chunsheng was a little older than me, about 28 or 29 years old. When he went abroad, he was not as lucky as A Guang. Not to mention getting married, he had never even been in a relationship. He was only 21 years old at that time.

Chunsheng is very handsome, the kind of handsome that can become a movie star, but unfortunately he is a little short, only about 1.7 meters. Otherwise, he is a standard handsome man. He always wears a black T -shirt and a hard leather belt tied on his jeans. He knows how to dress well.

" Yes, " he said.

" What about her? "

" I don't know. " He said, " We broke up a long time ago. "

I felt a little sorry, as it must have brought back some sad memories for him.

There were only two beds in this room. After Xiao D came, he always gave his bed to him and slept on the sofa. Sometimes if there were more people, they would sleep on the floor, five or six men sleeping on the floor together. Sometimes I would lend them my extra quilts.

" I know I'm stupid, " he said after a while, " I knew this woman was lying to me, but after she left, I still couldn't forget her. "

I was silent for a while, then asked, " What were you doing at that time? "

" Before I joined Brother Zhu, " he said, " I was working in the kitchen at a restaurant in Chinatown. "

" What about her? " I asked.

He paused for a moment: " She was the waitress in our restaurant, but she was also in school at the time, and she worked in the restaurant at night while studying. "

" Why do you say she is lying to you? " I said, " Maybe she really likes you. "

He was silent for a long time again, and then he said slowly: " I just feel so stupid. "

I didn't know what to say or how to comfort him.

" Is she beautiful? " I asked.

" She was just average, " he said. " She wasn't very pretty, but I liked her very much at that time. ... Later we lived together. "

I said, " Then why did you break up? "

He said: " I don't know why we broke up. That's why I feel stupid. At that time, she no longer worked in our restaurant. I worked from noon to midnight every day, and she had to go to school during the day. We spent very little time together. I don't know what she was thinking later. "

I listened quietly.

" Then one day, when I came home from work, I found that she had moved away. She only left me a note saying that she was gone. "

" Maybe she just couldn't stand the loneliness because you two rarely met each other, so she moved away. " I comforted him.

" No, she must have another man outside, " he said.

" Why? "

" Because she never contacted me again after that, " he said.

I find that sometimes I am really stupid, and I don't even understand women as well as a man in this kind of thing.

" I know I was deceived by her, but until now, more than a year has passed, I still can't forget her. " He lay on the sofa, his head resting on his arms, looking at the dirty spots on the ceiling, and said.

Refugee couple

The old Wei couple lived in the room directly opposite my downstairs. The difference was that their house was originally a dining room, which was connected to the kitchen and the back garden. It was a room that was forcibly separated by the second landlord. So the room first had no windows, secondly, it was next to the kitchen, and the cooking fumes all rushed into the house through the cracks in the temporary wall. Thirdly, there was a wall that was originally missing, which might be two doors built after the house was repaired to separate it from the back garden. In other words, living in such a room was cold in winter and hot in summer, and it was smoky and hot, but because they wanted to save money, the old Wei couple lived like this.

The old Wei couple are about thirty years old. The old Wei may be forty, but his wife Xiaoli is only thirty-four or thirty-five years old. Don't be fooled by her name " Xiaoli " . Although she is pretty and can even be a beauty with makeup, the problem is that she doesn't wear makeup. She always has a yellow face without any blood color, is thin and small, and has short hair. She looks like a stunted teenager.

Once, when Xiaoli and I were out, she proudly told me the trick she and her husband used to take the bus. Transportation in the UK is extremely expensive, not to mention taxis. We can't even afford to take the bus. A bus ticket costs 16 yuan in RMB, and the price has been rising every year. Now it is 19.2 yuan per bus ticket. Subway tickets are even more expensive. A day ticket (which allows you to take any subway or bus in a day) costs about 70 yuan . With such high prices, many Chinese people try their best to evade the fare. The method used by the old Wei couple is one of them. Because the UK takes care of women and children and encourages families to take the bus instead of driving private cars (to avoid traffic jams), a family ticket is specially set up for families. As long as an adult brings a child, he and the child can enjoy a discounted fare at the same time. The discount is also very large, and the fare for two people is even cheaper than a single adult ticket. The old Wei couple buys this family ticket every time they go out.

But there is a science to buying this kind of ticket, not everyone can buy it. For example, if you go to any subway station or official ticket agency, the ticket seller will not sell you a ticket if he sees that you are two adults and there is no child at all, and you will just ask for a lecture. Although it is in English, you can pretend not to understand, but that situation is really embarrassing, and the most important thing is that you can't buy a ticket, and you will get into trouble instead of trying to cheat. But the old Wei couple has been in the UK for many years and have figured out these tricks. They never go to subway stations to buy tickets, but go to small grocery stores run by Indians and

Pakistanis (we call them Acha stores). Some Acha stores sell tickets on behalf of others, because the government hopes to avoid the long queues at the subway station ticket office during peak hours by dispersing ticket sales points, and for the convenience of the public. But Indians and Chinese will cleverly use this convenience. When the old Wei couple went to Acha stores to buy tickets, they would say to the Acha (Indians) in their half-baked English (or just show them the sample of the ticket they bought before):

" Family ticket, one adult and one child. "

Although everyone can see that Xiaoli is definitely not a " child " under the age of fifteen , they will pretend not to see it and tacitly issue tickets to them. One adult, one child. Because only in this way can they welcome a steady stream of Chinese, Indians, Pakistanis, etc. who come to buy tickets. In short, it is none of the British's business.

" Every time I go out, I pretend to be that little kid. " Xiaoli said to me proudly, waving the children's ticket in her hand, and then pointed at her husband who looked like he had a big beard, " He just took the adult ticket. "

I asked her with some concern: " Won't there be any problems? For example, when you pass the ticket gate at the subway station ..."

" Sometimes the subway will honk, but only at some big stations, such as Liverpool Street, Victoria Station, etc., but we all know it, so we usually don't go to those places and just walk around them, " she said.

" What about buses? " Most buses in London don't have ticket sellers, and the driver checks tickets when you get on the bus.

The subway has machine ticket gates, but buses have manual ticket gates, so I think this stage will be more difficult.

" That's no problem, " Xiaoli said, " just go up when there are a lot of people, and be careful when you take the ticket, and cover up the word "children". "

" Oh. " I see. I admire their courage.

" But there have been times when I was caught, " Xiaoli saw that I was feeling guilty and told me, " There was one time when I was riding a bus and the driver found me and refused to let me get on. "

" What should we do then? "

" Oh, " Xiaoli complained, " That was my bad luck. I was so angry. My husband had already gotten on the bus, but the driver wouldn't let me get on. I had no choice but to let my husband get off the bus and wait for the next bus. "

" Didn't the driver say anything to you? " I was still worried.

" No! Who knows what nonsense he is talking about? Just pretend you don't understand these foreigners. They can't do anything to you. "

I have really learned a lot from Xiaoli.

Xiaoli and I are both talkative, and when the two women get together, they chatter endlessly. At such times, Lao Wei would just listen with a smile, saying nothing, and occasionally agreeing with his wife.

Lao Wei is a very kind man, his voice is not too loud, very soft and elegant, in this respect he seems like a real British. Lao Wei is also very gentlemanly in doing things, for example, when cooking in the kitchen, others are busy, but he is always leisurely, sometimes I see him squatting in the kitchen for most of the day just to peel a few potatoes.

" At your age, why would you want to go abroad when you haven't come here illegally and don't speak English? " I asked him once.

" Well, I used to work in a factory in China. I worked there for many years, but was eventually laid off. There was no way out for me. I would suffer the same hardships in China anyway, so I might as well come to the UK. At least, if I can get a status or something, I can still stay, right? " Old Wei said to me slowly.

Old Wei and his wife were both illegal immigrants. Later, Xiaoli's brother got lucky and obtained British citizenship (this story will be told later). With this identity, he became successful, so he helped his sister to change to a family visit visa. However, as a non-direct relative, he could only help her so much. But even such help was a big help. At least Old Wei and his wife now had an identity (family visit visa) and were no longer black. Then they could do things that people with identity could do, such as applying for refugee status.

" It's been two years since we submitted our refugee application, " Xiaoli said, " and it hasn't been approved yet. I don't know what will happen. "

I said, " Relax, there will be a result. At worst, you still have a British brother here, so you can stay here anyway. "

Xiao Li felt a little relieved and said, " But my brother can't help me with anything else. I've already thought about it. If it doesn't work this time, I'll try again. If I'm rejected the third time, then there's no hope at all. There's no point in me staying here to visit my relatives. I might as well save some money in the next few years and go home to start some business with my husband. Tell me, what's so good about the UK? Apart from the money, there's nothing to eat or live in, and everything is so expensive.

66

There's no one to talk to when I go out. I really don't want to live here anymore. "

Lao Wei echoed, " That's right. When my friends in China heard that you could earn 1 British pound for 15 RMB, they were so envious that they wanted to come here. But who knew that we were living this kind of life? "

Xiaoli said: " I can't even tell my relatives and friends. If I tell the truth, I will be sad, and my family will be even sadder. What can I do? "

Old Wei and his wife usually run a small business. They used to sell fruits in the open-air market, but later found that they were not making money. There were baskets of rotten fruits left and no one wanted them, so they changed their career and started selling pirated CDs. They first bought goods from other channels, also from a Chinese. The pirate gave them too harsh conditions and always made things difficult for them. The place where they bought the goods was far away and it was very inconvenient, but for the sake of their livelihood, they had no other way and had to continue doing this.

At first, they felt embarrassed and did these things in secret. Every day, they would sneak out with a small bag on their backs and come back with a half-empty bag at night. It was like a thief. But thieves don't do this. They always go out with an empty bag and come back with a full bag. It was the exact opposite of what they did. Most of the people in the building were doing illegal business, so they didn't ask each other about each other. Everyone was doing their own business and no one asked what others were doing. So, it was only after the old Wei couple got to know me that they used to go to the market every day to sell CDs.

" Oh, why didn't you tell me earlier? " I shouted as soon as I heard it.

" What's wrong? " The old captain suddenly looked very nervous. He was probably worried that I was an undercover agent sent by the police.

" Upstairs, " I pointed at the ceiling anxiously, " the store next door to me, upstairs they wholesale CDs! How come you don't know? And you buy from such a far place? They are the largest wholesale station in London! "

Amitabha! The old Wei couple were very grateful to the Bodhisattva for their protection. The next day, I got up and went to the bathroom to brush my teeth. With the toothbrush in my mouth, I heard the sound of someone walking outside the door. I looked out through the crack in the door and saw the old Wei couple carrying a huge cardboard box downstairs together, and they thanked old Zhu profusely for coming to see them off.

Old Zhu stood at the stairs, watching them go downstairs with a smile, leaning against the railing and saying, " Don't be polite, don't be polite, everyone upstairs and downstairs, just come back to me after you've sold out. If you have any films that are selling well, just come back and tell me, and I'll keep you posted if I have any new films in the future. "

Everyone is happy. I returned to the sink and continued brushing my teeth.

* * *

Two days later, perhaps to thank me, Xiaoli suddenly ran upstairs and knocked on my door, asking me if I was free on Saturday night. I threw away the book from the sofa by the window (this sofa was thrown in the back garden by the original Indian landlord, so I asked Xiao D and Chunsheng to carry it up for me, and covered the outside of the sofa cover with a layer of soft white cloth, which was just right for me to read), stood up, invited her to come in and sit down, and said, "You are free." Xiaoli stood at the door and said happily, "No, no, I still have to go downstairs to cook. You are free on Saturday, right? Come and have dinner with us tonight."

I then realized that they wanted to treat me to a meal, so I happily agreed. Xiaoli was also very happy and went downstairs to cook happily.

The next day, they really packed up their stalls early and came back with a lot of fruits and vegetables bought at the open-air market. They cooked in the kitchen with great fanfare. I ran downstairs to drink water and saw the couple busy like that. I said embarrassedly:

" Oh, don't make it so complicated. Just eat something simple. I'm a very casual eater. "

Xiaoli was chopping pork ribs with a large Chinese kitchen knife while waving at me: " Don't worry about it! You're not the only guest today. My brother is coming too. "

I see. If their own family members want to treat us to such a grand dinner, I won't say anything more.

" Well, do you want me to help you with anything? " You still have to be polite. This is the Chinese habit.

" No, no, " Xiaoli said happily, " Go upstairs and read a book! I'll come up and call you when I'm done. "

" Oh, " I listened, feeling a little guilty, thinking that such a small matter was not worthy of their grand invitation to this meal, but I couldn't say anything else, fearing to spoil their fun, so I had to agree to go. I poured a cup of boiling water from the kettle in the kitchen, and went upstairs amid the deafening sound of chopping bones.

Xiao D saw me coming up through the open door of their room and said with a smile: " Sis, you haven't cooked today? "

I held up the water cup and said, " No, no, the couple downstairs invited me to dinner. "

Xiao D exclaimed with envy: " Wow, sister, how come you are so lucky that even that couple wants to treat you a meal? "

What he meant was that they were both very frugal, but they were willing to spend money to buy spareribs for dinner. This showed how much I valued him.

I giggled and just took the cup of water into the house, then continued reading my book sitting on the tattered sofa I picked up from the backyard.

* * *

The old Wei couple worked in the kitchen all night, and finally called me downstairs to eat at eight or nine o'clock when I was almost starving. My God, if it weren't for this meal with them, I would have made a pack of instant noodles. Even eating instant noodles is better than being hungry, but since they were both busy in the kitchen for this meal, I had to starve in my room.

The couple arranged for me to sit in the house, and asked me to change into their slippers and sit in their best chair to watch TV. Their house was small, but there was a TV cabinet that Zhang Lai had picked up from somewhere. On it was a half-new color TV, which was playing the Spring Festival Gala broadcast in China half a year ago. ——For them, this was simply the best

TV program. Especially in the UK, I don't know where they transcribed this tape from, they regarded it as a treasure, and only played it when entertaining VIPs like me.

A small, low folding table was already filled with four or five dishes, all cooked by Lao Wei. Xiao Li never cooked at home, and at most she just helped him with the kitchen, washing vegetables, etc. Today she chopped pork ribs for me, which was unprecedented.

Lao Wei led me in and left. Xiaoli asked me to sit down and poured me a drink. I told her not to be polite and to do it myself, but she still insisted on pouring me a cup of Coke.

" Where's Lao Wei? " I only realized it when I took the Coke cup.

Xiaoli also poured herself a full cup of Coke and sat down on the carpet: " Don't worry about him, he still has dishes to cook. "

Oh my god, there are still dishes to be cooked? The couple had been cooking in the kitchen since 5pm, and they hadn't finished cooking for several hours? I couldn't stand their hospitality anymore, so I quickly said:

" Don't do it, don't do it. We can't eat all of this. Call Lao Wei back quickly. Save the leftovers for tomorrow. "

According to Chinese custom, no one can eat unless everyone is at the table. And I was really starving, especially when faced with a table full of steaming and fragrant food.

Xiaoli waved her hand decisively: " Don't worry about him, we will eat first, he still needs to make a soup. "

" Really, that's not necessary. Hurry up and ask him to come over to eat with you. If he doesn't eat now, the food will get cold. " I advised earnestly.

" He cooks his food, and we eat ours. He's going to cook a few more dishes, and my brother will be here soon. " At this time, Xiaoli fully demonstrated her supremacy as a woman in the family. " Come on, try this first, cold-mixed shredded vegetables. "

I sat there with great inner anxiety. Although Xiaoli served me food enthusiastically, I just couldn't move my chopsticks. So I didn't move at all.

" Hahaha ..." Xiaoli ignored me after picking up the food for me. She watched the skit on TV and laughed out loud, while eating half a handful of melon seeds in her hand.

" I like Zhao Benshan's skits the most, " she said to me with a smile as she watched them. " They are so funny. "

" Haha. " I smiled foolishly and drank Coke to suppress the hunger in my stomach.

" Ding Dong! " The doorbell rang.

" My brother is here! " Xiaoli jumped up immediately and ran to the door to put on her shoes, holding on to the door frame and shouting:

" Wait a minute! I'm coming right now! "

Half a minute later, Xiaoli led a middle-aged man who looked similar to Lao Wei in and introduced him to me very enthusiastically:

" This is my brother! "

I sat down with her brother after chatting. This brother was very aggressive. He walked into the room, and before he even put down his bag, he took one look at the dishes on the small table and said, " This is all you made? Who will eat it? "

Xiaoli quickly helped him put the bag away while explaining: " Don't be in a hurry, Lao Wei is still cooking in the

72

kitchen. - Sister, you two can chat first, I'll go to the kitchen to see Lao Wei. "

Then she left.

I was left alone in the room with her brother who was in his forties. There was really nothing to say.

Her brother was quite comfortable. He took the chopsticks from the table and poured himself a glass of white wine from the bottle (I don't know where they got the domestic white wine from). Then he sat down on the carpet, watched TV, and started eating the snacks with a sip of wine and a bite of chopsticks, while chatting with me casually.

" How old are you? "

" Do you go to school here? "

" What to learn? "

" Where are you from? "

I had no choice but to answer them one by one. I felt like I was sitting on pins and needles, anxiously hoping that Lao Wei or Xiao Li would come back soon. It was the first time I met this big brother, and he interrogated me like an inmate, while he could still watch TV and drink and eat.

Ten minutes later, Lao Wei and his wife finally showed up. Lao Wei was holding a large pot of boiling carrot and pork ribs soup, while Xiao Li was holding a rice cooker with a rice spoon hooked on her little finger.

" Come on, find me a place to put the soup! " said the old captain.

My elder brother didn't move at all, just watching TV by himself, as if he didn't hear anything. I quickly moved the dishes in the middle of the table to make room.

Thank God, we can finally sit down and eat together.

* * *

About a week later, I finally understood the real reason why the old Wei couple invited me to dinner that day. On the one hand, it was to thank me, but on the other hand, and most importantly, it turned out that they wanted to introduce me to Xiaoli's brother.

I understand that they did this purely out of kindness. You know, in their view, if a female student can marry a British man with a British passport like her brother, it would be a step to heaven. Her brother is a good man, has never been married, and has a passport. This is a golden husband that many women can't find even if they put up newspaper ads. They think I am a good person, so they introduced their only brother to me. They think that if a female student like me who has only been in the UK for a year can marry their brother, it will save them a lot of suffering. Difficult refugee applications, expensive lawyer fees, hard and tight lives, and long and endless waiting.

Unfortunately, I did not accept their kindness. To some extent, this is also a regret in their hearts.

Qi

Qi (琦) means a piece of fine jade. Few people use it as a boy's name, but there are many girls named Qi because people often think that beautiful jade refers to girls.

But when we say idiom "Face like a beautiful jade", we usually describe a man. And he must be a very handsome man, so that he is worthy of the description of "beautiful jade".

Qi is a very handsome man. Although he is only 17 years old, he is already 1.82 meters tall, with a good figure that can be a male model on the cover of a magazine. He is also very handsome. He can be said to be the most handsome Chinese boy I have seen in the UK. Even if he is a woman, his face would be a stunning beauty on any woman's face. So only a man like him can be described as " beautiful jade ".

After Apple and her boyfriend moved out, the room downstairs was vacant. It was vacant for a long time, and then one day Zhang Lai suddenly moved in with Qi.

" Hey, is this your brother? " Xiaoli saw a new tenant next door and couldn't help but ask Zhang Lai out of curiosity, standing at her door.

" No, no, " Zhang Lai smiled, " He's so handsome, how could he be my brother? A friend introduced him to me, and he's also looking for a house, so he'll stay here for a few days. "

" Why won't he stay longer? " Xiaoli asked.

" He's alone in this double room. I can't find anyone to share the room with him right now, so he's only staying here for a week or two. He'll move out when he finds a suitable house, " said Zhang.

Xiaoli looked at his back with some regret as he was busy moving luggage. He was about the age of her nephew in China.

" Why did he come out at such a young age? And alone? His parents are really at ease. " Xiaoli whispered to Zhang Lai.

Zhang Lai walked aside and lit a cigarette in the corridor outside Xiaoli's house. He took a puff and said, " Don't tell anyone else. This child is actually quite pitiful. It turns out that his family is very rich. They sent him out before he even graduated from junior high school and he went to study in the most expensive private school for the aristocracy in the UK..."

" Oh my! " Xiao Li cried out quietly, " How much will that cost? "

" This is the tuition alone for a year. " Zhang Lai quietly held up a few fingers, which scared Xiaoli. It was enough to buy a house in her hometown.

" Then what about now ... ? " Xiaoli meant, how come we can't even afford to rent a room like this now.

" Well, that's a long story. To be honest, I don't know much either. I just know that he is working as a waiter in a restaurant in Chinatown. " Zhang said, " Actually, a friend of mine introduced him here. I felt sorry for the kid, so I let him stay here for a few days. Basically, I didn't ask him for any money. Please help me take care of him when you get back. "

" Okay, okay, " Xiaoli didn't know why she was suddenly triggered by a maternal emotion. She looked at him and sighed, " Such a handsome child, just hanging out outside like this, not having enough food to eat. I don't know how sad I would be if I were his mother. "

Zhang Lai suddenly waved to her. Xiao Li was hesitating when she saw the boy walking towards them. He asked Zhang Lai:

" Excuse me, I need to go to the bathroom. "

" Upstairs. " Zhang Lai pointed upwards with his cigarette butt, then threw it on the ground and stomped it out. Xiaoli was about to remind him not to litter, but when she saw that he had already thrown it away, she didn't even say a word.

After the boy went upstairs, Xiaoli said with a look of regret: " This child seems to be quite polite, and hasn't learned bad things yet - unlike the couple next door who dress like that all day long. I think they are probably doing ..."

Zhang Lai winked at her, and Xiaoli immediately stopped talking. After a while, she said, " It doesn't matter. I know they are not at home. They just left and you came. "

The boy went downstairs after using the toilet.

Zhang said: " Okay, then you pack up first. I have something else to do, so I'll leave first. "

The boy said, " Okay. Thank you. "

Xiaoli said: " Judging from your accent, you are from the north, right? "

The boy hesitated and said, " I'm from Beijing. "

Xiaoli immediately looked at him with envy and said to Zhang: " I wish I could have a son as tall as you. "

Zhang Lai smiled and said to the boy: " This is the auntie who lives next door to you. You can just call her Auntie Li. "

" How are you? Aunt Li, " the boy greeted her.

Xiaoli was so happy: " What's your name? "

Zhang said: " Just call him A-Qi. "

Xiaoli said: " Okay, A-Qi, come to our house when you have time. If there is anything you don't know how to use in the kitchen, just ask me. "

A-Qi said: " Thank you, Aunt Li. "

* * *

After Qi moved into our building, apart from Xiaoli, only Abao and I who also lived downstairs had seen him. The only time I saw him was because he was using the toilet on the second floor and I was waiting outside for him to come out.

He was so busy and seemed so secretive. No one had ever seen him cook in the kitchen, and no one had ever talked to him. I guess Aunt Xiaoli was the only person in our building who talked to him during the first week after he moved in.

I heard about him moving in because one day Abao told me mysteriously: " Sis, there's a new handsome guy moving in downstairs, did you see him? "

Although she is younger than me, she is used to calling me sister, and I am used to it too.

I said, " Who is it? I didn't see it. "

Abao said: " He's a very handsome kid, he's also from Beijing, didn't you see him? "

Because I heard that he was also from Beijing, I suddenly felt an indescribable interest in him and wanted to meet him.

I didn't expect him to be so mysterious all day long, and I never saw him. I don't know what he is busy with.

Until one day when I needed to go to the toilet, I found that the toilet on the second floor was occupied. There was another toilet on the first floor, but it was too dirty, so Xiaoli, Abao and I didn't like to use it, so I waited at the railing of the corridor upstairs. Then I found that I had waited for a long time but no one came out, so I wondered if there was anyone inside, or if someone was careless after using the toilet and closed the door.

I was getting impatient and was trying to push the door stealthily when it suddenly creaked open by itself, giving me a fright.

A-Qi came out and was startled when he saw me. I noticed that he was wearing a snow-white shirt that was a little loose on his adult body. When I saw him, I thought to myself, no wonder a woman like Ah Bao, who has seen a lot of things, would say he is handsome. I was just afraid that Achang would be jealous.

When he saw me waiting outside, he guessed that I had been waiting for a long time. He lowered his head and said to me softly, " I'm sorry. "

" Ah, there's someone inside, " I said quickly, " It's okay, it's okay. "

He recognized my accent and seemed to hesitate for a moment, wanting to say something, but in the end he said nothing and went downstairs with his head down.

I quickly ran into the toilet and locked the door, thinking thank God! I could finally relieve myself after holding it in for so long.

* * *

The next time I ran into him was around five or six in the morning. I had insomnia that day because of an accident. I had planned to read half a book and then go to bed, but I ended up finishing the whole book without feeling sleepy at all. I looked at the clock and found that it was already four in the morning. I was in a dilemma. Should I go to bed or get up at this time? I struggled with it for a long time, but I didn't feel sleepy. Finally, I decided not to go to bed. I tried to stay up all day and go to bed at night. I didn't believe that this vicious cycle of biological clock could not be reversed.

So at 4 a.m. I turned on my computer and played some games, then watched a new Hollywood action movie that I had borrowed from Chunsheng. After the movie, I looked at the clock and saw that it was almost 6 a.m. A new day had begun, and I wanted to stretch my muscles, so I decided to go to the kitchen downstairs to make some breakfast.

Who knew I would be shocked when I entered the kitchen. It was early in the morning and I hadn't slept all night, but someone was up earlier than me. It was Qi, who no one had ever talked to.

" Why did you get up so early? " I asked blankly.

When Qi saw that it was me, she lost her shyness and said a little awkwardly, " I usually get home at two or three in the morning. I came back late today and didn't sleep. "

From what he said, he had just entered the house.

80

I saw him sitting at the outdoor dining table that connected the kitchen and the back garden. There was a piece of paper on the table. He seemed to be writing a letter here. The plastic dining table was also picked up by Zhang Lai on the roadside. When he picked it up, a corner was missing and it was so dirty that it could be described as dog shit. One day, Achang couldn't stand it anymore and bought a plastic tablecloth to cover it. At least the table looked like it could be used for eating. Finally, Zhang Lai hadn't forgotten us and kindly bought us two plastic chairs for eating. In this way, the dining set was complete. The problem was that there were more than a dozen people living in the building, so no one could sit on the only two chairs to eat. In the end, the dining table and chairs became decorations, or a place to sit when picking vegetables in the kitchen. For example, Lao Wei was a frequent visitor to that chair, often sitting there to peel garlic or something. It was the first time I saw someone writing a letter on that table.

I said, " It's okay, you continue writing, I'll make some instant noodles for breakfast. "

He held the pen in his hand, lowered his head and prepared to write, but he didn't write anything. It was as if he lowered his head to think for a while, and suddenly said: " Don't eat instant noodles. I have some snacks I brought back from the store. Why don't you eat them first? "

I was startled when I heard that, and immediately said with a smile: " No, no, this is embarrassing. "

He looked at me seriously and said, " Really? I brought it back because I couldn't finish it. I have to go to the store soon. It's useless to leave it there. You can eat it first and have lunch later. "

I was tempted and said, " What kind of snacks are they? Let me see. "

A-Qi said: " It's right there on the chopping board. I brought it back and haven't put it in the refrigerator yet. You can eat it while it's hot. "

As the saying goes, "A man's mouth will open to you if he eats your food." When I saw that the restaurant's disposable lunch box was filled with shrimp dumplings, I was immediately overjoyed and speechless. I didn't say anything, so I picked up the chopsticks, took the lunch box, sat on the plastic chair outside and started eating.

" Your restaurant is so good, and we serve you such delicious food. " I said while eating.

He smiled and said, " No, it's not every day. Yesterday it happened to be the birthday of our boss's little daughter. "

" Oh, oh, " I was enjoying my meal, but out of a guilty conscience I quickly asked, " You really don't want to eat anymore? "

" I'm really full, " he said with a smile, " I came back only after I was full. The food in this lunch box is what everyone asked me to bring back because no one else could eat anymore. "

That's great, I started eating without any worries and chatted with him while eating.

" You are from Beijing too, right? " I asked.

" Yes, you too, right? I heard it from your words last time, but I didn't have the courage to ask. " He smiled shyly. I think he is very cute.

" Yes, " I said while eating dumplings, " Which district are you from? My home is in Chaoyang. "

He smiled: " We live in Chaoyang too. We live in ... Huaqiao Apartment, do you know? "

" Ah? " I was shocked. The houses there were 2,000 to 3,000 US dollars per square meter, and they were the earliest foreign-related apartment buildings in Beijing. People who could afford to buy a house there had to meet at least two conditions. The first was that they had a net worth of over 10 million in the 1980s, and the second was that they must have overseas identities or overseas connections. Otherwise, it was impossible to buy a foreign-related apartment in the 1980s. When he said this, I immediately looked at him with new eyes.

No wonder, the temperament of a young man from a wealthy family is different. Even if he lives in such a shabby house, his every move still reveals an aristocratic temperament.

" Oh my god, how come your family is so rich? " I asked without knowing how high the sky was. After all, he was still a child.

He smiled, as if he had finally met someone who knew about the Overseas Chinese Apartment: " No ... My father and mother divorced when I was just born, and my father gave this house to my mother during the divorce ... Later, the money for my study abroad was earned by my mother's business, and she never asked my father for a penny after that. "

I could tell from what he said that his father was a very wealthy man. His mother wasn't as rich as his father, but she was also considered rich in Beijing.

" Did you and your father meet often afterwards? " I asked.

He shook his head: " I have never seen him since I was born. "

" Where are the photos? "

83

" Yes, my mother tore them all up. She told me to just treat him as dead. " At this point, he suddenly felt a little sad and lowered his head without saying anything.

I was silent for a while, eating dumplings in silence. After thinking for a while, he said: " To be honest, I often meet people from Beijing in the UK. I don't know why. Do all the people from Beijing go to the US? " I smiled.

Hearing this, he recovered a little, raised his head and said: " There are some who come to the UK, but not many, and most of them are still in school, so you can't see them. "

When he said that, I suddenly remembered: " Why don't you go to school? "

He lowered his head and played with the ballpoint pen he used to write letters: " I haven't been in school for a long time. "

" What are you doing then? What degree did you graduate from in your country? " I asked.

" I only studied up to the second year of junior high school in China. My mom heard people say that the earlier you send your child abroad, the better, because it will be easier for you to learn the language ... Who knew that I still haven't learned any language. I was only thirteen when I came out, and I hadn't taken many English classes in China. I couldn't understand anything in class here. "

I was anxious: " You have to listen even if you don't understand. Otherwise, how can you learn? Which school do you go to? "

He mentioned the name of a British school that I was not familiar with.

" It's a very good aristocratic school, and it's very expensive, " he explained to me. " The school is very strict, and it's a boarding school. But the problem is that the students there are all British children, and they can speak English. I don't even know the most basic English, and I just can't understand what I'm saying in class. "

I understood his situation and could not say anything to blame him.

" And what happened next? "

" I dropped out after half a year, " he said. " I dropped out. I thought it was a waste of tuition fees, so I might as well find a cheaper language school first. "

I nodded. He was still a good kid who cared about his mother and her money, which was rare. " What happened next? "

" As a result, I studied in a language school for more than half a year, but I still couldn't understand anything ... I completely lost confidence in my language skills. "

" So what are you going to do? "

" I had no choice but to go. If I didn't go to class, I wouldn't be able to get a visa, so I still went, but I have completely given up studying. " He was very honest.

At this time, I had finished all my dumplings, but I had completely forgotten how they tasted. I was just concentrating on listening to him tell me a story.

" What if you go back now, read junior high school and high school again, and go to a university in China? " I thought of a way out.

He thought about it, shook his head and said, " It's impossible. After so many years, I have forgotten everything I learned before. Besides, I am already so old, and I can't go back to junior high school to attend classes with students who are much younger than me. "

At that time, I thought to myself: Is such a good child going to be ruined like this?

But I would never say that out loud.

" Why don't you go home? I mean, if you go back home, at least your mother can still find a way for you. " I said.

He said: " My mother also asked me to go back ... But I'm used to living outside. There's nothing to do in Beijing, and I'm not free. Besides, I didn't bring anything with me, so what can I take back? - Although there's no point in staying here, it's better than going back. "

I am so sad that I can't say anything. If I were his mother, I don't know how sad I would be for such a son.

" Then why did you end up working in a restaurant? " I asked.

He looked up at the first rays of morning sunlight that had begun to shine in the messy back garden outside, illuminating the dilapidated and incomplete garden wall obliquely.

" Later, my mother found out that I didn't study here, and the tuition fees that the school had to pay were still in her international account. She called me to ask what was going on. I couldn't explain it to her clearly on the phone, so I simply said that I couldn't concentrate on my studies. As soon as she heard that, she wanted me to go back to Beijing. I said I didn't want to go back like this. " He said slowly. I know that because we are both from Beijing, he has regarded me as the only friend here with whom he can talk.

" Then what? "

" Then ... she cut off my financial support. "

I understood everything at once. What should I do? I really didn't know what to do. Even his mother couldn't help him, so what else could I do? Not to mention his mother or me, even he himself knew there was no way. No one in the world could help him. You can recover everything you've lost, but you can't recover your lost youth and time.

My heart was getting heavier and heavier. More and more heavy. Like him, I had no idea how this had happened. How could it have happened?

" How long have you worked in that restaurant? "

" Not long, " he seemed to sense my heaviness and tried to comfort me in his tone, " only two or three months. "

I nodded and said nothing.

He went on to say: " I was broke at the time, completely broke. I had to pay my rent, so I was anxious to find a job ... I went to every restaurant in Chinatown, but couldn't find a job ... I was so poor that I didn't even have money for a meal, and I really thought, if anyone could give me a meal, I would do any job for them. "

I nodded and said nothing.

" Later, there was a buddy working in a restaurant in the place where I lived at that time. He felt sorry for me and brought me a box of fried rice from the restaurant. It was the most delicious fried rice I had ever eaten. ... Later, my buddy took me to their restaurant to find the manager of the restaurant and told the manager that I just wanted a job with meals provided. The manager took one look at me and said to try him out for a few days. I helped the dishwasher wash dishes for a few days. A few days later, I didn't expect the manager to pay me and asked me to pay the rent ... Later, I worked there all the time. "

" Are you still washing dishes there now? "

" No, the manager later asked me to be a waiter and asked me to memorize the entire menu. " Qi said.

I nodded and said nothing.

We sat at the open-air plastic dining table between the kitchen and the back garden. It was already seven or eight in the morning. The bright sunshine shone brightly in the weed-covered yard. We heard a bird singing in the big tree in the next yard.

After a long time, I said, " Are you going to continue writing letters? "

He smiled, rolled up the letter paper with some embarrassment and said: " I won't write anymore. I was originally thinking of writing a letter to a friend of mine because I was bored and afraid I would fall asleep. "

I smiled slightly and said, " It's a girl, right? "

He hesitated and nodded.

I laughed.

He suddenly asked: " Do you want to see it? "

I was flattered: " Isn't it bad? "

He smiled: " It doesn't matter, I only wrote a few lines, you can read it and show me if there are any typos. "

I took the colorful letter paper with cartoon flowers printed on it from his hand with a smile and read it. It said:

" Xiaolin, are you okay?

I am doing well here. My classmates are very nice to me and my English is much better than before. I wonder how you are doing recently. Do you have any good news from your old classmates? It is almost autumn in London now, and the temperature is higher than that in Beijing ..."

Seeing me smile, he also smiled and said, " I was wondering whether the temperature in London is lower or higher than that in Beijing, and then you came. "

I put down the letter paper: " It's very good, there is no typo, but the handwriting is too messy. "

He laughed and said, " Well, I haven't written for a long time. I can hardly remember how to write Chinese. "

I said, " When do you go to work? "

He looked at his watch and said, " I have three more hours before I have to leave. The journey will take another hour. "

I know he didn't buy a subway ticket, and took a long bus to work to save money. It took nearly twice as long.

I said, " Are you really not going to get some sleep? You'll be working from 11am to 1 or 2am, can you handle it? "

He looked at me and smiled and said, " No problem, I'm used to it. "

I nodded, stood up and said, " Then you can continue writing letters - thank you for the shrimp dumplings - to be honest, this is the first time I have eaten dumplings since I came to the UK. Thank you. "

He smiled very happily, like the bright sunshine in the garden in the early morning.

" Thank you too. It's been a long time since anyone listened to me like this, " he said.

* * *

I didn't expect that it was our first and last conversation. After that day, due to our different schedules, I never saw him again. About two or three days later, one morning, I was sleeping and suddenly heard a crackling noise downstairs. I got up, squinted my eyes and went downstairs to see, only to find that it was Qi and a friend moving things. No one in the building came out, and I immediately realized that he was moving.

" Why are you leaving? " I asked in a daze.

He saw me and stopped, while his buddy continued to move things back and forth behind him.

" Yes, I found a house and live with this friend. It is also closer to where I work, " he said.

" Oh, really? " I looked at his friend, who seemed to be a very honest boy. There was no need to worry that he might be gay. But compared to him, the two of them looked like a prince and a beggar. It wasn't about appearance, it was purely about temperament.

" Then, " I thought about it, but couldn't think of anything to say, so I suddenly asked, "--Do you have a phone? "

" Yes. " He immediately took out a mobile phone from his pocket. It was obviously the most expensive model of NOKIA in China (British mobile phones do not have Chinese logos), but it was an old model, which was popular half a year ago.

I told him my phone number: " Just give me a call. "

When he got through, I immediately heard my mobile phone dinging upstairs. I ran upstairs, took the mobile phone down, and when he was about to drag the last box out of the door, I ran down the stairs and stood at the foot of the stairs and asked him:

" By the way, what's your name? "

He stopped, looked back at me, and said, " My last name is Lin. My name is Lin Qi. "

I quickly spelled his name on my phone.

" Qi is the one next to the slanted jade, means a fine jade. " He knew I wouldn't which word it was, so he told me again before leaving.

Those were the last words he said to me.

He walked so quickly, as if he was in a hurry to get to work.

" Got it! Take care of yourself and call your mother when you have time. Bye! " I said quickly too.

He had already left the house, but turned around and nodded at me from a distance as a response. I stood at the door and watched him and his friend who was helping him move. After that, I never heard from him again, nor did I see him.

Alun

One day I wanted to go online. A Chinese stranger on the street told me:

" Go straight along this street, and you'll see a Muslim church at the end. Go a little further down and you'll see an Internet cafe. It's the only Internet cafe on our street. Look for it, you'll definitely find it. "

That was the first time I walked in the opposite direction of this street since I lived here. In the past, I would turn right when I went out, walk through the open-air vegetable market in " Chinatown " , and walk a few minutes to the nearby subway station.

I walked and walked, following the advice of my Chinese neighbor who also lived on the street, and I felt that the road was almost deserted before I saw something that looked like a small church. If it weren't for the stars and crescent moons on the roof, I really wouldn't have realized it was a church.

Outside the church stood a lot of people wearing white robes and white hats. I knew they were all Muslims, but I was too embarrassed to ask them where the Internet cafe was. I searched and searched, and finally found a Chinese man who appeared out of nowhere.

" Hello, do you know where the Internet cafe is? "

This guy was a big fat guy who was much taller than me, and I felt like I had to look up to see him.

" You want to go online? Isn't this it? " He pointed to a shabby little house behind him. I looked in the direction he said and vaguely saw a few words written on the window glass: " Cheap long-distance calls, Internet cafes, photocopying, printing. "

I was very happy, like a rabbit that found a carrot. I said, " Thank you. "

" You're welcome. How could you not know? " He stood outside the Internet cafe, lit a cigarette, and said in the tone of Zhao Benshan, "Everyone on earth knows it. "

I quickly ran into the Internet cafe and plunged into the world of the Internet.

* * *

I surfed on and on until I finally got my fill. The time I had to buy with a few coins was used up. Then I sighed with contentment, turned my head to look around, stretched, and prepared to leave.

Who knew that when I turned around, I found that the Chinese man I asked for directions was sitting next to me. I don't know when he came back after smoking, and he was grinning at the computer screen.

" Huh? Why is it you? " I said.

He glanced at me, nodded nonchalantly and smiled: " I just went out to smoke a cigarette. I felt the urge to smoke. "

" Oh, " I said. It seemed that he was an experienced surfer here, and I could ask him many questions. Thinking of this, I immediately flattered him:

" Do you know where I can find computers that can type in Chinese? I want to write a letter to my friends in China, but I can only use pinyin - some of them can't read English. "

The fat man nodded and smiled again, still with that nonchalant look: " There's no computer here, you have to download it yourself from the Internet. It's very convenient, just the next Chinese Star or something like that. "

I gave up immediately: " Forget it, it's too troublesome, I'd better write in pinyin. " Otherwise, every time I go online, I have to spend half a day downloading some software, and it will be so slow minute by minute, and it all costs money.

The fat man comforted me and said, " This place is pretty good, because it's in Chinatown . At least the computers have Chinese language systems, and you can still read domestic news. Many Internet cafes elsewhere can't even read Chinese websites. "

I admired his profound knowledge: " Then can you tell me where I can download popular songs in China? "

He looked at me, and this time he was serious: " Damn, why didn't you tell me earlier? What have I been doing here for so long? " He motioned for me to look at what he was doing on the computer. I leaned over to take a look, and wow, it turned out that he had downloaded dozens of Chinese songs and even the latest version of Korean pornographic movies in just a few hours.

I was stunned: " How can you take so many files with you? How big a USB (mobile hard drive) must be to hold them all? "

The fat man smiled proudly and pointed at the computer host under the table and asked me to look at it: " Look here, I don't need USB at all . That little bit of memory is useless. It will be gone after downloading a few songs. This is a mobile hard drive I brought from China. How many megabytes of memory does your computer have? This must be several times more than the memory of your computer host. "

I was so impressed by his work that I quickly tried to curry his favor: " Oh my god, that's awesome ... Can you lend it to me later? I don't have to download it myself. I'll return it to you after I'm done copying it. "

The fat man smiled gently: " Sure, do you live far away? If I pass by later, I'll lend it to you to copy. It won't take more than a few minutes. The most troublesome thing is to download things from the Internet. You see, I've been waiting here for the whole afternoon. "

I quickly said, " I live on this street, near the vegetable market. You will definitely pass by it. "

" Oh, " the fat man looked at me again, " so our two families live quite close to each other. I live not far from the vegetable market. "

I laughed along, my face flushed with excitement. Since I moved to Chinatown , I was the only one in the building who used a computer, and I couldn't access the Internet, so my poor notebook could only be used for typing or watching two pirated DVDs . Now that I have made such a friend, my dear notebook is blessed: in addition to using it to write that damn

95

paper, I can also listen to music and watch plays, which is a lot of fun!

* * *

" Hey, your house is pretty nice, " the fat man said as he walked into the building with me. He had a cigarette in his mouth, and he was wearing shorts and slippers. He looked like a bandit entering the village. Later I found that he was dressed like this everywhere, and no one cared about him even if he walked into the luxury restaurant of a five-star hotel.

This kid is really powerful.

" Really? You think this is good? " I said, " but these broken stairs, broken carpets, broken wallpaper? I'll take you upstairs to have a look later. "

The fat man nodded all the way up the stairs and said, " Not bad, not bad, better than my place. You don't know, on our street, a house like yours is considered quite good - many houses are so dirty that they are unbearable to look at. "

I remembered: " Oh, maybe. This house was originally occupied by an Indian family. They bought a new house half a year ago and moved there. This house has just been rented out. "

The fat man looked around and said, " No wonder, no wonder. "

" I wonder how the houses Chinese people live in can be so clean. " He said as he walked into my room. " But this is just the beginning of your stay. You'll see, it won't be good in half a year. "

I took him to sit in front of my laptop. Since Zhang hadn't given me a chair, I had to move the table to the bedside and sit on the bed to write on the computer. He didn't say anything when he saw me, but sat down at the head of my bed, and then began to operate skillfully, turning on my computer and the power supply, and putting the huge mobile hard drive on the table to connect it.

" Oh, I forgot to ask, what's your name? " I suddenly remembered and said a little embarrassedly.

" You can call me Alun, " he said, occasionally freeing up one hand to smoke, and in a few seconds, the computer was ready.

" What do you want? Whose songs do you like to listen to? " Alun said leisurely while smoking a cigarette and looking at my house. " You have decorated your own little house quite well, even with curtains and so on. "

I smiled: " Yes, because there is a row of outdated cabinets behind it, which is very ugly, so I put up a curtain to block it. - Just send me all the songs of those singers from Hong Kong and Taiwan, and I will slowly delete them after you leave. "

He started to operate: " I'm afraid that your computer doesn't have that much memory. Look, your C drive is full, and D drive has only 20% left . Damn, what era of computer is this, and it still has such a small memory? It's okay to install a few songs, but you won't be able to watch movies. "

I listened to him talking nonstop, and he was more familiar with this computer than I was. I couldn't help but admire and respect this man even more: " Yes, yes, I bought this in China a few years ago. It's already out of date. I bought it just to type, but I didn't know that MP3 would be invented later , and there were small movies and so on. The little memory was used up in an instant. "

97

He nodded after hearing what I said, satisfied that his judgment had been confirmed. As we talked, the rain continued, and I could only see a piece of paper on my computer screen flying from one briefcase to another, just flying and flying.

I was afraid that he would be impatient because of the slow pace, so I took this opportunity to chat with him: " Are you here to study, too? "

He nodded and began to talk about his own affairs: " Yeah, what grade are you in now? I went to college for two years in China, but it was just a junior college. I didn't really want to study hard, so I came here before I graduated. Didn't they say that if I study here for another year, I can directly get a bachelor's degree in the UK? Damn, those overseas study agencies in China are really shitty. They have deceived countless people. "

" Why don't you do it yourself? " I said. " I did it myself, from applying to schools to getting a visa. "

He said: " Damn it! I can't even do it myself now, and you're talking about doing it when I was in China? If my English is so good, why would I come here? "

I think so too, this is how the agents make money.

" How old are you? " I asked.

He sat back on my bed and crossed his legs, filling the (single) bed. He blew a small smoke ring: " Twenty-three. "

" Then you are much better than many people I know, " I comforted him, " many of them are still studying languages at the age of 22 or 23, but you have already been in college for two years. "

" I studied in China, " Alun said. " When I came here, I first attended a preparatory course for university. How could I graduate with a British undergraduate degree if I didn't even

98

understand preparatory courses? Those agents are all bullshitting, all lies, just to trick you out so they can earn a little bit of agency fees and kickbacks from the school. "

" You seem to understand it quite well, " I said. " Why don't you study hard? You've already come out. "

" Damn, studying is useless. My dad has already told me to just hang out here for two years. I can even tell my relatives and friends in China that I'm attending university here. "

" And then? " I didn't understand.

" Then after two years, when my English is a little better and I can speak a few words, I can buy a diploma here and my dad will arrange a job for me when I go back. No one will check (the diploma) anyway, " said Alun.

Now I understand, his father is a high-ranking official in the local area.

But to what extent, I don't know yet.

" Then what do you do if you don't go to class all day? " I was worried about him.

" Eating, sleeping, betting on football, and surfing the Internet. " He answered very straightforwardly.

" Betting on football? " This is the first time I've heard of this. " Can I win? "

" I won over two hundred pounds last week, " he said, " but I lose sometimes. It doesn't matter, I'm just having fun. "

" Have you finished copying? " I looked at the computer.

" Almost there, " he said, moving the mouse casually, " It's already 91% , it will be done in a moment. "

I breathed a sigh of relief and stood up from the sofa: " Do you want to drink something? I'll go get you a glass of water. "

He thought about it and didn't refuse: " Then just give me a glass of iced water, tap water is fine. " (The UK has good disinfection facilities, and many British people drink tap water directly.)

I went downstairs to pour him a cup of Coke, carried the cup upstairs, and met the kid next door.

Xiao D asked me with a smile: " Who is it? "

I smiled and said, " A friend. I copied the MP3 music from him . "

" Oh. " Xiao D went back to the house with a smile.

* * *

Alun finished his water and said, " I'm leaving. "

I said, " Sit for a while. Your house is just across the street. "

Alun thought so too, but still said, " I have to go back now. I haven't finished reading the novel I read halfway this morning on my computer. "

" There are also novels? " My eyes suddenly lit up.

" Oh, yes, " he said as if he suddenly remembered something, " I often read novels online at home. They are all long novels, including martial arts and romance novels. If you want to read something later, just tell me the name and I'll download it for you. "

This guy is such a good friend. I immediately agreed and said, " Thank you so much, I'm just feeling bored. "

He said: " Why don't you buy a USB ? They are also sold in the UK. A small one is enough for downloading novels. "

I said, " It's too expensive. "

He thought about it, nodded and said, " Yeah, this damn place, everything is sixteen times more expensive than in China. "

He was referring to the exchange rate between the British pound and the RMB, which reached a high of 1:16 .

I walked him downstairs and made an appointment to meet again in a few days. He ordered me the movie "Xun Qin Ji" (a HK popular online novel) which I had specifically requested.

" I saw this eight hundred years ago, it's such an old story, " he said, " but if you want to see it, I'll show you. "

* * *

A few days later, the doorbell of my house rang. There were more than a dozen people living in the building, but no one answered the door because they all knew that no one was looking for them. And if it wasn't for them, such as the landlord or Zhang, then it must be British, and they wouldn't understand what they said if they opened the door. So they simply didn't open the door.

I didn't know who was coming, but it wasn't a good thing that the doorbell kept ringing, so I hurried downstairs to open the door.

It was Alun.

He had changed into cleaner clothes that day, but he was still dressed the same way: vest, shorts, and slippers.

"The 'old story' you wanted." He waved the huge mobile hard drive in his hand.

I at once invited him in like a VIP.

When Xiaoli saw someone coming, she probably still remembered her brother, so she secretly opened the door a crack and saw me and a boy going upstairs. But when she saw that he was a fat man who looked like a bandit, she felt relieved and secretly closed the door again.

Although she did it secretly, Alun still found out. When we walked up to upstairs, Alun deliberately asked me loudly:

" Have you had lunch? "

I was stunned, obviously not understanding the context of his question: "Of course? What time is it now? "

" I'll treat you to dinner then. " Said Alun.

I was almost crushed to death at the stairs by this pie that suddenly fell from the sky. " Oh? Great, great! " I said excitedly.

What a good day today is. I have online novels to read and someone is treating me to a meal.

After copying the novel for me, Alun really invited me out for dinner.

" Where are we going to eat? " I asked excitedly, and even sent Alun downstairs, closed the door, and changed into a pretty dress.

Xiaoli closed the door for us: " Go out, sister. "

I laughed and said, " Yes, yes, this is my friend Alun. He got rich today and he invited me to dinner. "

Xiaoli looked at Alun with a smile, and Alun immediately felt very proud and walked out with his head held high.

" Let's go to the real Chinatown! " Alun said proudly while standing on our street which was also called "Chinatown " .

* * *

But when we arrived at the real Chinatown, Alun didn't treat me to Chinese food.

" Let me treat you to a nice meal. " Said Alun.

Then he took me to a western restaurant near Leicester Square, the kind with a star. This was my first time in London to go to such a high-end restaurant. Strangely, he was dressed in a vest and shorts, but the concierge didn't stop him.

I followed Alun into the high-end restaurant with excitement, thinking to myself, my God, wouldn't a meal here cost me several weeks' worth of room money?

I was so broke at the time, with only a few hundred dollars left in my bank account. If it weren't for Alun, I would never have dared to eat at such a nice place.

Because it was still early and there were not many people eating, the waiter found us a table by the window. I sat down on the soft sofa and saw flowers and candlesticks on the table.

" Oh my god, how expensive are the things here? " I exclaimed.

Alun smiled and opened the menu brought by the waiter: " You will know after you take a look. "

With his encouragement, I also opened the menu.

My guess turned out to be correct; this meal would cost me two weeks' rent.

Fortunately, it's not my rent money, it's his.

So I just let him order.

" What do you want to eat? " Alun asked me.

" Me? Whatever. " I answered as if I were going to a Chinese restaurant, then suddenly remembered and said, " Just order whatever you want. I've never been to a place like this before, so I don't know what they have to offer. Just order everything for me. "

Alun smiled and shook his head, as if he felt sorry for people like me: " Do you have a boyfriend? Has he never treated you to a meal? "

I answered awkwardly: " Yes, but he is British, and we always eat at ordinary street restaurants or buy takeaways. "

This is the truth. The British are never as generous as the Chinese in eating and are not willing to spend money. Many of my British friends only have a sandwich for lunch, even if they are the boss of a big company.

Alun smiled smugly and continued to look at the menu: " What kind of boyfriend is that? Dump him right away. He hasn't even treated you to a decent meal. What do you think he is? "

I can't argue with that. Maybe he's right.

Aaron ordered a veal dish for me and a mixed meal for himself, which looked like steak, lamb chops, potato salad, etc. I was really shocked by his appetite.

No wonder he is so fat.

Because it was free, I ate it with great pleasure. After the meal, Alun ordered me a huge cup of coffee ice cream, which made me extremely happy.

Finally I said, " I just can't eat any more. "

There was still half of the ice cream in the big cup, and a little bit of meat on the plate.

Alun glanced at it calmly and said, " If you can't eat it, don't eat it. Just leave it there. "

Alun was really generous, giving the other person more than ten pounds in tips alone.

I thought, why not give it to me? A dozen pounds is enough for me to buy some food for a week. But I didn't have the nerve to say it out loud.

The waiter seemed to be used to seeing Chinese people being generous, and he didn't show any surprise or flattery. He just respectfully saw us out.

Alun made another move and casually gave a few coins to the old gentleman at the door. The old man smiled and bowed slightly to thank him.

Ha, no wonder he was able to come in wearing only slippers and shorts.

* * *

After having a good meal and a few drinks, Alun and I wandered around Leicester Square in the evening.

Alun said: " Girl, what else do you want to play? "

I said, " I don't want to play anything. I'm too full and I just want to take a walk. "

Alun said, " Girl, don't save money for me. My dad will send someone to fly over to give me the money as soon as I call him. "

I said, " I didn't mean to save you money, I just ate too much. There's a saying that goes, 'When you're full, you have nothing to do. '"

Alun amused me and said, " Girl, next time I'll take you to eat French food. "

Stowaway couple

Bro Qing lived in the room at the corner of the stairs on the second floor, next to the toilet. It was a very large room, the largest in the whole house except for Lao Zhu's room. But he lived there alone at that time, and I never saw him for a long time. I didn't know what he did all day, but he seldom stayed at home.

After Apple and Qi moved out, the downstairs room remained empty. After a while, Zhang Lai got anxious. He thought that the room was small and next to the kitchen, so it would be noisy when people cooked. So no one wanted to rent it. He discussed it with Bro Qing, and Bro Qing moved downstairs with his luggage. Two days after Bro Qing moved down, Zhang Lai rented the upstairs room to a foreign couple.

When we saw two foreigners living in the building, we all admired Zhang Lai's ability. When he came to collect the rent that day, I flattered him: " Zhang Lai, your business is getting bigger and bigger now. You have brought the letting business in Chinatown to foreigners!"

Zhang Lai smiled smugly, waved away the smoke that had been blown into my room, and said nonchalantly, " Well, they happened to be in this area and were in a hurry to rent a place. The house was empty anyway, so I let them live there. "

Then I realized that they were the ones who took a fancy to Bro Qing's room first, and it was Zhang Lai who persuaded Bro Qing to move downstairs.

But no matter what, at least I have someone I can speak English with. And after Bro Qing moved, he found a woman from somewhere, about 30 or 40 years old, to live with him in the room downstairs. I thought, ha, Xiaoli should have someone to talk to.

Unexpectedly, the woman ignored Xiaoli. Maybe it was because she was still a little bit pretty, so she ignored all the men and women in the building. I felt strange at first, but later I realized that the real reason was because she couldn't speak Mandarin.

" Everyone in my family speaks Fuzhou dialect. " She tried hard to explain to me once.

" I couldn't speak a word of Mandarin before I came to the UK. " Maybe she wanted to practice her spoken Mandarin with me, or maybe it was because she was too lonely being alone in the house, but one day when I was cooking in the kitchen, she actually came out to talk to me.

I was a little flattered and continued to cook.

" Really? But you're talking very well now. " I said, adding salt to the potatoes. I was going to stir-fry some green peppers and potatoes. There are so few vegetables here in the UK that there's nothing to cook.

" No way. " Bro Qing's woman said with a smile. Until then, I still didn't know what her status was in Bro Qing's eyes. No one knew the real relationship between the two of them. No one asked. Even a woman like Abao didn't care.

" Why are you home alone? " I asked casually.

The woman said: " Alas, men are always running around outside. Who can control them? "

When she spoke, she was always very gentle and soft, and her manners revealed the charm unique to a mature woman. In addition, she wore heavy and bright makeup all the time. If she didn't live with Brother Qing, I think she would be more like that kind of woman than Abao.

" Is Bro Qing working now? " I asked. I have never chatted with Bro Qing. Not to mention chatting, Bro Qing is like the president in the building. It is difficult to see him.

" No," the woman said immediately, "he doesn't know how to do any work. He is just lazy and eats all day long. "

I could hear a hint of complaint in her tone. I was very surprised and thought that these two people were very strange. Women said that men were lazy and greedy, but whether it was Bro Qing or Bro Qing's woman, I had never seen the two of them cook a meal in the kitchen.

" Who of you usually cooks? " I asked out of politeness, while picking up a shredded potato from the pot with a spatula to taste whether it was cooked.

" Cooking? " The woman said, " I never know how to cook anyway. A-Qing used to know how to cook, but then he came to England and worked in the kitchen for more than ten years. He got hurt, and now he says he won't go into the kitchen to cook no matter what. "

108

" Then what are you two going to eat? " From her tone, it turned out that she had been Bro Qing's woman before he went abroad.

" Let's make some noodles, " the woman said. " Sometimes we buy some noodles outside. "

" It's so expensive to eat out, " I said, continuing to stir the spatula, intending to scoop out the food with a few more turns, " you guys are rich. "

The woman laughed, then sighed and said, " What? He gambled away all the money. "

I nodded, deciding that the green pepper and potato shreds were completely cooked, and turned around to get a bowl from the cupboard to put the food in. As soon as I opened the cupboard, I shouted, " Huh? Why is my bowl gone? "

When the woman heard this, she hurried back to her room, took out a dirty bowl with half a bowl of noodle soup left in it, and said, " Oh, I didn't know this was your bowl - I just got here and I don't know anything about the kitchen, I thought it was A-Qing's. "

" Oh, oh, " I said, " nothing. "

The woman hurriedly tried to pour out the noodle soup and wash the dishes, but I quickly said, " Don't bother. It's OK as long as my bowl is not lost. I'll just find another plate to put the food on. "

The woman still felt embarrassed and was still busy washing the dishes, but she couldn't find the dishcloth. After searching for a long time, she finally found a dishcloth that belonged to someone else by the sink, and poured out the dishwashing liquid I had placed on the windowsill.

I pretended I saw nothing and found another plate from the cupboard to put the food on.

" Would you like to try some of the shredded potatoes I fried? " I wanted to relieve her mental stress of washing dishes at the moment.

" Oh, no, no, I just had my meal ... Can you try feeding me a little bit? I don't have my hands free now. " She was washing the dishes.

I used chopsticks to put a piece of food into her mouth. She ate carefully with her lips painted with thick red lipstick. I don't know if she was afraid of getting the lipstick on my chopsticks or the oil on the food on her newly applied lipstick.

After feeding her, I thought, okay, I have to wash one more bowl and one more pair of chopsticks later.

You could tell she was enjoying the meal, as if she hadn't eaten anything other than noodles for a long time.

" I didn't realize you were such a good cook, " she said as she chewed, " You're as good as my husband. "

"... your husband? " I was wondering if she had another husband?

" Yes, " she said, having finished washing the dishes excitedly, " A-Qing is my husband. " Then she suddenly bent down and smiled tenderly and charmingly: " You don't know yet? We are a couple. "

" Ah ..." I didn't react for a moment, holding the dish in my hand, still stiffly raised there. She had clearly moved in two months after Bro Qing moved in, so how could she be his wife? If she was his wife, and they were married in China, where had she been in the past two months, why didn't she live with him?

She is a very smart woman and she saw through my doubts at a glance.

" It's like this. Two months ago, he and I had a fight and wanted a divorce. He got so angry that he moved out by himself, " she explained to me.

" Oh, " so that's how it is.

" Why are you getting a divorce when nothing's going on? " I said, as I started to prepare to eat at the plastic dining table outside. It was still early and everyone was not back yet. In half an hour the kitchen would be packed with people.

Brother Qing's woman - now she should be called Mrs. Qing - Mrs. Qing leaned against the kitchen door frame, looked at me and said with a smile: " Alas, as a couple, it's inevitable that they don't quarrel. Once they quarrel and get excited, they will talk about divorce. "

" I thought you were Bro Qing's girlfriend. " I said bluntly.

Mrs. Qing's expression changed slightly, but she immediately smiled and said, " How could that be? They are already an old married couple. "

I started eating: " You have been following him for so many years? It must be so hard, why don't you stay in China? Many of their wives enjoy themselves in China, anyway, men here send money home as soon as they have money. "

Mrs. Qing sighed: " I used to live like this. After a few years, I couldn't stand it anymore. I missed him, so he found someone and spent hundreds of thousands of dollars to get me out. Who knew it would be like this? "

The " do it " she said meant smuggling. Finding someone meant finding a human smuggler.

" A couple. " I said something I didn't know where I heard it from. " They say a husband is a husband. If he is more than ten feet away, he is no longer a husband. "

She smiled happily, and her deep smile left deep wrinkles at the corners of her eyes. Only then did I become convinced that she and Bro Qing were a real couple.

She ran back to the house and showed me a photo of her son. It was a photo of a boy of 11 or 12 years old, dressed neatly in clothes, taken at an art photo studio in town, and it was a " star photo " taken with countless soft lights .

" The little guy is very handsome, " I put down my chopsticks and took a look at him. " He looks a lot like his father, not like you at all. "

Mrs. Qing smiled happily. At this moment, she was a truly happy woman. Or, a happy mother.

" You two have been away from home for so many years, what should you do with your children in China? " I said.

She put the photo away with care and said softly, " It's his mother who has been taking care of him all along. A-Qing wanted to wait a few more years, until the child was older, and then ask someone to get him out. "

My God, this couple has already embarked on this road of no return, and they want to bring their children over as well. I seem to see another Xiao D in a few years, and another spring in a few years.

" But what are we going to do with him? " I couldn't help asking.

The woman said: " No matter whether it is good or bad here, we are always together as a family. "

I finally understood what she meant.

112

After thinking quietly for a while, she continued, " Besides, in our place, everyone who has some connections in a village has come out. What else can we do if we don't come out? Don't you think so, sister? "

I said, " Yes. "

* * *

A few days later, maybe Mrs. Qing told Bro Qing that I had become friends with her. When I was cooking in the kitchen, Bro Qing ran out of his room for the first time and leaned against the door to chat with me, holding a big bowl of rice in his hand. Mrs. Qing was away, and this was the first time he talked to me after living here for a few months. I realized that the couple were more talkative than each other.

" Are you a student? " He asked with a smile. His wife smiled in the same way. On his wife's face, it was charming, but on his face, it was smooth and versatile.

" Oh, yes, " I said. I forgot whether I was peeling carrots or potatoes. It should be carrots. I couldn't eat potatoes for several days in a row.

" You know, I'm out all day long, and my wife is very lonely at home. When you have time, come down and talk to her more often. " He said sincerely.

I was a bit overwhelmed by what he said, and I was even moved by his words: " Oh! No, not at all. She has a nice personality and I like chatting with her! You know, I have nothing to do all day, and I always stay at home alone. There is no one in the building during the day, so she comes to keep me company. "

He nodded, took another big bite of rice, and holding his big bowl, he suddenly thought and said, " Why don't you go to class? "

I said, " I have finished my classes, and now I'm looking for a job. " I was running out of money at the time, and I was anxious to find a job. I wanted to work part-time to earn the rent first, and then earn some money to continue writing my thesis.

He was immediately startled and asked me seriously: " What kind of job are you looking for? "

I said, " It doesn't matter. Any job is fine. If you know of a restaurant that's short of staff, just let me know. "

He left suddenly without saying a word, and came back from his room a moment later with something like a flyer in his hand.

" Here, " he said, handing me the colorful sheet folded in three, " take this and memorize it first. Once you have memorized all of it, you can immediately go to work wherever there is a shortage of people. "

I put down the paring knife in confusion and reached out to take the list. It turned out to be an ordinary Chinese restaurant takeout menu, but the difference was that this menu was printed in Chinese and English. Under each Chinese name of the dish was the English name and English ingredients. I remembered the recipe Qi told me about. It turned out that he memorized this one.

" What ... is this for? " I couldn't help but ask.

" Hurry up and memorize it, " he said hurriedly, as if he was very worried about me. Maybe he misunderstood that I had no money left. In fact, I had thought it through at that time that if I really had no money, I could use my credit card and the bank to borrow money to get by for a while, until I found a job and earned money.

" You have to memorize it first before you can find a job. No one will hire a student like you who has never worked in a restaurant before. You have to say that you have worked in a restaurant before to have a chance, but if you can't memorize the menu, you will be exposed as soon as people ask you a few questions. " He told me these tricks in an experienced way, saying, " Memorize it quickly. "

Then he took another big mouthful of rice from the bowl in his hand. He chewed slowly and said, " If you have any questions, just ask me. I have cooked all these dishes. "

" Oh, " I admire you very much, sincerely.

" Thank you, Brother Qing. " I said.

He chuckled, and this time he really laughed, a happy laugh: " Don't be so polite, we all live in the same building, upstairs and downstairs. I'm giving you this list, take it back and memorize it slowly. "

I put the menu away as I was told, thinking to myself, it turns out there is so much to learn about working in a Chinese restaurant. It's not as simple as I thought.

* * *

One day, someone came to visit the Mr. Qing couple. He was wearing a tattered jacket. When I opened the door for him, I thought he was a salesman from somewhere.

" Brother Qing, someone is looking for you! " I opened the door and knew he was coming for Bro Qing, so I called to the inside of the building. People living on the first floor already got used to have me, the "little sister" who lived upstairs, running down to open the door whenever there was a doorbell ringing.

After a while, I was in my room upstairs watching the latest American blockbuster that I had borrowed from the next door, and Mrs. Qing came running upstairs. This was the first time she came upstairs to see me.

" Little sister, are you free? If you are, come down to eat watermelon! " She invited me enthusiastically.

" Okay, okay! " When I heard about eating watermelon, I didn't want to watch any movie anymore, no matter how good it was. At once I followed her downstairs.

"He's my husband's friend," she told me as she came downstairs, "he used to live with us, but now he has moved out and found a place in the south. "

I said, " Oh. "

I didn't care who that person is at all, but she said that just to thank me for opening the door for their friend.

Then we sat together in their room and ate watermelon.

" Thank you, little sister. I stood outside and rang the doorbell for a long time. I almost thought no one was home, " said Qing's friend. " So you two are here. "

Bro Qing said: " Why didn't you call before you came? "

His friend said, " That costs money. I was just passing by today and came to see you. If you weren't home, I would have left. "

I silently ate the big piece of watermelon they gave me, and occasionally said a few words to Mrs. Qing.

When Mrs. Qing saw that my hands and face were covered with watermelon juice, she took out a new roll of toilet paper from the cupboard to wipe my hands.

" Thank you, thank you, " I said as I wiped and ate. Then I realized that their watermelon juice was all smeared on a rag whose color could no longer be seen.

After eating the watermelon, I chatted with Mrs. Qing, and she showed me a thin album of photos of her son. Perhaps because I was not an outsider, the friend started talking to Bro Qing about serious matters.

" How much of the stuff you gave me last time do you have left? " He said.

Bro Qing looked a bit embarrassed: " Even I have nothing left. You know, the inspections have been strict recently, and the people who gave me the goods have gone into hiding. "

The man said: " What should I do? I can't break off the relationship here. I have several brothers. "

Bro Qing said: " Let me think of a solution, I will come to you in a few days. "

I guessed that people who do this kind of business would not dare to say anything over the phone. They had to talk face to face.

" And my nephew, how long do we have to wait? " The man asked again, " I'm so anxious about him - why is he still in Vietnam? It's been almost three months, right? "

Bro Qing said: " You must not rush this matter. Not to mention the UK, even France is investigating strictly recently. Are you more anxious to see him or to see him in jail? Let him choose for himself. "

The man stopped talking.

" If his family members dare to take the risk and sail on the cusp of this storm, if you dare to do it, I dare to do it too." Bro Qing said, glancing at his face and said, " Your nephew is my

117

nephew, isn't he? We are all family children, that's why we need to be so safe. "

The man was convinced.

He nodded, wiped his mouth without saying anything, stood up and said: " You guys go ahead and do your work, I'm leaving first, come to my house in a few days. "

Mrs. Qing quickly put down the album she was showing me, stood up and said with a smile: " Hey, why are you in such a hurry to leave? Stay for dinner. "

The man waved his hand and said, " No need to trouble you. I have already made a lot of trouble to Bro Qing. "

Bro Qing stood up and said with a smile: " No at all! It's just a piece of watermelon. - Eat dinner before you leave. The little sister is not a stranger, she will eat with us too. "

I quickly stood up and said, " No, no. Thank you Bro Qing, you guys go ahead and do your work. I'll go upstairs now. "

Then I said goodbye to Mrs. Qing and went upstairs. I heard them chatting for a few more words downstairs, and then the door downstairs opened and closed again.

* * *

I asked Bro Qing: " Are you talking about heroin? "

Bro Qing laughed and said, "What do you know, kid? If it was heroin, I would have had someone arrested long ago. It's not that stuff, it's a drug called K powder, which is not addictive."

Although I didn't believe him, I still asked curiously: " Is K powder derived from marijuana? "

Bro Qing smiled and said, " No, but they are similar things. You know marijuana is not addictive, we all smoke it. Do you smoke? "

I quickly said, " I don't smoke. "

Bro Qing said: "K powder is not a cigarette, nor is it marijuana. It can be taken as medicine. "

I said: " It's not addictive, it's not cigarettes, why should I take medicine? "

Bro Qing laughed again. He knew I was teasing him, but he still patiently explained to me: " It's always good to grow something. You don't know if you haven't tried it. You will know when you try it. "

I said, " What does it feel like to eat K ? "

Bro Qing immediately perked up: " Oh, I'm just happy. No matter what worries you or how unhappy you are, they will all disappear after you eat this. I just feel happy. I am very happy. "

I said, "K is happy? "

He said: " Yes, isn't happiness the best thing in the world? "

I thought so too.

Bro Qing said: " You know, life is very annoying. There are so many troubles every day. Why not make yourself happy? "

I murmured, " Yeah. Life is boring enough. "

Bro Qing said: " Whenever you want to try it, just come to me and ask for it. I won't charge you for it. "

I nodded and said, " Okay, thank you, Brother Qing. "

But I didn't ask him for it. Because I knew I would still be unhappy if I ate it. It was just something they used to deceive people.

I was in a daze at that time, just because I thought of Chunsheng.

119

Chinatown

* * *

A few days later, Bro Qing suddenly disappeared. Just like when Mrs. Qing didn't come before, he suddenly disappeared. I didn't see him for several weeks, as if he had evaporated from the face of the earth.

Mrs. Qing said that he had gone out to do business.

I don't know what kind of business she was talking about. I just felt that Mrs. Qing was bored at home alone. For a few days, she even found a woman of her age from somewhere and lived in her room downstairs for a few days. The woman's makeup was heavier and more gorgeous than hers. Mrs. Qing introduced me as her old friend, who would come to accompany her every time her husband went out.

I wondered if Bro Qing had gone out to find another place to live, or was he really doing business?

After about two or three weeks, one night, I was sleeping in my room when I was suddenly awakened by a shocking noise. I opened my eyes in a daze and saw that it was three o'clock in the morning by the moonlight outside the window. Outside my open window facing the back garden, I heard a man chasing a woman and cursing her viciously, and the woman crying like a ghost. He cursed in Fujian dialect, so I couldn't understand a word. I only heard him and the woman crying like pigs being slaughtered running from one side of the backyard to the other, and then back to the room downstairs, and then there was a sound of a whole wooden table being overturned and falling to the ground, and then something huge fell to the ground and broke into pieces, the woman cried heartbreakingly, the man roared with the most vicious words, and occasionally I could hear the crisp sound of whips or belts hitting flesh.

I closed my eyes and went back to sleep.

I knew it must be Bro Qing and his wife.

Xiao Chen

Lao Wei asked me: " Girl, how old are you this year? "

I said, "27 , what's wrong? "

I thought to myself, isn't Xiaoli's brother's matter already over?

Lao Wei said: " I have a very, very good friend who is working in London now. He has a valid identity. His company has applied for a work visa for him. He will be able to get permanent residence in two years. "

I said, " Oh. "

The old lieutenant said: " He is a very nice person, tall and energetic. You will definitely like him when you meet him. "

I said, " Oh. "

Lao Wei said: " Although he is my friend, he is much younger than me. He is only 31 years old this year. "

I said, " Where's Xiaoli? "

Lao Wei said: " She went out to buy groceries. "

I said, " Take your time picking the beans here. I'm going upstairs to the bathroom. "

* * *

On Friday, Xiaoli suddenly came upstairs to see me in a hurry.
" Sister, are you there? " Xiaoli said through the door.
I shouted at the top of my voice: " The door is open, come in. "
Xiaoli came in and saw me sitting on the bed playing poker on the computer. After Aguang left, there was no one to play cards with us anymore.
" Sister Xiaoli, please sit down. " I said crisply while getting off the bed.
Xiaoli grabbed my lower arm and said, " Come here, I want to tell you something. "
" What's wrong? " I was puzzled as she pulled me to the window away from the door.
" Sis, listen to me, " Xiaoli said eagerly, " Last time, I know you were unhappy. Although my brother is a good person, he is too old and not worthy of you. This time, Lao Wei has really found a suitable one for you. You must meet him. "
I was shocked: " Ah? " What is going on?
Xiaoli continued saying: " Little sis, don't you think about it? You are already 26 or 27 years old. You are out there alone. You even need others to help you move a sofa. How hard it is. Besides, you are a student now. What will you do when you finish school? You will have no identity. I am worried about you. You should be more realistic. Women should find a good support for themselves while they are young. "

I was extremely grateful for Xiaoli's heartfelt words, and I was deeply moved, but I just didn't know how to refuse her kindness: " Hey, hey ..."

Xiao Li said: " I know you are alone in a foreign country, without your parents, relatives or friends, and no one can make decisions for you. Let me tell you, listen to me. No matter whether you like this person or not, you should go out and meet him. At least you can make more friends and have more options, right? "

I had no choice but to say, " Yes. "

She was right. I didn't know how to refute her. I even lost the courage to refute her.

The meeting was thus decided.

Lao Wei hurriedly called someone, and then Xiaoli ran upstairs extremely excitedly and told me that they had agreed to meet at the Leicester subway station next to Chinatown at six o'clock tomorrow afternoon.

The next day, just like last time when they wanted to treat me to dinner, the old Wei couple came back from the market early after closing their stall. Then Xiaoli came upstairs and told me to hurry up and get dressed.

" Today is Saturday, and I'm afraid there will be traffic jams on the road, " Xiaoli said, " We should leave early so as not to be late. "

I nodded hurriedly and agreed: " Okay. Okay. " I hurriedly dressed up according to her instructions and put on high heels that I hadn't worn for a long time.

Seeing me start to move, Xiaoli hurried downstairs to prepare herself. She said, " Come down to meet us when you are done. We will set off in a quarter of an hour. "

I agreed and said, " Okay. Okay. " While combing my hair with the horn comb I brought from home.

Ten minutes later, I appeared at the door of the old Wei couple downstairs on time.

" Old Wei? Xiao Li? " I knocked on their room like a thief. Old Wei and his wife and I had been doing this in secret. I was afraid that other people in the building would know that I was going on a blind date and laugh at me. They were even more afraid that people would say that they were bored and did this.

But no matter what, I am still grateful for the kindness of Lao Wei and his wife. Although I later learned that they had twisted the whole thing around, it turned out that Lao Wei's friend couldn't find a girlfriend in the UK, and cried and begged Lao Wei to introduce him to one.

" How do you know him? " I asked the old captain on the bus to Leicester Square. " So he is more than ten years younger than you. "

Lao Wei said: " This is a long story. I met him many years ago when I was in Africa. "

" What? You've been to Africa? " The image of Lao Wei, a typical traditional henpecked man from Jiangsu and Zhejiang, was completely shattered in my mind. I never thought that Lao Wei had such an adventurous and legendary life.

Lao Wei smiled proudly, sitting on a rickety double-decker bus in London with me and his wife: " Yes, seven or eight years ago I was still in South Africa. "

" In South Africa? What for? " I was completely stunned.

" Gold panning, " the old captain said politely, " South Africa has gold and diamonds, you should know that, right? "

" I ... I know, " I stammered, even though I didn't learn geography very well in junior high school, " but how did you come up with the idea of running from a bankrupt factory in Jiangsu to South Africa? "

" To make money, " said the old Wei, in a tone that showed he had experienced many hardships, " to survive and develop. "

" You hadn't met Sister Xiaoli at that time, right? " I asked with a blink.

Xiaoli and Lao Wei both laughed.

Xiaoli said coquettishly: " I was still in China at that time, who knew him? "

I know that Lao Wei and Xiao Li were both married and divorced in China. They met and got married after going abroad.

" I met Xiaoli after I came to England, " said Lao Wei happily, and he did not forget to teach me: " So this is fate. We will meet each other after traveling thousands of miles. "

My face turned red, I lowered my head and stopped talking.

Seeing this, Xiao Li said happily: " Yes, yes, that's why it's fate. If Lao Wei hadn't stayed in South Africa for a few years, how would he have known Xiao Chen? If you didn't live upstairs from us, how would we have known you? "

I was so excited that I suddenly choked on my own saliva and started coughing violently on the bus without paying attention to everyone. I coughed so hard that I almost rolled my eyes while holding my chest.

The old Wei couple was anxious: " Don't worry, don't worry, we will arrive at the station soon. When we get to the station, we will go with Xiao Chen to find you some water to drink. "

I struggled to utter a few words in between violent coughing: " No ... cough, cough, cough ... use it. "

Xiaoli ran up behind me and started slapping my back violently.

I coughed even more.

* * *

After getting off the car, I was still coughing like crazy, but I felt much better now and could finally breathe.

The old Wei couple were watching me nervously and looking around, when a tall and thin young man appeared.

" Brother Wei, Sister Wei, you are here. "

" Oh, it's Xiao Chen, hurry up and find some water for this little girl, " Old Wei grabbed Xiao Chen as if he had found a treasure, " She suddenly lost her breath while talking and choked. "

I thought that if he didn't explain, people might think I had tuberculosis.

But I didn't even bother to greet him, I was still coughing awkwardly. I held Xiaoli and my chest hurt from coughing.

Seeing me like this, Xiao Chen also got anxious: " Don't worry, let's go find a cafe. "

When I heard that, I grabbed Xiaoli's arm tightly like chicken claws and used all my strength to utter: " I ... cough, cough, I can't drink ... cough, cough, cough! Coffee ..." I bent my waist and struggled desperately.

After listening for a long time, Xiao Chen finally understood and said quickly: " It's okay, it's okay. If you can't drink coffee, go somewhere else. There is also a place to drink tea next door. "

Then the old Wei couple helped me into a tea restaurant run by the British, just like they were helping a patient.

Xiao Chen sat down and said to the waiter who came over without even looking at the menu: " Please bring this lady a glass of water as soon as possible. "

Fortunately, he could speak some English, so I didn't have to speak. I fell on Xiaoli's shoulder, covering my chest with one hand and my mouth with the other, rolling my eyes and coughing so hard that I couldn't breathe.

The water finally came. Give them a tip for that.

I took the cup from Xiaoli and drank it down without thinking, like a camel seeing water.

After drinking a glass of water, my throat felt better immediately.

I regained my composure in an instant and breathed a sigh of relief. I turned around and saw the three of them still looking at me in panic, and even I began to suspect that I was acting.

" It's okay, it's okay as long as you stop coughing. " The old lieutenant said with a sigh.

Xiao Chen immediately straightened his chest and pulled in his stomach, opened the menu and said naturally: " Come on, order anything you want. "

Mr. and Mrs. Wei suddenly realized at the same time that they had made a serious mistake: just now, because they were in a hurry to find me some water, they went into a tea restaurant closest to the subway station - there was nothing to eat here except cakes and snacks. And they had originally come to Chinatown to have dinner tonight.

Xiao Li looked at Lao Wei, and then she opened the menu and said angrily, " I want to try the cheesecake made by the foreigners. "

I was immediately in awe of her: she actually knew such a profound word as cheese.

Xiao Chen seemed to suddenly realize the couple's original plan and said, " No, let's have some drinks first and then go to Chinatown for dinner. I just got off work and haven't eaten yet. "

The old Wei couple were very happy when they heard this. I was impressed and couldn't help but look at this young Chen with a new eye: Don't underestimate this young man, if he becomes a public relations manager, he will definitely be able to get along with everyone and thrive.

Lao Wei suddenly remembered something and said impatiently: " Why don't we go to the restaurant and have some drinks? It's so expensive to order drinks here, we might as well go to a Chinese restaurant and order a pot of tea. " It sounded like he wanted to save money for Xiao Chen.

Xiao Chen thought for a moment and said, " No, no, we've already come in, and they even brought water to the little girl, so we have to buy something before we leave. "

After hearing what he said, Mr. and Mrs. Wei let it go.

Xiaoli then happily ordered a large cup of ice cream coffee. A round ball of vanilla ice cream was stuck with a delicate little flower umbrella, and a thin half-slice of lemon was embedded on the edge of the goblet. When Xiaoli saw the drink she ordered was served, she was as happy as a three-year-old child, clapping her hands and laughing, " Oh, it turns out that the foreigners make drinks so beautiful! "

I asked for a cup of English milk tea, saying that I had been coughing for a long time and couldn't drink anything cold. Xiao Chen looked at me and said, "Okay, drink some milk tea to moisten your lungs."

When Old Wei saw us singing the same tune, and his wife enjoying such delicious ice cream, he smiled so much that his brown face blossomed, his nose and glasses wrinkled together like a yawning cat.

I drank my tea in silence. I had stopped coughing.

Xiao Li ate the ice cream and began to exercise her responsibilities and obligations with satisfaction: " Xiao Chen works at the Chinese supermarket next door as their delivery driver. Because he has a driver's license and can speak English, his boss immediately gave him a work permit. Hey, you see, he is so lucky. If Lao Wei had half of his ability, I wouldn't have to live such a hard life. "

Old Wei laughed and showed his good side again: " That's right, Xiaoli has suffered a lot with me these years. If she had a better vision and found a man like Xiaochen who is capable, has a formal job and British citizenship to marry, she would definitely be living a much better life than now. "

Xiaoli looked at him with a blush on her face, and the two of them seemed to have returned to the state of their first love: " So, you are a person with a conscience. "

The old lieutenant laughed and stopped drinking his orange juice.

I lowered my head and said nothing.

Xiao Chen glanced at me, then smiled and interrupted the old Wei couple, saying, " You two are an old married couple, and you are still making fun of me here. "

Good job, Xiao Chen, he resolved the situation with just one sentence.

Now I know I have to speak up, or I will be sorry for the efforts of Mr. and Mrs. Wei. I looked up, looked at Xiao Chen who was sitting opposite me and said calmly: " How many years have you been in the UK? "

The old Wei couple immediately breathed a sigh of relief.

Xiao Chen smiled and said, " Three years. I have one and a half years left on my work permit before I can apply for a British passport. "

" Look, look, " the old lieutenant said, patting the coffee table, " how capable this young man is. "

I was really fed up with their double act, but because Xiao Chen invited me to tea and almost saved my life, I had to let them continue the show.

" What time is it now? " I asked casually.

Xiao Chen took off the phone on his waist and looked at it: " Seven thirty, - How about it, have you all finished drinking? Otherwise, let's go eat first. "

" Drink, drink. " Old Wei and his wife nodded in unison.

* * *

I followed the old Wei couple and Xiao Chen on the pedestrian street in Chinatown. When passing by Leicester Square, a ragged beggar was sitting outside the huge cinema with bright lights. In front of him was a small broken bowl with a few cents. Xiao Chen walked over, took out a one-dollar coin from his trouser pocket, and threw it into the bowl of the British tramp.

I glanced at him for the affectation.

" Every time I see them, I give them some money, " Xiao Chen said to me casually, " It's not easy for them either. They are really pitiful. "

131

I thought to myself, we are even more pitiful than them. After all, they are still British. They don't do any work all day but still receive government welfare and relief. Why are we still pretending to be poor and generous?

But of course I wouldn't say that out loud.

But I can't be too enthusiastic towards him. Otherwise, he will misunderstand me. It's hard to strike the right balance between being too cold and too warm.

That's why I get a headache whenever I mention blind dates. To be honest, I did this to satisfy the wish of the old Wei couple to have a meal: although I know Xiaoli's brother was innocent last time, I somehow feel like I owe them a favor. So even though they told me it was a blind date, I still came anyway. In fact, it's nothing, it's just a meeting. If I really said that I didn't even meet, Xiao Chen would probably be even more sad.

Thinking this way, I felt that I was really hypocritical. But in my behavior, I couldn't help but continue to play the role of the woman in this blind date game. If it were up to me, I would rather go home and cook a pack of instant noodles.

But now that things have come to this point, I am in a dilemma.

* * *

We entered a Chinese restaurant in the middle of the road in Chinatown. Xiao Chen told me with some pride but pretending to be casual that he worked in the Chinese supermarket across the street. Every morning from 6 am to 12 pm. Overtime is also paid extra. Lao Wei glanced at the supermarket across the street, which was still operating in full swing, and then looked at him with envy, saying nothing. Indeed, this is much better than them

132

selling pirated CDs in the open-air market all day long with fear and trepidation. It is simply a world of difference.

Because it was the weekend, all the restaurants in Chinatown were packed with people, as if eating was free. We lined up downstairs for half a day, and finally waited until someone finished eating and a palm-sized table was vacated.

" Is it you four? Come on, hurry upstairs! " A manager-like man greeted us in front of the long line at the door, looking very impatient. It seemed like he was treating us to a meal.

At his urging, we went upstairs in a dusty state, walked around among the crowded tables and people, and finally found a seat in the corner and sat down.

" What do you want to eat? " The waiter threw a menu over like a flying saucer, and it landed exactly in the middle of the table. Seeing his superb skills, I suddenly wondered if A-Qi was working here.

Thinking of this, I couldn't help but take a second look at the waiter standing there waiting to take the names of the dishes. He was certainly not A-Qi.

" Hurry up, hurry up, " the waiter impatiently flicked the pen in his hand, " If you haven't made up your mind yet, I'll come back later. "

" You guys order. I'm not very hungry. Just a small meal will be fine, " I said.

Xiao Chen looked at me, then at the old Wei couple, and said to them: " Then you can order what you like. I don't mind eating anything either. "

The old Wei couple excitedly picked up the only menu on the table and began to study it with great interest, just like studying a piece of music. Their heads were almost pressed together, head to head.

It's rare that this couple loves each other so much. I think they are at least much better than Bro Qing and his wife.

While they were discussing the order, I finally had a little free time. I drank a sip of tea and turned my head to look out the window at the dim lights. The night was filled with people, and looking out the window on the second floor of the restaurant, the prosperous Chinatown was bustling with people, and the neon lights were flashing chaotically, a scene that seemed like the prosperous Tang Dynasty in ancient China.

" Am I in London? Am I in England? " This strange thought flashed through my mind in an instant.

" What are you looking at? " Xiao Chen next to me suddenly asked me. He could see that I was in a daze.

" Ah, nothing, " I said. My train of thought was interrupted. I turned my gaze away from the window and returned to the bustling and brightly lit restaurant: "... are the dishes ready? "

" It's almost done. " Xiaoli said, while continuing to study the complex, ancient and long-standing Chinese recipe with Lao Wei.

Snakehead Lao Zhu (1)

Lao Zhu was actually the first friend I met in this building, and he was also the one I was closest to. A-Guang, Xiaodi, and Chunsheng all knew me because of him, and it was because of the good relationship between Lao Zhu and me that they took extra care of me. Even when Lao Zhu was not around, it was the same. If there was anything delicious, they would come to me and ask me to bring them. If there was any good disc or new movie, they would be the first to come and ask me to watch it, as if they treated me as a member of their family. One time, I suddenly remembered that I wanted to watch an old Hollywood movie that was released eight hundred years ago, and asked them if they had it. Of course, they didn't have such an old movie. I forgot about it as soon as I said it, but a week later, Chunsheng got the Chinese subtitled version of that movie from somewhere, and handed it to me without any expression, saying:

" Old Zhu asked me to give it to you. "

135

I was so grateful that I quickly put it away like a treasure. That night, as soon as Lao Zhu came back from outside, I ran to his room and said a lot of words of gratitude to him in front of everyone.

" What are you doing here so late? " Old Zhu yelled at me with a fierce look on his face, " Go back to sleep! "

It was already one or two in the middle of the night, but I knew they always went to bed at two or three in the morning and slept until noon the next day.

" Why are you so mean to me? " I cried aggrievedly, " I'm just waiting for you to come back and say thank you. "

" Thank you, thank you, thank you for nothing! I need you to say thank you to me? Go back to bed quickly! I've been outside all day and you little girl come to bother me when I come back. Are you afraid that I won't be annoyed to death by you? " Lao Zhu said viciously, while taking off his T-shirt in front of me, patting his round belly, sitting on the bed against the wall, with his legs raised on the cabinet beside the bed, fanning himself with a cattail leaf fan, finally making himself comfortable and breathing a sigh of relief.

Chunsheng was playing computer solitaire on the sofa at the side, with a half-burned cigarette on the ashtray next to him, still smoking slowly. When he heard what Lao Zhu was scolding me, he couldn't help but pursed his lips slightly, wanting to laugh but not wanting to.

Xiao D was so sleepy that he fell asleep two hours ago. Once he was asleep, not even a thunder could wake him up.

" Forget about my thanks, " I muttered, " Who do you think would want to say thank you? Humph, I'll return the disc to you tomorrow after I finish watching it. "

In fact, I knew that they would not be able to use the disc even if I returned it to them, as it was originally given to me by Lao Zhu from somewhere, but I was just being angry at the time and had to say that on purpose to piss him off. Who knew that he would not answer me after hearing that, but just fanned himself with a palm-leaf fan and closed his eyes to rest.

I was so angry that I turned around and left, went back to my room and closed the door, thinking to myself: I will never pay any attention to this stupid pig again.

* * *

To be precise, although Lao Zhu's surname is Zhu, he is not a pig head, but a snake head. However, he also holds several positions at the same time. He is the largest Chinese pirated wholesaler in London's " Chinatown " area, and the iron brother of some underworld boss. Once, the landlord Zhang Lai angered the Fuqing Gang, one of the largest underworld gangs in the UK. They threatened to take one of his legs within three days. Zhang Lai was scared and finally asked Lao Zhu to come forward to help him settle the matter. So when it comes to seniority in the underworld, Lao Zhu can't be considered big, but he is not small either.

Old Zhu seemed to do everything, yet he seemed to do nothing. Sometimes I saw him lying in the room all day, basking in the sun with his belly bare, fanning himself with a palm-leaf fan, with the stereo playing sad popular songs from Hong Kong and Taiwan, and he would lie there all day. Sometimes I didn't see him for days in a row. Only Xiao D and Chunsheng were left in the room, depressed, dependent on each other, waiting foolishly

137

for the boss to show up. Sometimes I wanted to wait for Old Zhu to come back to play cards, but he didn't come back after waiting for a few days. I got impatient and grabbed Chunsheng's phone to call him. Chunsheng saw me dialing Old Zhu's number and didn't stop me. He just said coldly:

" It's no use fighting you. "

What he said was right. Lao Zhu's phone was either busy or turned off. Anyway, I have never been able to get through to him since I met him. Or even if I got through, no one answered. I had to give up.

The business that Lao Zhu does in the UK is really varied. As long as it is Chinese business, there is nothing he cannot do. However, after being with Lao Zhu for so long, I guess there is only one business he does not do, which is white powder. Unlike A-Qing downstairs, although he occasionally uses a little, I have never seen him and his men do business with anyone in this area.

Lao Zhu and his friends all treat me as their best friend and never hide anything from me. Even when they go to SOHO to look for girls, they will come back and proudly tell me which country's girls have big butts and which country's girls have small breasts. If they go out not to look for girls but just to have fun, whenever they have such group activities, they will definitely call me to " go with you, go with you! " From my personal feeling, I don't know why, although Chunsheng is the most handsome among them, and Lao Zhu is the ugliest, he really looks like a pig, with small eyes, fat face, bald head and thick mouth, but I always like to talk to Lao Zhu the most, and I feel most comfortable with him. As long as Lao Zhu is at home, I like to run over to their place to tease Lao Zhu and chat with me no matter what. Sometimes Lao Zhu is happy and says a few words to me, and when he is unhappy, he ignores me, and he will not get angry no matter how I tease him. I often clap my hands and laugh: " Haha, Lao Zhu is the most fun! "

He was leaning on the bed with his eyes closed, resting. When he heard what I said, he opened half of his eye to look at me, laughed from the bottom of his heart, and then closed his eye again.

Since Lao Zhu found out that I can speak English, he often asked me to do something for him and give me some small favors. For example, he would find me a disc, treat me to a meal, ask Xiao D to bring me a hot barbecued pork bun, or buy me some chestnuts (candied chestnuts are also available in the UK, but there are few places to buy them and it is not easy to find them), which made me feel like a monkey. Fortunately, the things that Lao Zhu asked me to help were very simple, such as calling an English-speaking foreigner to ask him when it would be convenient to meet, or helping him call the Royal Mail Company in the UK to ask when a package someone in China sent to him would be delivered, or helping him read a notice or letter written in English, and so on. I guess doing these small favors is not against the law and it is fun to help others. Lao Zhu is a very loyal person. You can't see anything at ordinary times, but when it comes to the key, you will feel that he is really good to you, and even if you do a small thing for him, he will definitely return it, so I am always willing to help him with these things sincerely.

Later, Lao Zhu gradually discovered that I not only spoke English, but also had the talent to be a human smuggler. From then on, he began to have evil ideas about me, always trying to trick me onto a pirate ship and ask me to help him smuggle someone across the border, promising a generous reward.

One day I went to Lao Zhu's place to play. Lao Zhu was talking to someone on the phone. He was speaking in Fujian dialect, and I couldn't understand a word of it. I didn't know where Chunsheng had gone. Xiao D was squatting on the ground, putting the packaging covers of pirated CDs together. Pirated CDs and black plastic boxes were piled up next to him.

Lao Zhu was talking loudly on his mobile phone by the window, as if he was bargaining with someone. After talking for a long time, he sighed impatiently and said, "Okay, okay, let's do it." I understood the last sentence because he hung up the phone after saying it.

Then Lao Zhu stood in front of the window for a while, then suddenly turned around and said to me:

" Little sis, do you want to make some money? "

" Make money? " I was so excited that my eyes turned green. Why not take advantage of such a good opportunity? " Sure, sure! " I said happily, " What do you want me to do? "

Lao Zhu thought for a moment and said with a smile: " It's actually quite simple to explain. Do you have your passport here? "

I said, " In my room. "

Lao Zhu said: " Go and bring it to me. "

I went there obediently and showed him my passport. Xiao D was silently putting the cover of the box on the side, as if he didn't hear anything.

Lao Zhu opened my passport and took a look. It said that it was a student visa and it would expire in nine months.

Lao Zhu returned my passport to me and said, " Well, I'll buy you a plane ticket for tomorrow, and you can go to Malaysia for free. After everything is done, I'll give you another 3,000 yuan, not RMB, but British pounds. "

" Ah? " I was so surprised that my eyes popped out of my head. How could there be such a good job in the world? " Okay, okay! " I said, " What do you want me to do? "

Lao Zhu said: " Sis, listen carefully: you take the flight to Malaysia at 2 o'clock tomorrow afternoon, and don't go through customs. There will be someone to pick you up at the airport. I will tell you where to meet him then ..."

I listened to his explanation as nervously and excitedly as if I were watching an exciting police and gangster movie, nodding my head like a chicken pecking at rice: " Okay, okay, okay, what next? "

" After you meet that person, he won't talk to you, but will put something in your backpack. Don't open it or look at it. Go to the restroom in the airport right away. ..."

I thought to myself, this is easy. " What next? " I asked.

" Then you go into the toilet, lock the little door, take off your pants and go to the toilet. You must really poop, even if you can't poop. After you're done, take out the thing that person stuffed in your backpack. Don't open it or look at it. Then throw it into the toilet along with the toilet paper you used to wipe your butt, and then flush it away. That's it. "

" This is even easier, " I said. " It's just going to the toilet. Anyone can do it. No problem! "

" After you rinse, check again to make sure everything is clean. If it's not clean, rinse again. "

I thought to myself, my god, when did this old Zhu become so nagging? He has to talk for so long just to go to the toilet?

" What happens next? " I was still looking forward to a more exciting and thrilling plot. " Where do I go after using the toilet? Is there anyone else I want to contact? What is the code for contacting? "

" No, just go through customs normally after using the toilet, and then use the money I give you to have fun in Malaysia for a few days. When you've had enough fun, just buy a ticket to come back on any day, and that's it. " Lao Zhu said.

" Ah? " I was immediately disappointed, "——Is that the end? "

" Ah, I told you that what you are going to do is very simple. " Lao Zhu said, " But don't underestimate these simple things. If any mistake is made in the middle, it will be all over. "

I suddenly felt an inexplicable fear in my heart. At this moment, I suddenly truly experienced the " thrilling " feeling in the movie plot.

" What will happen when it's over? " I asked timidly.

Lao Zhu looked at me and suddenly said with determination: " No. You little girl, you still can't do such a thing. I can't find you, I have to find someone else. "

I suddenly cried out in despair: " Old Zhu, you just said I was fine! "

Lao Zhu shook his head and dialed the mobile phone. Before the call was connected, he said to me: " No, no, you have no experience. I still don't trust you with such a big thing. "

" Oh my god, it's just a toilet, isn't it? " I cried out in grievance, " You don't even trust me to go to Malaysia to use the toilet? Ah? You damned old Zhu, I will never talk to you again! "

Before I could finish, Lao Zhu had already walked to the window and started speaking Fujian dialect to the person on the other end of the phone. I immediately stood there like a fool again.

I looked angrily at Xiao D who was sitting on the ground:

" Xiao D, do you think your sister is okay or not? "

Xiao D raised his head, looked at me with a strange smile, and said: " Sister, do you want to hear the truth or a lie? "

" Nonsense! " I cursed.

Xiao D laughed and said, " Isn't it easy to listen to nonsense? Go to the street and find an old man or old woman, I guarantee you will listen to it all day long. "

Now even Xiao D dares to make fun of me like this. I really don't want to live anymore.

I returned to my room. I wanted to hang myself but there was no rope. I wanted to commit suicide but there were no pills. I wanted to slit my wrists but there was no blade. I wanted to jump out of the building but the hole in the window was not big enough. Finally, I thought, it turns out that dying is so difficult.

There was no way out. The three thousand pounds were gone, the two-way flight to Malaysia was gone, and the exotic tropical travel adventure was gone. All gone in an instant. From then on, I hated Lao Zhu.

* * *

" Lao Zhu, old pig,
 A lazy pig.
 Eat and then sleep.
 Worse than a pig! "

Ever since Lao Zhu offended me about the toilet trip to Malaysia during our threesome, I made up this song for him and sing it to him every day when he takes a nap after eating.

Lao Zhu was lying on his bed with his bare chest, leaning against the quilt, fanning himself with a big fan and closing his eyes, pretending not to hear.

Xiao D said: " Sister, do you want to eat fish balls? There are some in the pot downstairs. If you want to eat some, I will go and get you a bowl. "

I looked at him sideways in surprise and said, " Hey? Why did the sun rise from the west today? When did you learn to respect your sister? "

Xiao D laughed and said, " I have always been very filial to my elder sister, but she has always looked down on me and has not noticed my sincerity. "

My teeth were almost broken by his words: " Oh my god, you should stop using those corny words. You should use your flattery skills in a proper way, like fanning this old pig and spanking him. "

Lao Zhu suddenly laughed out of his sleep and said, " He gave you fish balls just to shut you up. Gossip girl, go back to your room. Old Zhu, I'm full and I'm going to sleep. "

" I won't let you sleep. I won't let you sleep! Unless you let me go to Malaysia! " I said hatefully.

Lao Zhu suddenly opened his eyes, sat up suddenly, and yelled at me fiercely: " Go back now! If you don't leave, I will rape and kill you, little girl! "

I was so frightened by him that I ran away like a mouse seeing a cat.

* * *

" Sister, brother Zhu is calling you. " Xiao D came over and said excitedly, smiling at me all the time.

I was playing on the computer and didn't even look at him: " Why do you think of me again? "

" How would I know about you and big brother? " Xiao D said something that immediately became ambiguous. He laughed and said, " Maybe big brother missed you. - You don't know, he has been talking about you all morning today. "

I went there with great joy in my heart.

" Please help me call the foreigners. " Lao Zhu said as soon as he saw me.

I turned around and glared at Xiao D: " Is this what he's been talking about all morning? "

Xiao D smiled and said, " How would I know what you want, big brother? "

I sat down, took the phone from Lao Zhu, and said, " Go ahead, what do you want me to say to them? "

Lao Zhu said: " Ask him how much his film costs? "

I asked, and a British man who was almost inaudible what he was saying shouted for a long time before telling me the price.

I told Lao Zhu: " He said two pounds and a half. "

Lao Zhu grinned: " Why is it so expensive? "

Xiao D explained to me flatteringly: " Our films are only sold for two pounds and three cents. "

I don't care: " Then how should I tell him? "

Old Zhu walked around the room, thought for a moment and said, " Ask him if he'll sell it for £1.80. If he says the price is good, I'll buy more, five thousand at a time. "

I told the Englishman what Lao Zhu said. Before I finished speaking, the Englishman suddenly said, " Wait, wait! "

I held the phone and waited, confused, but still listening.

Then I heard the man enter some place and mutter something to himself, and then after a while, a loud urination sound came from the phone. I frowned and was about to put the phone away when the man's voice on the phone rang again, accompanied by a huge flushing sound of a toilet (I imagined the water in the toilet was swirling):

" What? He didn't drink? One pound eight? "

" Yes, yes, " I said quickly, " listen to me, what he means is that if you give him a good price, he will buy 5,000 tickets from you every time. "

" Oh. " The English man walked out of the toilet and said, " How about this, five thousand, and the minimum is two pounds and three cents. "

I told Lao Zhu, and Lao Zhu waved his hand and said, " Hang up. "

I said goodbye politely to the British man and hung up the phone.

" I didn't expect them to be more corrupt than us. " Old Zhu laughed and said, " It seems that in the future we can not only do business with the Chinese, but also with the British. "

I know he was talking about selling pirated CDs wholesale to British vendors. But I never thought that there were people in the UK doing this. I always thought that only Chinese people did pirated CDs.

" Where do you get your movies from? I think your discs are better than the genuine ones sold outside? " I have always been puzzled. How can these people who sneaked in from the rural areas of Fujian get absolutely authentic original movie discs earlier than the major cinemas in the UK? Because they live next door to me, I borrow discs from them every day and know that their discs are of very good quality, and there is no difference at all from the genuine ones. In some aspects, they are even better than the genuine ones, such as the optional Chinese subtitles. And let alone the Hollywood blockbusters in the United States, even the domestic blockbusters have not been released in the cinema yet, but I have already watched them in this room on the second floor of the " Chinatown " in the UK . Their business is global.

" What do you know? If we sell it later than the movie theaters, who will buy it? " Lao Zhu told me about their business philosophy. " It's not that we sell it cheaply, it's the one-week time difference. Once the movie theaters release it, no matter how cheap you sell it, fewer people will buy it. "

" But how did you get the original master tape so quickly? " I didn't understand.

Old Zhu waved his hands impatiently: " It costs money! What can't be done with money? Just make a phone call and it will be airlifted directly from the United States. "

I can't help but deeply admire their strict and scientific piracy operation system.

" Haha, you guys are awesome. I've seen a movie called 'Traffic'. When I have time, I will definitely write a movie called 'Traffic'. " I said with a laugh.

Old Zhu looked at me strangely; he knew I was talking nonsense again.

" Anything else? " I wanted to leave.

Lao Zhu thought for a moment and said, " Do you have anything to do tonight? "

I said, " No. "

He said, " Then come hang out with us. I'm going to have some friends over later in the evening. "

I immediately became excited and my eyes lit up: " Great, great! What time is it? "

Lao Zhu said: " Ten or eleven o'clock, I'll ask Xiao D to call you in the evening. "

Snakehead Lao Zhu (2)

In the evening, several of Lao Zhu's friends drove over, had dinner at his house, and chatted for a while. After discussing business, Lao Zhu began to arrange for everyone to go out and have fun .

" Let's go, let's go! " Xiao D ran over to call me hurriedly.

I hurriedly put on my high heels, grabbed a coat and ran out after them, afraid that I would be late and miss them and they would drive away on their own.

My friends drove two cars. Lao Zhu, Chunsheng and I sat in one, and Xiao D and a few others sat in the other.

" Boss, where are we going? " The friend who was driving asked Lao Zhu while steering the car with a cigarette in his mouth.

" Let's go to the disco run by the foreigners near Chinatown! I know the security guard there and we can go in without a ticket. " said Lao Zhu.

Everyone is happy.

I thought to myself, Lao Zhu is really very powerful. How come he even recognizes the British security guards? How can he speak (British) to them (the British)?

When we arrived at Chinatown, it was Friday night and the entire Soho Street was packed with people. We couldn't find a place to park. We drove two cars in a row around Chinatown for several rounds.

" What should I do, boss? All the parking spaces are fucking full. "

Lao Zhu thought for a moment and said, " Then let's go to Afeng's restaurant. I'll ask him to make room for two tables. "

The two cars drove to a Chinese restaurant on the edge of Chinatown. Lao Zhu got out of the car and went in for three to five minutes. He came back and got into the car and waved his hand and said, " Let's go. I've already told A Feng. Let's go around to their backyard from this path. "

The car finally stopped in the restaurant owner's private backyard, and it was free. Old Zhu showed off his skills again.

" Let's go, the dance hall is right next to the subway station. " Old Zhu gave an order, and everyone got out of the car. A group of people marched through Leicester Square, just like a gang of hooligans.

I was the only woman in the team. I was very proud of this and walked among them with my head held high. Perhaps because of my special status in the team, those fellows who didn't know I was Lao Zhu's neighbor didn't dare to confirm my identity with Lao Zhu when they saw me. They all respectfully called me " Mrs. Zhu " .

" Haha! " I thought proudly, " I'm going to be ' Mrs. Zhu ' too ! "

Although he was pleased with himself, he warned them solemnly:

" Who is Mrs. Zhu? I'm his little sister! "

" Haha, haha. " They just laughed, obviously not believing it but not saying it out.

I was very depressed about this. I thought, starving to death is a minor matter, but losing one's chastity is a major one. It's a pity that my good reputation has been ruined just like this, and a beautiful flower has been stuck on an " old pig " !

The more I thought about it, the sadder I became. I had no choice but to scold Lao Zhu: " Hey! Did you hear what they were calling me? Where are your pig ears? Tell them to stop calling me that! Who wants to be called ' Mrs. Zhu ' and smell pig odor? "

All his brothers laughed out loud. Lao Zhu also laughed, but he didn't say anything about them or me, he just laughed there.

When we got to the nightclub that Lao Zhu mentioned, Lao Zhu walked over and patted the foreigner who looked like the security guard or admission manager, and said with a smile: "Ten ! How much ? "

Ha, I didn't expect he could speak a few words of English.

The fat and short foreigner took a look at our group of lumpen proletarians and said to Lao Zhu with a smile: " Are these all your people? Ten of them? All right, all right, go in! "

My god, the tickets here should be at least ten or fifteen pounds (on weekends), but Lao Zhu just said a word, and this Englishman let us all in for free! I stared at him with wide eyes, he could even deal with the English, I thought he was a miracle.

" Come in, come in! " Lao Zhu waved his hand and said to our group.

A group of people filed in. I followed Lao Zhu and was the last one to go in. I saw Lao Zhu quietly put two banknotes into the foreigner's hand before entering. It was too dark, so I couldn't see clearly whether it was ten pounds or twenty pounds.

So the British can also be bribed? Old Zhu really broadened my horizons.

It was almost ten o'clock when we entered. This disco is different from other discotheques. Other discotheques in London are usually open until twelve or two at the latest, but this one is open all night, until five in the morning. So this is when there are many people, and everyone is just starting to have fun. As soon as I entered, Lao Zhu asked someone to buy drinks for everyone, beer by the bucket. Lao Zhu asked me what I wanted to drink. I thought about it and said:

" Orangeade. "

Actually, it's just orange juice. But I don't know why, when I'm with them, my way of speaking changes, as if I would feel awkward if I say " orange juice " instead of " orange water " .

The boy bought me a glass of orange juice with ice and asked me for a straw. I drank it with great interest, watching the people dancing on the dance floor to the beat of the dance music.

All the people dancing here are foreigners. Just by looking at them, I can't tell whether they are British, European, or descendants of British colonists from British colonies. Anyway, they are just a bunch of foreigners with high noses and cat eyes. We are the only group of Chinese in such a big disco.

" Let's go dance? " Xiao D asked me with a smile. So far, no one in our group has dared to go down and dance.

I understood that Xiao D wanted me to start this: " Okay, okay, now that we are here, what's the point of just sitting here? Lao Zhu, come on, let's go dance together. "

Lao Zhu didn't go, but the other brothers went down together at our invitation. We gathered at an area on the edge of the dance floor to dance.

" Wow, little sister, you dance very well. " One of Lao Zhu's friends no longer called me " Mrs. Zhu " but called me sister.

I smiled triumphantly amid the blaring music. I was the worst dancer in Beijing's top nightclubs, but here, with so few Chinese people around, I became the dancing queen that everyone was paying attention to. Haha, I laughed out loud with joy.

Keep dancing.

We danced for a while, sweating profusely, and when we returned to the table to rest, we found that everyone at the table was gone, and only Chunsheng was left there, drinking alone.

" Where are they? " I shouted to Chunsheng over the music, " Where have they all gone? "

Chunsheng was already a little drunk. He raised his head and glanced at me lazily, then looked under the table.

Oh my God, there were already two or three people sitting under the table, on the floor of the ballroom, or leaning against the wall, and they were just shaking their heads with their eyes closed, not knowing anything.

I know they all took the medicine, but we were all dancing down there, so we didn't know when they took it.

Old Zhu has disappeared.

I also noticed this, and he followed my gaze to look for him, and soon found that he was standing next to the bar counter with the young boy who had driven us, holding a bottle of wine. The two seemed to be talking loudly (it had to be loud, otherwise you couldn't hear the loud music).

I knew they were talking about business, so I ignored him, drank some orange juice, took a break, and continued dancing with them.

The DJ was also dancing wildly to the music, occasionally holding the microphone and shouting:

" Come on everybody, it's time to go higher! "

Then came the crazy spinning electronic dance music, which sounded like a metal gear in a factory that was put out of place, twisting with a steel bar and spinning wildly at a high speed.

We are like the misplaced gear, spinning madly in the dance music.

" Oh yeah... oh yeah... oh oh yeah..." said the voice in the dance music.

In the darkness that was changing at the same speed, with the colorful lights of the dance music, I was almost exhausted from dancing. Or maybe I was tired.

" Oh yeah ... Oh yeah! " I heard a voice in my heart say.

* * *

" Let's go, " Lao Zhu returned to the neon-lit streets of London's SOHO at midnight and waved to the brothers walking behind him, " Awei is already waiting in the car. "

I got into the car with them in a daze. I was completely exhausted.

" Old Zhu, where are we going? " When I came to my senses a little and found that the road outside the car window was not our way home, I couldn't help but ask suspiciously.

Old Zhu, sitting in the front row, laughed and said, " It's still early (it was three in the morning at that time). If we go back, we'll disturb their sleep (he was referring to the other tenants in our building). Let's go sit at Awei's place first and go back after daybreak. "

I didn't know what they were going to do at that time, but I felt relieved after hearing what he said.

The car traveled through the city of London for most of the night and finally drove into a typical wealthy area on the hillside at four in the morning.

As our car slowly drove into the community street, I saw Mercedes-Benz and Ferrari parked outside the doors of the houses next door.

" Awei, you are so rich. Why do you live here? " I said ignorantly.

Ah Wei smiled at ease: " What, little sister? I don't have any money. This is all from my big brother. You will know when you see him later. "

Old Zhu suddenly remembered something, turned around and told me with a bit of worry: " Awei's elder brother is a very good person, but when you go there later, you won't understand our business, so don't talk too much. "

When Ah Wei heard this, he immediately changed his tone and said with a smile: " Mrs. Zhu is such a smart girl, there's no need for you to remind her. I think she understands everything better than you do. "

He was wrong. I really didn't understand anything now. I was so sleepy that I just wanted to find a place to fall asleep, even if it was on the floor.

At first I was wondering why Lao Zhu suddenly became so kind. Just to avoid waking up the people in the building, he brought his brothers to such a far place in the middle of the night, and even went to someone's home, just to wait until dawn to go home?

It was not until I arrived at Awei's or his elder brother's house that I realized what he wanted for this.

" Not bad, not bad, " Lao Zhu said hurriedly, sniffing, " I know your place is just right. "

The eldest brother of Awei, whose name I don't know, said: " Don't you see where I got my stuff from ? I'm not bragging, but you can't find such pure stuff even in the whole of London. "

I know they are talking about drugs. Although Lao Zhu is not in this business, he occasionally goes to the house of a big brother who is in this business to satisfy his addiction.

As the eldest brother spoke, he lazily sat up from the soft chair he was lying on, picked up the straw on the glass, tapped it twice, and inhaled it from beginning to end in one breath along a white line that had been drawn.

Lao Zhu laughed and said, " Boss, I think you should be more careful. You use so much . "

The elder brother lazily lay back down. He looked very kind and amiable, wearing a snow-white shirt, beige trousers, and his face was white and clean. He was a veteran elder brother who had already achieved a high level of success. If you didn't know his background, people who met him would think he was a kind-hearted man, and would never have thought that he was the famous Chinese drug lord in London.

" Well, I don't have much time to live anyway, so why not live happily while I'm still alive? " he said, still lazily lying on the soft chair.

Then they all fell silent.

I was watching blankly from the side, and when I saw that they were getting excited, there was nothing else to see, so I ran to the kitchen to cook noodles.

" I'm hungry. " I said to Awei who met me in the corridor.

" The kitchen is over here, " Ah Wei immediately took care of me enthusiastically and took me to the kitchen at the back. " Here, what do you want to eat? There are instant noodles here, there is a cabbage there, and there are a few eggs in the refrigerator. "

Before I could say anything, he had already arranged everything I wanted to eat: egg instant noodles with boiled cabbage.

I followed his instructions and worked in the kitchen for most of the day. I was so busy that I didn't feel sleepy anymore.

At five in the morning, I walked out with the cooked noodles and returned to my eldest brother's living room to have breakfast.

The living room was filled with smoke, as if someone had just set off a smoke bomb. Everyone was motionless, and it was unclear whether they were comfortably asleep or lying on the sofa.

I sat at the table in the living room, trembling with fear, and finished my noodles while holding my breath. Then I quickly ran out with the bowl and went to the kitchen to wash it.

" How is it? Are you full? " A Wei came to the kitchen and asked me with a smile. He looked at me frantically washing the dishes and said, " Don't be afraid. Lao Zhu and the others are asleep in there. "

" Oh, " I said without looking up from washing the dishes, " I know. "

" I'll go and call them to take you home. " said Awei.

" No, no, no, " I said quickly, " let them sleep a little longer. "

Then I said, " Don't worry about me. I'll go out to the garden for a walk. "

" No, no, " Awei said, shaking his head. " There are dogs in the garden. If they see you, they will bite you and even bark. "

After thinking for a while, he said, " Why don't you go to my room? You can play video games there. "

I thought about it and there was no other way, so I said: " Well, it happens that I haven't played games for a long time. "

* * *

I played Super Mario in Awei's room for more than an hour, and finally around seven or eight in the morning I heard Awei calling me downstairs:

" Mrs. Zhu! Come down and leave! "

I hurriedly turned off the game and ran down the stairs in a panic.

Because there were only a few people from Lao Zhu's side going back, Awei drove a car to accommodate us.

This time, Lao Zhu let Xiao D sit in the front, and he, Chunsheng and I squeezed into the back.

Awei also didn't sleep all night, but he was still in great spirits and drove us home.

I was so sleepy that I couldn't even speak. My only dream was to go home and sleep. Because of this, I was determined not to hang out with Lao Zhu anymore. Even if it was a thrilling nightclub, a drug lord's lair, I couldn't stop sleeping. I was so sleepy that my eyelids kept fighting when I was playing games.

It was already nine in the morning when I got home. The birds were singing on the treetops, and the sun had already come out, smiling quietly behind the clouds. I didn't sleep all night.

A few days later, Xiao D came running to me excitedly again and called:

" Sister! Lao Zhu asked if you want to go out with us tonight? "

I turned over in bed and said, " Tell him I'm asleep. "

Sleeping is really the happiest thing in the world, ah..

Prostitute Abao (I)

At the age of seventeen, Abao was attending high school in a small city in the northeast. In her second year of high school, she met a boyfriend at school. The boy was a student at a technical school outside. He was hanging out with a bunch of people, drinking, and fighting. He had a bad reputation. Abao's parents were afraid that their daughter would learn bad things from him, so they discussed and decided to send her abroad to go to college.

Abao was not called Abao at that time. Her name was He Tingting, which means graceful and elegant. When she was born, family planning had been implemented for many years. The He family had only one daughter, and they loved her dearly. So her mother gave Tingting the nickname Abao.

When He Tingting was 17 years old, she was indeed a graceful lady, 1.68 meters tall, with a good figure, fat where it should be fat, thin where it should be thin. The aunties in the neighboring houses were envious and praised her, saying that your daughter can be a model in the future.

He Tingting didn't dare to think about being a model. She just thought about how to leave that damn school, and leave the terrible senior year and college entrance examination. So when her parents told her about studying abroad, she agreed without a second thought.

Her parents wanted to send her abroad, partly because they heard about her boyfriend who was not doing well, and partly because they were influenced by other rich people in the city who sent their children to study abroad. The town is not big or small, but there are many rich people. Nowadays, parents only have one child, who is the baby of the family. They want to spend all the money in the family on their children. Therefore, many parents have more spare money. They don't need to buy a house or a car. The house is already available, and the car is not used. It is more convenient to take a taxi to get around the city. In addition, with the encouragement of the newly emerging study abroad agencies, they are willing to send their children to study abroad, gild themselves, and get a foreign diploma. Not only will they have face in front of relatives and friends, but they can also find jobs in foreign companies. Moreover, it sounds good to say that they are from the United States or the United Kingdom.

It was during this wave of studying abroad that Tingting's parents spent all their savings to send their child to study abroad. Going to the United States requires English scores and visas are difficult to obtain, while studying in the UK does not require language skills and is easy to obtain. When you return, you can speak authentic British English, which is much better than Australia and New Zealand, so they decided to go to the UK.

Tingting's father runs an Internet cafe in a small town. As soon as the Internet became popular, Tingting's father saw the potential market because of his quick mind. He borrowed tens of thousands of yuan from his friends to open the first Internet cafe in the town. Unexpectedly, the business was so popular that the storefront doubled in half a year, and the original snack bar and bicycle repair shop next door were merged to open an Internet cafe. After two years, Tingting's father paid off his debts and had a net of 600,000 yuan left in his bank account.

The study abroad agency introduced the complete study abroad plan they designed for Tingting to Tingting and her parents in detail: Tingting is now in the second year of high school in China, and after going abroad, she can use the time in the third year of high school in China to study language for one year. If the language is not up to standard in one year, she will study for two years, staying among the British every day. After two years, even a fool can speak English. Besides, Tingting is so smart, maybe she can pass the language in one year? After studying language, she will have to study for one year of preparatory course. Tingting's academic performance in China is not very ideal. She is only in the middle of the class. She has a poor foundation. If she goes directly to undergraduate studies, she will definitely not be able to keep up with the progress of British students. Therefore, it is best to lay a solid foundation first and study for one year of preparatory courses that local British students also study. Moreover, the tuition fee of preparatory courses is half cheaper than that of undergraduate studies.

After successfully completing the foundation course, with a good educational background of graduating from a British foundation course, it will be much easier to apply for a prestigious British university. Of course, this also depends on

Tingting's grades at that time, but no matter what the grades are, it is still no problem for her to apply for an above-average university after completing the foundation course. If the grades are excellent, it is not difficult to apply for Oxford and Cambridge. Didn't someone's child in a small town get admitted to Cambridge University? Chinese students are famous all over the world for their hard work. As long as she is willing to work hard, she will definitely not be worse than others.

In this case, the next step is to study for three years of undergraduate studies, and after three years, you can get an undergraduate diploma from a British university. If you parents still want your child to continue studying, you can let her study for another year to get a master's degree. It takes at least three years to get a master's degree in China, but the good thing about the UK is that the study time is short and you can get a master's degree in one year. So in total, your child has graduated with a master's degree, while her classmates in China are still studying for an undergraduate or master's degree.

After all, the study abroad agency designed the plan professionally, and considered all aspects of the problem according to the child's situation. Tingting's parents nodded repeatedly, and Tingting's eyes lit up. Thinking that she was going to the UK soon, she would be an international student after all, which was much better than staying in this crappy place. The family made a decision immediately and did it.

The lady working at the agency kindly advised Tingting's parents: It's best to exchange all the tuition and living expenses for the child for several years at once. Otherwise, when she goes abroad in the future, firstly, it will be troublesome to exchange it for pounds, and secondly, the current exchange rate is low, and it will definitely rise in the future. Even if you don't give it to the child, it's better to take this opportunity to exchange the savings into foreign currency than to keep it in RMB. When the parents heard it, they thought that the other person had experience dealing with foreign currencies every day, and everything he said was right. Anyway, the family store is still making money every day, so why keep so much savings? The child needs money for studying abroad, so just exchange it all for her.

Tingting's father left 100,000 yuan for working capital, and exchanged the remaining 500,000 yuan for British pounds, which was about 40,000 pounds at the exchange rate at that time. The agent calculated and said that it was enough, and that this money was enough for your daughter's three-year tuition and living expenses in the UK. After three years, she will also go to college, and you can save money for her future college education in these three years.

My daughter is leaving, and as a mother I am so heartbroken. I almost cried when I was preparing clothes for her for all four seasons.

" Abao, there will be no one to take care of you outside, so you have to learn to take care of yourself. You are still growing, so you must eat well, sleep well, and don't be reluctant to spend money. If you run out of money, call your mother and I will find a way to send you more money. " said the mother.

" Okay, okay, have you said enough? I've heard you nag me a hundred times. " Tingting said, while thinking about which pairs of boots to bring. I heard that the weather in the UK is cold and gloomy, and it rains a lot in winter, so leather boots are a must-have luggage.

On the day of departure, Tingting's father asked Uncle Li, an official in the municipal government, to send his special car and full-time driver to take them to the airport. Carrying dozens of kilograms of luggage, Tingting's father decided to fly to Beijing with Tingting and took her to the plane from Beijing to London.

" Tingting, don't play around when you get there. Study hard and finish your studies early and come back. " Tingting's father finally advised his daughter.

" Dad, don't worry, go home and say hello to my mom. You should go back quickly, the plane will take off soon. " Tingting hugged her father for the last time and followed the chaotic crowd to the boarding gate.

The moment he walked out of Beijing International Airport, Tingting's father suddenly felt that he was old. It was a kind of ruthless old age that came from the bottom of his heart. He finally realized that his daughter had completely left him and her mother and was about to start a completely independent life. His daughter had grown up.

Haha, England! What a fresh and wonderful life that would be. Sitting on the plane about to fly to London, Tingting couldn't help but laugh out loud with excitement.

* * *

What the study abroad agent said was absolutely right. English teaching here is in the British style. All the teachers are British with standard accents. Classes are small, with only eight to ten students in each class. The language school where the classes are taught is located in downtown London. The dormitory provided by the school is also not far from the school.

Among the vast number of international students, Tingting is already quite lucky. She was not sent to a private language school in a remote village in Scotland far away from the town, where she learned authentic rural English with a small town accent. She also did not meet " British " teachers who were black or Indian . She did not find out that the language school she attended actually charged three to five times more than other language schools with the same conditions. She did not have to stay in a temporary hotel because she could not find a place to stay, spending a lot of extra money.

He Tingting did not encounter any of these problems. She is really a lucky girl.

Tingting had a very happy time in the first days of her arrival in the UK. It is said that children who have just arrived in the UK for the first year are likely to feel language barriers, unfamiliarity with life, and emotional loneliness, but Tingting did not encounter any of these problems. Because the school was introduced by the agent, the teachers and staff of the school were all British, but all the students in the class were Chinese, except for one boy from Nigeria. No one could understand what he said, including their English teacher, so no one talked to him.

After Tingting came here, she found out that the world is really big, but also really small. Many of her Chinese classmates came from the same city as her. The others were also from the north, either the sons of the vice governor or the daughters of the bosses of state-owned enterprises. Now the leaders are all young, so the kids who are studying abroad are also young. Because everyone speaks Chinese, Tingting quickly got to know them. They soon became good friends who could talk about anything. After class, they would go out to play together - they went racing together: the governor's son bought a top-of-the-line Ferrari two-seater convertible sports car in the first week after coming to the UK, and other students who could drive followed suit, fearing that they would be outdone. Anyway, cars here are dirt cheap. I heard that some people from other classes think they are " too " cheap and buy two at once. We go to a Chinese restaurant in Chinatown to eat together. We order a big table of dishes just like in China. A meal costing hundreds of pounds is no big deal. We eat half and leave the other half. We never pack up. " Don't embarrass yourself. I never pack up food in China. Why would I pack up here? Let's go . " Drive to a coastal city for a self-guided tour on weekends: " Driving in London is so awkward, there are so many traffic lights! It's faster to drive on the highway. Why drive if you don't race? " Go to bars and nightclubs in SOHO to dance: " Damn, why is London so old-fashioned? Why do even the discotheques look like antiques from the 1930s? " The music is not as exciting as in China, but the foreign wine here is not bad, and there are many beautiful foreign girls, so just make do with it; go to watch a live Premier League game together: " How much is a ticket? It's not even enough for my dad to open a bottle of foreign wine in China! " Go shopping at the most expensive brand store on Old Bond Street: If she takes a Hermes , you will feel embarrassed to take a LV ... Anyway, they have plenty of money and plenty of time.

However, they soon discovered that they all had one thing in common: they could not understand a word the teacher said in class.

What if I don't understand? Should I still go to class?

Chinatown

Go ahead, at least you can still see these classmates, and you're free anyway. But the problem is, trouble comes as soon as the class starts. If you don't understand, you can pretend to be confused, but their British teachers are very serious and responsible in teaching, and they are all very dedicated, especially for small classes with high tuition fees. The teachers really hope that every child can learn English well. There are only seven or eight people in the class, and the teacher is also responsible for every student, fearing that someone can't keep up, so he often asks repeatedly without getting tired:

" Do you understand? Do you know what I mean? "

She didn't understand anything and was embarrassed, so she just nodded randomly.

The teacher was very happy and continued to patiently enlighten: " Then can you tell me when this adverb can be placed in this position? "

She was completely confused. She had no idea what the teacher was saying. It was like listening to a foreign language. She only vaguely felt that the teacher was asking her a question. She couldn't answer it, and looked at the students next to her for help.

But none of them knew. They were all like her.

The teacher saw that she didn't understand, so she patiently and slowly repeated it to her word by word: " Do you know when this adverb can be placed in this place? "

Her face turned red, as red as a big tomato. She knew the teacher was speaking to her at the slowest speed, but she still couldn't understand.

This time, she was finally completely desperate.

Chinatown

* * *

Are you still going to class?
What else are you going to do?

* * *

There is no need to go to class. Some of my friends have learned a solution from their senior classmates: Why go to class? When it is time to renew your visa at the end of the year, you can just spend some money to buy attendance from someone, and then put more money in your bank account to ensure that your visa will be renewed. There is no problem at all! What the senior classmates said was absolutely right. They all went through it this way, and some have been here for three or four years.

Fortunately, Tingting's visa was successfully signed at the beginning, and the visa officer gave her three years at once. That was according to the visa materials prepared by the agent for her, which said one year of language, one year of preparatory course, three years of undergraduate study, and one year of master's degree. According to the agent's estimate, such a plan should have given her at least five years, but giving her three years was acceptable. After three years, she could renew her visa, and the renewal procedure was not troublesome.

Therefore, she didn't even have to worry about her attendance rate. He Tingting felt that she was really lucky. She soon fell in love with a boy from another class. The boy was very handsome, his family was also in business, and he was also very rich. He often went out to eat with Tingting, and the tip alone was ten pounds for the waiter - equivalent to the money you can earn working in McDonald's for two hours. But at that time, they had no concept of these things.

The boy had a nice name, Qin Ping. Because his last name was Qin, He Tingting always called him Qin. Qin was half a year older than her. He had been in the UK with her for a year and was studying in the same language school. Qin said that the students in this language school were basically the children of high-ranking officials or wealthy people in China, because firstly, the tuition here was more expensive than other schools. Although it was not an aristocratic school, the tuition was not something that ordinary families were willing to afford. Secondly, the teaching here was very formal, and parents wanted their sons to receive the most authentic British education. Thirdly, most of the Chinese students here were brought here by agents, and their families were either rich or powerful, so they dared to go to such a school.

Qin and Tingting soon moved out of the small and inconvenient dormitory building at school and rented a large villa outside. There were three bedrooms, a living room, a dining room, a parking lot in front, and a small garden in the back. Living in such a large house, the two teenagers, aged 17 or 18, lived like gods. Because the house was too big and lonely, Qin thoughtfully bought Tingting an authentic British noble pet dog. Tingting loved it very much, and because it had black fur, she named it " Xiaohei " .

Xiao Hei thus became the symbol of Qin and Tingting's love. They took him with them wherever they went. This breed of dog never grows up, and is always the size of a full-moon dog. It looks small and very cute. Tingting began to act like a noble lady from a wealthy family. Every evening after dinner, she would walk on the tree-lined path near the villa, holding Xiao Hei in one hand and Qin's arm in the other. Tingting felt that she had never been so happy in her life. It was as if she was really in the love world of a prince and a princess in a fairy tale.

It turns out that life in the UK is so wonderful, Tingting thought blankly but happily.

It was her first time having sex with Qin. It was her first time, and Qin's first time too. Both of them were extremely nervous. At first, she was afraid of the pain, and Qin didn't know what to do. He was so nervous that he was sweating all over. The two of them tossed and turned on the huge double bed in the bedroom all night, but Qin didn't really get in. When daybreak came, both of them were exhausted. Qin fell on the bed and said, I didn't expect sex to be so difficult.

Fortunately, they were much better the second time. Tingting gritted her teeth and endured the pain and let him do it for a while, and then slowly it got better. Then they got better and better. Both teenagers were doing this for the first time, and they became more and more impulsive and could not control themselves. Sometimes they even stayed in bed for a whole day, and when they were hungry, they would get up and call to order pizza to be delivered downstairs.

This went on for more than half a year. One day, Tingting suddenly found that she only had a few thousand pounds left in her account.

" How come I've almost spent all my money in less than a year since I arrived? " Tingting felt strange.

Qin listened and went to the bank to check his account. When he came back, he looked a little nervous: " I only have a few hundred pounds left. "

171

Fortunately, the rent for the house was paid in one lump sum for a year, so they don't have to worry about housing for the time being.

" It doesn't matter. A few hundred pounds is just a few hundred pounds. Your money plus my money is enough for food. " Tingting comforted him, " In the future, we don't have to go to fancy restaurants to eat. If we save some money on tips, we can eat takeaways. "

They continued to live their carefree lives.

Until one day, Qin told her with a pale face that the hundreds of pounds in his account had been spent.

" It doesn't matter. I still have money. Use mine first. " She said generously, " I'll ask my mother for more when I'm done. "

Although she was a little worried, she was worried that her family would ask her why she spent all the 40,000 pounds in one year.

" Never mind for now, we'll talk about it when the time comes. " She heard a small voice in her heart say.

Maybe Qin let the cat out of the bag when he called home. Qin's mother was the first to know that her son had no money in the UK. Without saying anything, she immediately booked a flight to London a week later. Qin's father runs a foreign trade company, so it is very convenient for his family to travel to various countries in Europe and America.

" What? Why did you call your mother over? " Tingting got anxious when she heard it. " Why did you call her over? Didn't I tell you I still have money? "

Qin stammered, " I, I didn't ask her to come. She insisted on coming here ... I didn't even mention the money to her. "

Tingting knew that it was useless to be angry, so she calmed down: " Does your mother know about our relationship? "

" I know. " Qin said, " When she said she was coming to London soon, I was afraid she would ask me where I lived, so I had to tell her everything. "

" What did your mother say? " she asked.

" She ... she didn't say anything. "

Tingting threw her hands and went upstairs: " Then you just wait for her to come. It will be a good show when she comes. "

With a woman's keen intuition, she was right.

Prostitute Abao (2)

On the day when Qin's mother came, Qin asked a classmate who had a car to go to the airport with Tingting to pick her up. The classmate was a fellow villager of Qin, and his father was the director of the Construction Department of a city in China. He drove a new cream-white Mercedes-Benz.

Tingting seemed a little uneasy in the back seat of the car, and she held Qin's hand tightly.

" What should I say to your mother when I see her later? " she asked. " It's really awkward. "

The classmate who was driving in front laughed and looked at them in the rearview mirror: " An ugly daughter-in-law will always have to meet her parents-in-law. Don't be nervous. "

Qin also smiled: " That's right, don't be nervous, my mother is very kind, just call her aunt when you see her. "

The director's son said, " What do you mean by 'Auntie'? You two are so close, you still have to call me mom, right? "

Tingting turned her head and said, " I don't call her mom. I can't even call my own mom, why would I want another one? "

Qin Xiaoxiao: " It's up to you, you can call me auntie or mom. Anyway, my mom is a very nice person, you will know when you meet her. "

When they arrived at the airport, the director's son couldn't hold it anymore and went to the bathroom, so Qin and Tingting were left alone.

In the spacious waiting hall, Qin gently brushed away a strand of hair from Tingting's face - that was her hair that she had just had done at the hair salon last week, the latest style of long hair dyed in purple and red. Tingting smiled and raised her head towards him, giving him a playful smile.

" Mom will definitely like you ..." Qin said with a smile.

Before he finished speaking, he heard a sharp female voice shouting: " Xiaoping! Xiaoping, come and help your mother get something! "

The two men panicked and headed towards the direction of the sound, and saw a middle-aged woman still wearing a brown short-sleeved shirt in the style of the 1980s, dragging two heavy boxes and walking towards them from a distance.

" Mom! " Qin rushed over in one step. The director's son also came back from the bathroom at this time and ran over to help pull a box.

" Hey, Auntie, what treasures did you bring? Why is this box so heavy? " the director's son said jokingly.

" Well, these are all food for Xiaoping! " Qin's mother said hurriedly while organizing the other large and small bags on her back. " I know you are so pitiful here and have nothing to eat, so I bought him a lot of his favorite snacks and local specialties.

When he was leaving Beijing Airport, he almost couldn't pass because of the overweight, and I was fined more than a thousand yuan! "

" Ah? Mom?" Qin turned around and said with a smile, "More than a thousand dollars? You might as well just throw all that stuff away at the airport. No food is worth a thousand dollars. "

" Oh, what's money? The most important thing is that you eat well and have a healthy body! " Qin's mother complained, "Look at you, you are taller than last year, but thinner! When you get home, I will cook you a good meal! "

Qin and his classmates put their luggage into the trunk.

" Wow, your classmate drives such a beautiful car? " Qin's mother said enviously, " Why don't you buy one too? "

Qin looked at Tingting awkwardly and thought, I don't even have enough money to eat, let alone buy a car.

" By the way, Mom, this is the He Tingting I told you about. We live together now. " Qin then remembered that he had forgotten to introduce her.

" Oh, " Qin's mother glanced at her with a little displeasure, but didn't say anything. Instead, she asked with concern, " You are Tingting. I've heard my son mention you many times on the phone. Where are you from? "

" From the Northeast. " He Tingting said shyly, lowering her head. Although she had already sensitively sensed that Qin's mother had some bad feelings towards her.

Four people got in the car. Mother Qin wanted to sit in the back with her son whom she hadn't seen for a long time, so Tingting had to sit in the front seat without saying a word.

The director's son asked Tingting in a considerate and gentle voice: " Do you want to listen to music? "

Tingting bit her lip and said, " No thanks. "

* * *

Tingting didn't know if she was too sensitive or if it was just the truth, but after Qin's mother came, she felt that everything had changed for her and Qin.

Mother Qin first questioned her son about the whereabouts of the money. " Didn't I change hundreds of thousands of RMB for you? How come it's gone so quickly? " Mother Qin asked her son in the bedroom with the door closed. Tingting was watching TV alone in the living room downstairs.

" Tell me, where did you spend all the money? Did you eat, drink, or play? "

Qin was cornered by her and couldn't answer a single word.

Mother Qin suddenly poked her son's forehead with her finger with a malicious expression, full of resentment:

" How come you are just like your damn father! You spend a lot of money on women at such a young age? "

Qin said aggrievedly: " Mom, this is none of her business! We both use our money together. My money is gone, and she only has a little money left. It's the same for both of us! "

" It's the same, so why is she still rich while you are? " Qin's mother said, " How dare you protect that wild woman and lie to your mother? - How could I give birth to a son like you who is exactly like your father! "

Then she sat on the bed and started crying. Because family disgrace should not be made public, and she didn't want He Tingting downstairs to hear anything, she sat cross-legged there and wiped her tears, crying her eyes out.

177

Qin was used to his mother's habits. But in the past, such scenes were played between her and his father. Now it was his turn again.

" Tell me, your father lives with that wild woman outside and doesn't come home once a year. You don't learn anything good, why do you only learn this from him? " She cried and snotted, as if all the suffering she had suffered for so many years was for Qin. " Tell me, when I came here, I saw you lifting that woman's hair. Your mother's hair has turned white because of missing you. When have you ever come to lift my hair? "

Qin made her speechless. He knew in his heart that his mother and his father had suffered a lot over the years. It was not material suffering, as the family had enough money for her to go from China to the UK. The suffering was all spiritual. He had been dependent on his mother for so many years, and he was still very filial to his mother in his heart.

" Mom, don't cry. If you start crying as soon as you get here, what will Tingting think if she hears you ..." He said distressedly while sitting on the sofa. He was only nineteen years old and really didn't know how to face such a situation.

" Now you only think about Tingting and don't care about your mother's life or death? " Qin's mother shouted angrily, " You don't want your mother when you haven't grown up yet? Huh? Have you forgotten that your mother came all the way here just to give you money?! "

Qin immediately became depressed. Like a deflated ball, he lowered his head and said nothing.

Even Tingting, who was watching TV downstairs, heard her last shout. Although she didn't hear clearly what Qin's mother said, she guessed about 70% of it.

Xiao Hei suddenly came running over from somewhere, jumped lightly onto the sofa where she was sitting, and dived into her arms happily, rolling around.

She stroked Xiao Hei's smooth and soft fur absentmindedly, and murmured, " Xiao Hei, our good days are over. "

* * *

Qin's mother lived with them in the UK for more than four months. At first, the two of them were just bickering with each other in a veiled way, but later it developed into a face-to-face quarrel. Qin, at such a young age, played a role that a middle-aged married man would usually play, and the three of them were miserable.

One day, Tingting couldn't help but say, " Qin, I think your mother is definitely a pervert. "

Qin said, " Don't say that about my mother. "

Tingting said: " Can you ask her to go back quickly? Is she okay in China? "

Qin said, " You know the situation in our family. She stays at home when she goes back. She is not allowed to interfere with anything in Dad's company. Now Dad lives with that woman. She must be lonely at home alone. "

" She can't just stay here and mess with us all day, " Tingting said gloomily, " I won't talk about the quarrels and tantrums. Just tell me how many times we've made love since she came here? "

Qin shook his head helplessly: " But she's leaving, who's going to give me the money? "

Tingting stopped talking.

179

" Besides, no matter what, she is still my mother. What do you think I should do? " he said miserably.

Tingting was holding Xiaohei, and suddenly she had an inexplicable idea. She didn't know where this terrible idea came from, but she suddenly had a very scary feeling. It was like a chill rising straight from the soles of her feet and rushing straight to the top of her head.

But she said nothing. It was too horrible, and she was too frightened by her own thoughts to speak.

* * *

This day has finally arrived.

After dinner, she took Xiao Hei out for a walk. Now it was her job to walk the dog alone. Qin had to stay at home with his mother to wash the dishes, otherwise his mother would not wash the dishes or cook. Qin's mother always threatened Tingting with a strike. Tingting felt that this woman was really pitiful and ridiculous. She once accidentally heard Qin's mother calling Qin's father in China. She actually said to the person on the phone in an unusually flattering and even almost flattering tone:

" Thank you so much for taking care of my husband. Could you please ask him to answer my call? "

Tingting felt so disgusted that she almost vomited.

Living with a woman like this, Tingting suspected that she would become mentally ill sooner or later.

So she would rather go out alone to walk the dog than stay at home in a restless state.

It was an autumn evening, the afterglow of the setting sun shone through the clouds in the sky, and the whole city seemed to be coated with a layer of light yellow. There were few pedestrians in this residential area of London, and only occasionally some passing vehicles came and went.

Tingting took Xiaohei for a walk on the tree-lined street.

Because it goes out like this every day, Tingting never ties it with a leash, and Xiaohei is also very obedient. If you tell it to go east, it will not go west. If you tell it to pee in the south, it will not go north.

She didn't know what had happened that day. Even now, when she thought about it, she felt that it was her fate. Everything was arranged long ago, not too early or too late, it would definitely happen at that time.

A dog named Xiao Hei was running in front of them, circling the street happily. Tingting walked slowly and sadly behind it, because it always ran faster than her. From time to time, Xiao Hei would stop after running a distance, look back at its little master, then slow down and walk around, waiting for her.

Tingting was so preoccupied with her own thoughts that she didn't notice that Xiao Hei had already run across the street. When she looked up to look for the dog, she found that Xiao Hei was sniffing a small blade of grass on the curb across the street.

Tingting turned around and clapped her hands at it: " Xiaohei! Come here! "

Xiao Hei was startled, turned around and saw his mistress calling him, immediately wagged his tail and ran towards her happily.

In a flash, the road was originally quiet and there was no car, but suddenly a car came out from nowhere, and the driver was driving so crazy for some reason that it was not accurate to say that he was speeding. He was simply playing with his

181

life. - Tingting was so scared that she shouted on the road: " Xiao Hei, don't come over! Don't come over!! " But this time, Xiao Hei was disobedient for the first time and tried his best to hit the car.

Tingting shouted: " Brake! Brake! There is one of my dogs over there! "

Xiao Hei looked at his little master excitedly and rushed over from the middle of the road without hesitation.

Of course the driver heard nothing. With a " wooo " sound, it was unclear whether it was the sound of a car's wheels or a dog's barking, the speeding car flashed by, and the road was empty, leaving only the body of a small black dog.

Tingting hurried over to pick up Xiao Hei and anxiously asked passers-by how to get him to the hospital. But before she could ask anyone who knew how to get him to the veterinary hospital, Xiao Hei had already opened his bloodshot eyes in her arms, looked at his master with resentment for the last time, then rolled his eyes and died.

Tingting cried bitterly on the street while holding Xiao Hei who had died heroically.

She knew that her love with Qin was definitely over. She didn't know why, but she felt that way at that moment.

Although she doesn't know how it will end yet.

* * *

Tingting returned home dejectedly, first found a shoe box to put Xiaohei away, then slowly went upstairs to find Qin. Because of the accident today, she came back much earlier than usual.

The whole building was covered with the finest carpets, and she had taken off her shoes, and because she was too sad to walk, no one heard her when she came in.

Tingting weakly pushed open the bedroom door and was about to say to Qin: " I'm back, Xiaohei was hit and killed by a car ..." She was suddenly stunned by what she saw.

Mother Qin sat cross-legged on their bed, her son lying in front of her with his head buried between her legs.

" Ah ————— ! " Tingting screamed hysterically, almost like crazy. The piercing sound passed through the roof, and she rushed down the stairs like crazy, tightly holding her chest that could hardly breathe, and struggled to rush out of the entire building.

* * *

He Tingting moved out with her remaining bank savings and luggage, and with the help of a classmate, she found a shared house, a long way from where she originally lived.

" The farther the better. " Tingting thought.

Although she shared a house with several people and the rent was much cheaper, Tingting's money was still spent quickly. During this period, she was mentally stimulated and went to nightclubs to buy alcohol at night. Or she went to nightclubs with some friends from school. Although she knew she had no money, she was used to spending lavishly before, and she didn't know how to save money at all. The money in her wallet was still spent one by one like water.

Friends all knew that she and Qin had broken up, but no one knew why they broke up, and no one asked. If she didn't tell them, no one would try to pry into her personal life, which was one of the advantages of being in the UK.

She still spent her days drinking and partying with her friends, and she still spent her days having fun with people she knew and didn't know. She also slept with one or two friends when she was drunk a few times, but she forgot everything after she sobered up. She only remembered that one of them was to drive to the airport to pick up the son of the fucking director.

Later, she gradually ran out of money. At first, her friends didn't mind her and even paid for her to go out and play. Later, they found out that she really couldn't even afford a bottle of beer, and gradually everyone distanced themselves from her. It wasn't that anyone deliberately distanced themselves from her, but they felt that going out with such a friend made everyone feel a little guilty and they couldn't have fun.

She was quickly left out.

Only then did she begin to realize how important money was.

On her twentieth birthday, she used the last few coins in her pocket to buy herself a small chocolate cake at a street shop. " Just wish myself a happy birthday, " she thought, " there will always be a way. "

" Twenty years old. " In her little room, she turned off the lights, put a small candle on the small piece of cake, lit it with a match, but took a long time to blow it out.

" What wish should I make? " She thought blankly, looking at the bright candlelight.

* * *

She began to think about finding a job. For the first time in her life, she thought about earning money to support herself through work. This idea had never even crossed her mind before.

But she didn't know how to find a job. She couldn't speak English. After more than a year in the UK, she could only say the simplest hello and goodbye. However, she also learned how to call a taxi, how to go shopping for clothes, and how to pick up packages at the post office. However, these were all skills for spending money. She had no idea how to make money. Apart from these basic daily expressions, she didn't know anything else. It was really difficult for her to find a job in the UK. Many PhDs and masters who studied in the UK still couldn't find a job. They still washed dishes in Chinese restaurants. Even for such jobs, they might not be able to get in unless they were introduced by acquaintances.

Tingting wandered back and forth in Chinatown for two or three days. At first, she was too embarrassed to ask. One time, she mustered up the courage to walk to the door of a restaurant. Just as she was about to go in and ask if they needed anyone, the doorman standing at the door recognized her at once, greeted her with a big smile on his face and said:

" Hey, you're here? Long time no see! Today we have a new pork bone soup, which is perfect for you girls' skin care ..."

She suddenly stood there in great embarrassment, blushed and smiled, and said: " Oh, no, - I made an appointment with a friend to meet here, and he hasn't arrived yet. "

" Oh, it's okay, it's okay, " the concierge greeted her politely and warmly as usual, probably because he still remembered her generosity when she gave him tips in the past. " Please sit inside, please sit inside. "

Chinatown

She quickly turned around and left: " No, I'd better call him first. " Then she slipped out of the main street of Chinatown like a thief, ran to a crowded corner next to the subway station, lit a cigarette for herself, and it took her a long time to recover.

" Damn it, what is going on? " she thought angrily.

After going around a lot, she found a few small restaurants she had never been to before, but none of them wanted anyone. Only the manager of one restaurant looked her up and down and said, " We don't need waiters, but we can't even fill the positions right now. But I know a friend who is looking for nude models. If you want to go, I can introduce you to him. "

She was so scared that she quickly shook her head and said, " No, no, I don't know how to be a model. "

" Oh. " The restaurant manager, who had a slightly fat belly and was wearing a shirt and tie, looked at her and said nothing more. He just smiled and said, " But let me tell you the truth. We can meet more than a dozen girls like you who come to our restaurant every day to look for work. I'm not trying to discourage you, but you can't find a job on this street. Not to mention you, I've seen many PhD and Master's students. How can it be that easy to find a job? This is in the UK, little sister. There is only one Chinatown in the whole of London. Do you think this is your home? "

But for many Chinese living in the UK, this narrow Chinatown is their home. It is also the only place where they can find people like them in a foreign country far away from their homeland. When Tingting wanted to find a job, the first thing she thought of was this familiar Chinatown.

After hearing what the manager said, Tingting lowered her head in despair: " Well, then what do you think I should do? "

186

" Don't even think about working. Even if you do, this isn't a job for humans, " the restaurant manager said, as if he suddenly had a change of heart. " To be honest, my daughter is about your age. If I were in China now, I would never send my child to work abroad and suffer like this. "

When Tingting heard this, tears started to fall.

" Little girl, go home quickly. " The manager said his last words and left.

Tingting wiped her tears and turned away. She didn't know whether the home he was talking about was the small house she lived in London, or the home in China that seemed so far away like a dream.

* * *

But she didn't want to go back just like that.

After finally leaving the country and spending so much money, she has become accustomed to the free and easy life here. Besides, what's the point of going back? She still has to look after her parents and relatives. So she decided to stay in London and look for a job.

" I'd better give it one more try , " she thought. " There is always a way out. "

But she no longer had money to call home. She had already sold her mobile phone.

She had borrowed money from her neighboring classmate several times, and she felt embarrassed to ask for more.

The landlord also owed her six weeks' rent, but he knew she couldn't pay it, so he didn't come to ask her even if she came.

He Tingting sat alone in the room all day, just sitting there in a daze.

" What should I do? " She thought.

She stole a potato from someone's refrigerator in the kitchen, put it in the microwave for a few times, washed it with water, sprinkled some salt on it, and went back into the house to eat it voraciously.

But I'm still hungry.

At this moment, she remembered the ten-pound tip she had given to people at restaurants before. " It would be great if someone could give me ten pounds at this time, " she thought.

She thought of the director's son. After all, she had slept with him. She could always borrow some money from him.

She borrowed her neighbor's mobile phone and called him. No one answered the first time, but someone did the second time. A young girl's clear voice said:

" Hello? Who are you looking for? "

" Oh, is this Xiaodong's phone? Did I call the wrong number? "

" Yes, " the girl said, " he is driving now. Who are you? "

She was stunned for a moment: " Oh, I'm his former classmate. I haven't contacted him for a long time. I called to say hello to him. It's nothing. Let him concentrate on driving. "

She hung up the phone.

She finally knew what she should do.

" I should go home. "

Prostitute Abao (3)

She went home.

When her mother heard her say that all the money was gone, she almost fainted.

" That's half million yuan! How could it be all spent in one year? " Tingting's mother was worried, " And you haven't paid any tuition fees, where did the money go? "

Tingting huddled on the sofa in the living room, with her head down, not saying a word.

"Your father will be so mad at you if he finds out when he gets home!" Mom said, "Not only him, but also your grandparents, your great-grandparents ... The whole family thought you were studying hard abroad, but look at you, what have you done? You didn't study for a single day, and you spent all your money! "

Tingting finally couldn't help but get anxious: "Alright, alright, stop arguing! I flew all the way back from England just to hear you say this? I sat on the plane for eleven hours and haven't slept for a whole day and night. I didn't even have a sip of water when

189

I got home, and all I hear is you talking about money, money, money! Talk and talk! I'm so annoyed-- ! " She suddenly covered her ears with her hands and screamed loudly, then continued to curl up on the sofa, covering her head with her hands, motionless.

Tingting's mother looked at her daughter, angry and sad, with tears in her eyes, and said in a trembling voice: "Tingting... what's wrong with you? "

" If you keep talking like that, I'm going to go crazy. " She whispered to herself softly, quietly, and almost inaudibly, covering her head on the sofa. " I really think I'm going crazy. "

* * *

She fell seriously ill the day she got home. She had a high fever, refused to drink, and lied on the bed talking nonsense. Tingting's parents were almost going crazy. They didn't care to say anything and quickly called a taxi to take her to the hospital.

In the hospital ward, Tingting woke up from her sleep while receiving an IV drip. She opened her eyes and looked around, then said weakly:

" Where am I now? "

Her mother held her hand and burst into tears beside the bed.

* * *

" Tingting's mother, I heard that your child fell ill and was hospitalized after returning home? What's wrong with her? What's wrong with her? " asked the aunt next door.

190

Tingting's mother quickly replied: " It's nothing serious. She was just tired from the flight back. She didn't get enough rest, so she caught a cold and had a high fever. She's recovered in the hospital now and is fine now. "

" Oh, it's really hard for this child to study abroad. She's so old and can't take care of herself. Fortunately , she got sick after returning home. What would she do if she got sick in the far corners of the world without any relatives around her? Oh, Tingting's illness has made me worry about my son who is studying in Germany. You see, what parent doesn't worry about their children? "

" Yes, yes, " said Tingting's mother.

" Oh, by the way, why did Tingting come back suddenly? It's neither winter nor summer vacation now, and my son is still taking classes there. Why would Tingting want to take leave to return home? " Auntie suddenly remembered and asked.

" Ah ..." Tingting's mother was stunned for a moment, and quickly said, " No, no, Tingting's school curriculum is not that tight ... and Tingting has always been very hardworking, she has finished this month's lessons by herself in advance. You know, she hasn't been home for more than a year, and the child suddenly missed home, so she ignored everything and flew back. "

" Yes, yes, " the aunt echoed, " Nowadays, these children are too spoiled. Once they miss home, no one can stop them from coming back. You don't know, my precious son often calls me from Germany, saying that he misses home every day and wants to come back and eat the braised pork I make for him. If I hadn't kept stopping him on the phone, this kid would have come back eight or ten times! "

The aunt said, " Let me tell you a joke. A colleague in our company has a child who is also studying in Australia. That child is so funny. He relied on his father's money and flew back home on Friday during a weekend! He only stayed at home for a day and a half, and flew back to Australia to attend classes early on Monday morning! "

" Ah? " Tingting's mother had never heard of this.

" There's nothing we can do. The child misses home! " The aunt sighed and shook her head. " The child said that even if he comes back for just one day, it would be enough to eat the meals cooked by his mother. You see, what a poor child. It's really not easy for them to be out there. "

" Yes. " Tingting's mother murmured in a daze.

* * *

During the days when Tingting was sick and hospitalized, all her relatives and friends came to visit her and asked her about her life. Tingting and her mother had agreed to tell her relatives and friends that she was still studying in the UK and that she had just skipped classes and came back because she missed home.

Tingting's father already knew everything, but when he saw how sick his daughter was, he couldn't bear to tell her anything.

" Mom, is Dad okay now? " Tingting asked her mother softly when no one was in the hospital that day.

Tingting's mother was tidying up the cakes and fruits sent by the neighbors on the table. When she heard her question, she hesitated for a moment and said, " Tingting, what are you going to do in the future? "

Chinatown

Tingting opened her eyes in confusion, looked up at her and said, " I, I don't know. "

Tingting's mother sighed: " Tingting, there are some things that I haven't told you since you went abroad because I was afraid you would worry. "

Tingting suddenly tensed up. She struggled to sit up against the headboard and said, " Mom, what's the matter? Tell me. "

Tingting's mother said: " You don't know, just two months after you left, your father's Internet cafe was closed by the Industry and Commerce Bureau. "

" Ah!? Why? "

" They said someone was browsing pornographic websites, " Tingting's mother shook her head and said, " That's what they said, but in fact it was mainly because someone used a pseudonym to post some reactionary political remarks in your father's Internet cafe. "

"...... ? " Tingting was completely confused.

" To put it simply, the Internet cafe was closed down and its business license was revoked, " said Tingting's mother. " Your father was very worried about this matter. I don't know how many connections he had to make and how many gifts he gave. It took him nearly half a year to reopen the closed Internet cafe. "

"...... Then what? "

" But you also know that when your father opened the Internet cafe, he was the only one in the whole city. Now if you walk around the streets, you can find two or three Internet cafes on any street. " Tingting's mother sighed, " So even though your father's Internet cafe has resumed business, the business is completely different from before. "

Tingting was shocked: " What about Dad? "

" So, " said the mother, " he was worried and anxious, but what could he do? He just had to keep doing what he did. He had been worrying about how to save up money for your tuition in the next three years. You know, hundreds of thousands of dollars is not a small amount for him - who knew that you would suddenly come back by plane without even saying hello ... and end up like this now. "

Tingting lowered her head and finally understood her parents' situation.

" If you say he's angry, how can he not be angry? " Tingting's mother said, " But look at him, when he saw you, did he say anything harsh to you? Did he scold you? In fact, seeing you like this, he felt worse than anyone else! "

Tingting's eyes suddenly turned red, with two big red circles hanging on her face. She pursed her lips and lowered her head, trying hard not to let her tears fall.

Tingting's mother wiped her eyes, sat by the bed and comforted her, saying: " It's okay, it's okay, as long as you come back safely. Money doesn't matter. It's a blessing for the family to be together and live in peace. "

Tingting paused, then took a deep breath and said:

" Mum, I want to go back to England. "

* * *

This time, Tingting's parents completely ignored their daughter. They knew that their daughter had grown up and they could no longer control her. It was like a dragon ascending to heaven or a snake going to hell, so they could only let her go. It was not that they didn't want to control her, but that they had no way to change it.

Tingting stayed in China for less than a month. She found that she was completely out of tune with her original life in the small town. When all her old classmates saw her, the first thing they said was: " Hey? Why are you back? Aren't you studying in the UK? " In addition, her parents' relatives and friends kept asking about her life abroad, not letting go of any details, partly because they cared about her, and partly to accumulate experience for their own children when they go abroad in the future. Every time Tingting repeated and made up beautiful lies in front of these people, she became more and more aware that she no longer belonged to this world.

Now, her hometown has become a completely strange world to her, and she can't even find a way back here. She can't turn back anymore.

All the He family's social connections still believed that He Tingting was still studying in the UK, studying for a language , a foundation course , a bachelor's degree , and a master's degree. Tingting herself didn't know why she and her parents had come up with this big lie. Everything seemed to be tacitly understood.

Her parents had completely given up on her because they knew there was no other way. They couldn't even afford to give Tingting a few more months of living expenses when she boarded the plane back to the UK.

When she said goodbye at the airport, she looked at her father's gray eyes and prematurely gray hair. At that moment, she suddenly understood the vicissitudes of life. It was an unspeakable pain. The pain in her heart.

" Tingting, why don't you not leave? Stay here. Mom will cook for you and you can help Dad run the Internet cafe. " Tingting's mother suddenly started crying again.

Tingting shook her head.

" Dad, Mom, you don't have to worry. I have a classmate who works at a Chinese travel agency in London's Chinatown. When I go back this time, I'll ask her to introduce me there. If nothing else works, at least I can be a typist. The minimum wage is ten pounds an hour. You just don't have to worry. I won't study for the time being, but I can make one day's salary in the UK equivalent to a month's salary for college students here. Once I've worked for a few years and earned my own money and my English has improved, I'll go back to school. " Tingting said to her parents.

The father looked at her and nodded. It was no longer important whether he believed her words or not. What was important was that everything had to go on. The family tacitly performed a common myth in the small town. A myth about Britain.

"Tingting, you will be alone outside... remember take care of yourself." When her mother said these last words to her, her tears could no longer be stopped from flowing down.

" Don't worry, Mom, I can take good care of myself. " Tingting said.

Tingting hugged her mother and then her father, then dragged her suitcase into the airport immigration checkpoint.

She knew that this time, something had been completely left behind.

* * *

Chinatown

The little money she brought from home was used to pay off the rent owed to the landlord for several months, to pay off the plane ticket she borrowed to buy when she returned home, and to buy vegetables and fruits for a week. Basically, there was not much money left. Abao sat on the bedside of her room and smoked. When she boarded the plane, she bought a few cartons of cigarettes from the duty-free shop at the domestic airport (she didn't want her parents to know that she had learned to smoke), which was enough for her to smoke for a while. Abao sat cross-legged on the bed and smoked one cigarette after another, with an old newspaper next to her, which was covered with cigarette ash.

This month's rent is due soon, and she wondered what to do.

She exhaled a long string of smoke, which drifted into the room.

The sunshine outside the window shines brightly on the lawn outside the building. It is already spring again.

* * *

She leaned against the snow-white wall dejectedly, sitting in the empty room in a daze. She had finished all her cigarettes and had no money left.

There really is not a penny left.

She couldn't even borrow money. The classmate who used to live with her in the same building had moved out. She had asked everyone she could. Everyone avoided her like the plague. All her friends had disappeared.

She leaned against the cold wall, staring blankly out the window. She hadn't eaten for the whole day.

She no longer felt hungry, but just a little weak.

She wanted to get up and go to the kitchen to pour herself a glass of water.

When she stood up, she suddenly felt dizzy like never before. She wasn't hungry at all, she just felt a little dizzy.

She wanted to sleep. She wanted to lie down on the bed and have a good sleep. Even though she had been sleeping for several days. At one moment, she even thought of a very scary thought. She thought, will I never wake up again if I fall asleep like this?

She held her dizzy head and went to the kitchen to pour a glass of water. There was no one in the kitchen. Everyone in the building had gone out, either to school or to work. She was left alone at home, sitting on the bed in a daze. The cups in the kitchen were all dirty, so she had to pick up a dirty cup that someone had drunk from, wash it under the faucet, and then pour water into it.

Why is it so troublesome to even have a glass of water, she thought.

She recalled the time when she was in a Michelin-starred Western restaurant, where she would be poured chilled French red wine by the touch of a hand, the purple-red juice flowing into the crystal clear wine glass.

She took the glass of water and returned to her room.

" I really don't have a penny this time, " she heard herself say to herself.

" What are you waiting for? "

* * *

She soon discovered the advantages of this line of work. First of all, it was easy to make money. She used to run around Chinatown begging for help, just to find a job washing dishes or doing odd jobs that paid two or four dollars an hour. Now she could make a hundred pounds in a matter of minutes by just lying on the bed with her eyes closed, not counting tips.

Because she was a novice, the boss loved her very much after trying her out and gave her the highest price among all the girls in the brothel. If there were foreign customers, whether from Eastern Europe or South Africa, the boss would smile and say to them in half-baked English:

" Sir, we have a new lady here. She has an absolutely first-rate figure, with a curvy figure and a nice body . But if you want to order her, you have to make an appointment in advance. She is new and has just started working. She can only receive a few customers a day. The appointments are already full. If you want to order her, you have to be patient. "

In fact, she hadn't received any customers at that time, but after the boss introduced her, she quickly became the most popular lady in the yard. After a week, she really became a must-see and she even needed to make an appointment in advance.

Another advantage is that all brothels provide food and accommodation, so she can save even the rent. The money in her hand is almost always in, and she will be rich again in a few days. Because she is new and the boss's Miss Hong, she earned 10,000 pounds in the first month without feeling tired. " It turns out that making money is so easy. " She thought, " In a few months, I can return the 40,000 pounds my family gave me to my parents. " In the past, she was so hungry that she had to steal potatoes. Now?

199

She can go to the high-end restaurants in Chinatown and order a table of dishes as before, or treat her sisters to a nearby Western restaurant for a steak if she is in a good mood. Now she spends all the money she earns, and all of it is given by men who like her. She feels very comfortable and at ease when spending it.

" Thank God, I am finally alive again, " she thought.

" Abao, Abao, you are really the boss's treasure now. " When there are no customers or when she is taking a break, her colleague's girlfriend often says this to her half-jokingly and half-jealously.

" Look at her figure, she's born to be a prostitute, " another lady looked her up and down with envy, " Silly sister, you said you've been in the UK for more than two years, why are you only starting now? If you had started earlier, you would have at least two or three million in savings by now. "

" Two or three million? " Although she already felt that it was easy to make money in this industry, Abao was still shocked by the number the sister said. She never thought she could make so much money.

" That's right! " The lady named Yanyan pouted at the lady next to her who was applying makeup in front of the makeup mirror and said, " Look, she started doing this two years ago, and now she has more than three million in her bank account in China. "

" Ah? " Abao looked at her and said with infinite admiration, " I didn't realize you were so good at making money. You are my senior after all. "

" Hey, this is nothing, how much money do we earn? The boss gets ten times this amount! " Yanyan said, " Just think about it, there are more than a dozen girls in the yard, and he takes 55%

of each girl's salary. They are the ones who make big money! What's more, they are getting more and more prosperous, while we are only young, and we only earn money through hard work in the past few years. In a few years, it will be gone - you will know when you have worked for a long time, nothing is easy. "

Po lowered her head and wondered what they meant by saying these words to her.

" There's no point in me saying all this, " Yanyan is also a very smart woman, especially in observing people's words and expressions, not to mention things in bed. " Abao, I just want to tell you that it's good to be in this industry, but it's a pity that you got into it too late, and you won't be able to do it for a few years. You know, those Thai girls and Malay girls started working at the age of 15 or 16! By the time they were 20 years old, you were your age, they had already made enough money and retired. I'll also remind you, even though your boss treats you like a baby now, the good days won't last for a few years. When you're old and can't work anymore, and wrinkles appear, no man will want you, and no one will pity you! "

Ah Bao was having a great time, but her words were like a bucket of cold water poured down his body from head to toe: " Sister Yan, what do you think we should do? "

" What should I do? " Yanyan glanced at her with a faint charming smile, " Do you know what young ladies in ancient China did? Make money quickly while you are young and beautiful, and when you have made enough money, pick a man who treats you well, and when you find him, stop and marry him - it's the same in ancient times and modern times. For us young ladies, the best fate is to marry the right man. "

201

"Get married?" Abao had never thought of this. She originally thought that since she was in this line of work, she would not get married again. Moreover, once she got married, she would have to meet her parents-in-law, and she didn't want to meet another Qin Mama.

But because she remembered what Yanyan said to her, from then on, although she was still engaged in the flesh trade, she also began to pay attention to the men around her, to see if she had the chance to meet someone who was really willing to marry her.

But she gave up soon. The simplest thing was, what kind of men came to her? Even the good ones didn't like her. Not to mention the Chinese, even if foreigners were more open-minded, they wouldn't think of marrying a prostitute. She gradually realized the difficulty of doing this business, so she gave up completely, didn't think about anything, and just made her money honestly.

Life went on like this until half a year later, when she met Achang.

Pimp Achang

Achang is also from Fujian. He smuggled from his hometown to the UK three years ago and quickly settled down in London. When he met Abao in Lao Gen's brothel, he had been a pimp and pimp for more than two years and was thinking about opening his own shop.

Lao Gen is Achang's fellow countryman and the owner of the first brothel that Abao opened. Lao Gen has been in the UK for thirteen years and has been very experienced in this business. He considers all kinds of people as his brothers. Achang is no exception. After hearing Lao Gen bragging that a new lady from Northeast China has come to his yard, whose breasts are so plump that they are comparable to those of foreign girls, Achang passed by Lao Gen's brothel one day and thought that he hadn't seen Lao Gen for a long time, so he went to see how he was doing.

" Achang, where have you made your fortune recently? Why haven't I seen you for a long time? " Lao Gen greeted Achang with a smile.

Chinatown

Achang had been in the UK for three years, and was only about 21 or 22 years old at this time. Achang was handsome and tall, and looked like a boy who blushed easily. People who didn't know him well didn't know that he was in this business, and he had been doing it for two years. The brothel owners all liked him because he could always introduce them to a lot of Chinese business. Most of them were young illegal immigrants or refugees who had sneaked in from Fujian like him.

" No way. " Achang took a cigarette from Lao Gen shyly and lit it with the lighter in Lao Gen's hand.

" The police have been checking too closely recently, so many people can't come here. Business is bad everywhere. " Achang said, " It's not so bad here. The girls are so busy that I can't see any of them. Business is much better than other places. "

Lao Gen laughed out loud: " No, no, it's all thanks to my brothers. Actually, my life here is not easy either. "

" How is it? Are there any new people? " Achang knew as soon as he saw the sign behind the door.

" Yes, yes, yes, Achang, do you want to try it? " Lao Gen took the opportunity to promote his product. " Of course I'll give it to you at the most favorable price. "

Achang smiled lightly and said, " Call it here so I can take a look first. " He had seen many chickens before and might not decide which one to like.

" Not now, " Lao Gen looked up at the clock on the wall and said, " She is still receiving customers. Wait a moment. She should be out in half an hour. "

" It's okay, you guys go do your thing, I'll come next time. " Achang said as he was about to get up, " I just have to rush to Chinatown, I still have some money to give to Ah Ming, I agreed to go and get it today. "

" That's good. It won't hinder your fortune. " Lao Gen rubbed his hands and laughed, " Next time you come, give me a heads up so I can prepare for you in advance. "

Achang looked at him, suddenly smiled, patted Lao Gen on the shoulder and said, " Brother, let me say something I shouldn't say. I am the only one who chooses women, and it is not the turn of women to choose me. "

" Of course, " Lao Gen said sternly, " You, Achang, are a famous handsome guy in London nightclubs. You are young and promising. Many girls are eager to get you. I know that you, Achang, have no eyes for women. "

Achang smiled proudly, put out his cigarette in the ashtray on the table next to him, patted Lao Gen on the shoulder, stood up and said, " You go ahead and do your work, big brother. I'll come back another day. "

Lao Gen said with a smile: " Do you want Ah Xiang to come out and see you off? "

Achang said coldly: " This woman is very cheap. Since you mentioned her, I would like to trouble you to tell her something: tell her not to call me again in the future. "

Lao Gen was startled, then he immediately smiled and said, " The sun really rises from the west. Our Ah Xiang actually has the same idea as you! Hahahaha, okay, I will definitely tell you about your words later. "

* * *

When Achang came to Lao Gen's brothel for the second time, he met Abao. Because Lao Gen knew in advance that he would come to collect money, he had left Abao for him in advance.

Achang came, collected the money, and was about to leave when Lao Gen quickly called Ah Bao out from the inner room: " Ah Bao, come out and meet the guests! "

Ah Bao came out from inside with sleepy eyes. She had just finished serving a customer half an hour ago and didn't know it would be her turn again so soon, so she was taking a nap in the room. When she heard Lao Gen calling, she rubbed her eyes and came out.

" Isn't the next one Ah Xiang's? " Ah Bao said as he walked out. " She's been waiting for a long time. "

Lao Gen led Abao over with a smile, and said to A Chang: " Come, let me introduce you to this. This is Abao, the newcomer to our Lovers' Courtyard, and this is my best friend, A Chang, who is also my fellow villager. "

" Oh, hello. " Abao looked at him in confusion, not understanding why the boss wanted to introduce this person to her so solemnly.

Achang barely even looked at her, as if he was trying to look for something on the ground with his head down: " Well, OK, Lao Gen, I've seen your people. Don't worry, I'll make sure to bring you good guests next time. "

The good customers he mentioned were those who could afford a good price. He knew without even looking at his face that Abao was the top customer at Lao Gen.

Even though Lao Gen was well-informed, he was stunned to see him looking down in such a depressed state. He thought he didn't like it, so he quickly said, " This Abao is new here and doesn't know the rules yet. She came out to meet the guests without combing her hair or putting on any powder. But if you had time today, you would immediately know her merits. "

Hearing this, Achang raised his head, smiled at Lao Gen and said, " Brother, you don't have to say anything. I don't have time today. Let's come next time. "

Two days later, the "next time" that Achang mentioned came. Lao Gen arranged for him to go to Ah Bao's room as usual and asked him to try it first. Unexpectedly, an hour later, and then half past, Achang still hadn't come out. Lao Gen sat on the sofa in the front reception room and smoked. As he smoked, he laughed to himself, shook his head and said:

" This Achang, it turns out that he has taken a fancy to this treasure. "

* * *

However, to Lao Gen's surprise, two hours later Achang came out. Lao Gen knew at a glance that Achang had not even touched Abao, and insisted on paying Lao Gen the full amount for two hours. He would not do it if he was charged a penny less.

" If you don't accept it, it means you look down on me as your brother. " Said Achang.

Lao Gen could only accept the money in great annoyance, and took out a bill from the bank, stuffed it into Abao's pocket and said, " This is an extra gift from me. From now on, I will not charge you a penny for tea from this little brother. Do you understand? "

Lao Gen meant that Abao was not allowed to ask him for tips in the house, and Abao agreed. But what surprised him was that

207

when he stuffed the tip into her pocket, Abao's face turned red, and she didn't even raise her eyelids, looking at her toes on the ground shyly.

After Achang left, Lao Gen asked Abao: "What did you do in there for two hours? Why didn't he touch you? What happened? "

Abao turned his head and said, " How would I know? He just sat opposite me and chatted with me for two hours. "

" Chat? " Everyone knows that Achang is the most taciturn person.

Abao said: " He asked me when I started doing this business, how long I had been doing it, how my customers were doing, and so on. "

This is the topic that pimps usually talk about with prostitutes. But Lao Gen still felt something was wrong. After working in this business for so many years, Lao Gen knew the mentality of men and women very well. But when they bought the hourly rate but didn't have sex and only talked about work, Lao Gen couldn't figure out what Achang was thinking.

" Either he drank too much the day before, or he just tried out a new girl in another courtyard this morning and he is out of energy. " Later, Lao Gen thought so. When he thought of this reasonable reason, Lao Gen's heart immediately settled down. Anyway, Achang hadn't touched her yet, and he would touch her sooner or later.

* * *

Achang had never been in a relationship before he came to England. All the girls in the village knew that he was handsome, and many of them secretly liked him, but at that time he was so focused on sneaking out that he had no interest in women at all. He didn't even bother to look at those girls.

When he was 18, he borrowed a loan shark and spent 180,000 yuan to the smuggler to escape. Half a year after arriving in the UK, he followed a gangster and started a pimp business. He was smart, trustworthy, and good-looking. From clients to prostitutes to brothel owners, everyone liked to deal with him. A year later, he paid off the loan shark and started saving money to open his own shop.

After coming to England, because he started out with this business, he had no feelings for any woman from the beginning. He had seen all kinds of ladies. What kind of women had he not seen? It was just one word. Fuck. Especially since he was still young and full of vigor, the more the ladies liked him, the less interested he was in them. He just thought they were cheap and tried every means to please men, all for money.

He himself couldn't explain what was wrong with him. From the first time he saw this woman, Abao, he inexplicably had a special feeling about her. It was a very, very strange feeling, very wonderful, but hard to explain. He himself didn't know why he had such a feeling about a new prostitute.

"Don't tell me that's what love is," he thought. "It's all nonsense."

He actually chatted with Abao for two hours that day, which he himself did not expect. But in fact, he did not feel that two hours had passed that day. He just felt comfortable sitting there. The sofa in the room was very soft. The woman opposite him was lazy and seemed to have no interest in talking to him. She sat there to accompany him only because he bought her hourly salary.

" She doesn't think I'm incapable, does she? " He suddenly thought of this. He even laughed at the thought.

It's not that he couldn't, but he really didn't want to have sex with her at that time. He just wanted to sit there and talk to a woman, just a few words, just a casual chat, that's all.

However, he couldn't understand why it was her and not other women.

After a few days, he felt upset for some reason, as if he couldn't muster the energy to do anything. Even when his elder brother, with whom he usually drank and played mahjong, called him to come over, he said he was not feeling well and would not go. He sat in the room in a daze, wondering what was going on.

Slowly, he suddenly seemed to hear a small voice in his heart talking to him. He couldn't hear or feel what it was saying. But he seemed to feel that there was something there, trying to remind him to do something.

He put out the cigarette in his hand, even though he had only smoked half of it.

" I should go to Lao Gen's shop, " he thought. " I haven't been there for a long time. I might as well go and sit with him. "

Although he didn't know why he wanted to see Lao Gen so much. " I'm not a gay. " He wondered along the way.

* * *

Just like that, he started to go to Lao Gen every few days. He no longer called Ah Bao's place or chatted with her. Every time he went, he would just look for Lao Gen, sit for a while, chat with her casually, and then pat his butt and leave.

" Why is he hiding from Abao now that he's here? " Lao Gen was secretly puzzled. He didn't know what happened in Abao's house that day.

After a month or two, Achang seemed to have formed a habit of going to Lao Gen's brothel once or twice a week. He did not want any other prostitutes, but only talked business with Lao Gen, doing his job as a pimp.

Seeing him like this, Lao Gen thought that he had no interest in Abao in the first place, and maybe he was just bored that day and didn't have the energy to do anything, so he bought her clock to chat with him. So gradually he didn't take the matter of the two of them to heart and continued to attract his customers and do his business.

One day, Lao Gen went to Scotland to find a brother. As soon as the boss left, the girls in the yard immediately stole a day or two of leisure time. They were too lazy to do business and went shopping with their sisters in groups of three or four. " Just think of it as your period coming, " they said, " No matter what kind of work you do, you still have a day off. In our line of work, we work 365 days a year. "

Because Abao had the least experience and she was very tired that day and didn't want to move, she volunteered to stay in the store with another sister, Axiang. In case Lao Gen suddenly remembered and called, there would be someone to take care of him.

On such a lazy afternoon when no one was around, Achang suddenly came over again.

" Huh? Why is there no one here? " Achang asked as he came in. " Is Lao Gen closing down his shop? "

Ah Xiang smiled, stretched out a finger and touched her lips and said: " The boss went to Scotland for work, so the sisters went shopping secretly. "

" Oh? So comfortable. " Achang sat down on the sofa, crossed his legs, lit a cigarette and said, " Are you alone here? Is Ah Bao here? "

Ah Xiang smiled charmingly and said, " Others say that you come to see Ah Bao every day, but I don't believe it. It's rare that even Lao Gen was fooled by you. Forget it, I don't expect anything from you now. If you really like Ah Bao, be nice to her. Don't bully her like you did to me. "

Achang smiled faintly and said, " Call her out. "

Ah Xiang pointed to the room inside and said, " She's in there. There are no guests right now. Go call her yourself. "

With a cigarette in his mouth, Achang walked to the door and knocked.

" Come in. " Abao said from inside.

Seeing that the person who came in was Achang, Abao was slightly surprised, but soon got used to it and immediately smiled skillfully and charmingly: " It's you, you are here again, do you want to buy a watch today or just chat? If you just want to chat, don't buy a watch, anyway, Lao Gen is not here today. "

Achang said: " How do you know I just want to chat with you? "

When Abao heard this, he looked at him in shock, not knowing what he meant.

" So ... do you want to buy my clock? " Her voice suddenly trembled slightly, and she herself didn't know why.

Achang looked at her and sat down on a chair in the room without saying anything.

Abao stood there blankly for a while, and seeing that he didn't say anything, he slowly sat down next to the bed.

The door closed slowly and automatically.

Neither of them spoke, and the room was strangely quiet, as if one could hear one's heartbeat.

" How could this happen? " Abao wondered in surprise, " He just wants to have sex with me, right? Why am I suddenly so nervous? "

Achang smoked slowly, without looking at her or saying anything, just sitting there smoking by himself.

" Do you still want to do this job? " He suddenly asked after a moment of silence.

" Ah? " Abao didn't quite understand what he said. " What do you mean by wanting it or not? If I don't do this, what else can I do? " She said with some resentment. It was as if something she hadn't thought about for a long time had suddenly been touched upon.

Achang said, " Come with me. "

Abao looked at him and suddenly laughed: " Good brother, don't play such a joke on me. You know that people like us are worthless and can't stand your teasing. "

Achang said without moving, " No, I'm serious. If you want to leave, I'll say hello to Lao Gen later. From now on, just follow me. "

Abao finally understood: " Oh, so you want to open your own shop? " She felt relieved and dared to believe what he said.

Achang smoked his cigarette expressionlessly: " Yes. - Do you want to come with me? I'll only ask you once. "

Ah Bao looked at him, her heart pounding. She didn't know whether there was a cliff or flowers ahead. She didn't know whether he wanted to play with her or wanted her. She didn't know if his business would be good or bad, and whether he would have money or not if she followed him.

At this moment, her mind suddenly went blank and she knew nothing.

But she said: " Achang, I ... will go with you. "

* * *

The place where Achang used to live was full of his brothers who were involved in the pimp business. In order to get Ah Bao to move out of Lao Gen's place as soon as possible, he found out from his friends that Zhang Lai had a house to rent out. He called him and casually asked about the situation of the house. Without even looking at it, he said:

" Tell me the address and we'll move there tomorrow. "

Zhang Lai had never met someone who rented a house like this before, and was a little scared. He said, " You have to come and see the house first, right? "

Achang said succinctly: " To be honest, I've been having some trouble here lately, and I just want to move as soon as possible. "

Zhang Lai felt relieved upon hearing this. He immediately agreed on the phone, " Okay, okay, no problem. I'll get someone to clean up the house tonight. What time will you come tomorrow? Call me when you get there. Also, both the deposit and rent must be paid in cash. "

" No problem. " Achang said, " I'll call you as soon as I get on the bus tomorrow. "

* * *

So, the next day, Achang moved into the house with Abao and their luggage, and lived in the best room on the first floor facing the sun. The price was much higher than other rooms, but they didn't care at all.

The day after moving, Chang and Bao bought a one-month-old purebred pug at an open -air market in Chinatown . Just as they were buying pots and pans and passing by the dog seller, the little guy suddenly barked at Bao twice in the arms of the old British woman. Bao turned around and saw a snow-white long-haired lion dog. Suddenly she remembered Xiao Hei.

It seemed as if it happened in the previous life.

Achang saw her staring at the puppy in a daze, so he pulled her back to the old British woman.

" Ask her how much the dog costs. " Achang couldn't speak a word of English. After all, Abao had gone to school for two days, so he was better than him.

" Five hundred pounds, " the British woman said, " This is a purebred British noble dog. I'm not a dog dealer. This is the child of our own pet dog. I just want to find a good owner for it. "

Abao didn't understand a word of what was said afterwards. She only understood the three words "five hundred pounds". But that was enough.

" It's too expensive, let's go. " Abao pulled him and said.

" Woof, woof! " The puppy seemed to understand human nature and barked at Abao twice.

" Tell her I'll buy it for three hundred pounds, " said Achang.

" Ah? You really want to buy it - forget it, I'm just taking a look. " Said Abao.

" Do you like it or not? If you like it, buy it. " Achang doesn't like to talk nonsense.

Abao lowered his head and said nothing.

Achang held up three fingers to the British woman and said, " Three hundred, OK ? "

The British woman looked at the two of them, thought for a while in embarrassment, and finally nodded: " Well, I think you two are really a happy couple ... OK , three hundred is three hundred, as long as my little baby can find a happy husband-in-law, I will be satisfied. " She reluctantly handed the puppy to Abao's arms.

" Give it a name, " he said on the way home. He could already sense the joy in Po's heart.

" Look at its cute white fur. Let's just call it Xiaobai. " Abao said as she walked behind Achang, holding the puppy that lay obediently in her arms and didn't move.

" Okay. " Achang said, " You know, I will be out a lot in the future. When I'm not around, you can stay at home with Xiao Bai and have a good time to relieve your boredom. "

" Yes. " When Ah Bao heard this, she suddenly felt sad and happy for some reason, and almost cried. It was the first time she knew that he wanted to live with her.

" Achang. " She walked behind him and called him very softly.

" What? " Achang turned around and stopped, still looking at her expressionlessly.

She held tightly Xiaobai, who was looking at them strangely with his eyes wide open, in her arms, and walked over. After a pause, she said, "... Nothing, let's go. "

The two continued to walk home on the busy and crowded sidewalk outside the " Chinatown " open-air market, passing through the market, and then walking a few dozen meters ahead was their new home. At this time, the sky was gradually getting dark and the sun was setting.

Landlord Zhang

Speaking of Zhang Lai, he is definitely a legendary figure. When I first met him, he was wearing a shirt that was half new and half worn, and the original color could no longer be seen, a pair of obviously worn jeans and plastic sandals, and nervously introduced me to the rooms in this empty house upstairs and downstairs. Perhaps he was afraid that I would not be satisfied and said I would not rent it, so he almost gave me the cheapest price in the whole building. When I officially moved in a week later, Zhang Lai confided to me his deep regret for keeping this room for me. " If I had known earlier, I would not rent this single room to you. Your room is so big that you can rent it as a double room. In this way, I can charge at least 25 pounds more per week, and 100 pounds more per month. " Zhang Lai calculated the bill for me in detail, showing how much I should be grateful that he kept his promise for the sake of this little money and kept this room that later became very popular for me.

" But if one more person lives here, you will have to pay more for water and electricity, right? " I said. I thought, you are only concerned with making money and don't care about the lives of the tenants in the building. As it is now, there are already thirteen people living in a four-bedroom house, and you want to add more people? Then not only will you have to queue up to cook, but you will also have to queue up to go to the toilet.

" How much is the water and electricity bill? " Zhang Lai said frankly, " One week's price difference is enough. But you were introduced by my friend, and you were the first to make the reservation. Forget it, I won't ask you for more. "

Oh my god, it sounds like he is planning to raise the price with me.

When I first met Zhang Lai, I judged that he was a newcomer who had never been a sub-landlord. Later, it turned out that this was indeed his first time as a sub-landlord. However, this person was very lucky, and he was born to give people a sense of insecurity and trust . Insecurity means that he seemed to be erratic. When the kitchen light was broken, I called him ten times a day but couldn't find him. When it was time to collect the rent, he would automatically show up. The sense of trust came from his baby face and his eternally young personality. When I first met him, I thought he was still a student, 21 or 22 years old, still in high school or A-LEVEL here . Later I learned that he was 31 years old, but he was short and couldn't tell. So he gave people the feeling that he would never bully his tenants and deduct their money for no reason . So his house was rented out very quickly. Basically, everyone who saw the house decided to live there immediately.

With the successful experience of selling all the houses in one week, Zhang Lai became more and more courageous, and his life began to change dramatically. A week after I moved in, Zhang Lai came to help me carry my luggage upstairs. This was the second time I met him, but I was scared by his new look. I didn't expect that he would be reborn in a week, like a completely different person: that day he was wearing a brand new grass green shirt (I didn't see the label on his neck, but it should be a small brand name), a pair of snow-white pants, and a pair of equally brand new Nike sneakers. When I saw him, he was standing on the lawn outside the front door of the house, wearing a pair of fashionable black sunglasses on his nose, which almost covered most of his face. He looked like a small gangster leader in the movie, or a mistress kept by a woman.

" Are you ... Zhang Lai? " I hesitated.

He smiled, proudly took off his sunglasses with one hand, looked at me and said with a smile: " Why, you forgot after just one week? You are such a forgetful person. "

" No, no, " I said quickly, " You are just dressed so handsomely today. You are such a handsome guy. "

Zhang Lai smiled even more proudly and began to direct two brothers, whom he found from somewhere, to help me carry the heavy box upstairs.

" How come it's full so quickly? " I was shocked when I entered the house again.

" I'm still talking, " Zhang Lai said as he led me upstairs, " You're the last one to move in. Yesterday, three people came to see the room you wanted to stay in, and two of them wanted to pay me on the spot. I thought I couldn't leave you, a little girl, without a place to stay, so I kept it for you - but if you don't come today, I will definitely rent it to someone else tomorrow. I can even rent it to someone else for the price of a double room. "

I was so scared that I didn't dare to say anything. I just kept smiling at him, as if I hadn't paid the deposit and rent a week ago.

The two boys threw all my luggage on the floor of the room and clapped their hands.

Zhang Lai stood in the middle of the room, looked around like a leader, and said, " Okay, if you need any help, just give me a call. If I don't answer, leave a message. I live on the other side of the street anyway, so I can walk there in five minutes if you need anything. "

I nodded and said, " Okay, okay, okay, thank you. "

Zhang Lai waved his hand and two people went out with him.

I thought to myself, Zhang Lai was born in the wrong family. He should have been an officer a hundred years ago, at least commanding a platoon. Being a sub-landlord on this shabby street in England is really an injustice to his talent.

* * *

Zhang Lai originally came here on a student visa. According to Lao Zhu, he " saved 200,000 yuan for nothing. " But this was also due to the fact that Zhang Lai had a baby face and really looked like a student. And the most important reason was that Zhang Lai was not from Fujian.

After coming to London from Henan, Zhang Lai soon found that it was meaningless to study hard and get a doctorate degree here. He could not make money and could not get a status to stay. He was young and smart, and soon he learned the best experience

221

of living in London by working in the circle of Chinatown. He first made friends with a close friend of a Chinese company's office in the UK, treated him to meals and drinks, and became sworn brothers. Then he asked that friend to help him get a staff identity of the Chinese office in the UK. Don't underestimate this identity, it has solved Zhang Lai's biggest problem: now he can stay in the UK indefinitely with this identity, and he no longer has to worry about visa issues.

After resolving his identity, Zhang Lai began to think about how to make money here. He opened a company and started a business, but all ended in failure. After all, what kind of business could he do in London as a student who came to the UK to " study " without even graduating from a junior college in China ? A few years passed like this, and gradually he got to know more people and made more friends. From their various ways of living, he gradually figured out: If you want to make money in the UK, you can only find a way to make money from the Chinese. Want to make money from the British? Except for opening a restaurant and doing illegal business, there is no hope!

Zhang Lai's first successful business was renting out the house in " Chinatown " where he was living from a British landlord. The house was originally rented out by another Chinese boy who rented it out to others. Later, the boy finished his studies here and his visa expired, so he returned to China. Zhang Lai took over the house. This was his first time as a sub-landlord. In fact, he did nothing, just signed a contract with the landlord on behalf of the boy who had left. But in this small transaction, he had tasted the sweetness and began to discover that there was a huge business opportunity and market here.

It's very simple. Having lived in the UK for six or seven years, and having been admitted to a junior college in China, Zhang Lai's English is good enough for general conversation and dealing with British landlords. In the UK, most Chinese people are unwilling to rent a house directly from a British person, but prefer to rent a house from a Chinese sub-landlord. There is only one reason for this: they don't speak English and are simply afraid of dealing with foreigners.

A few months later, he heard that an Indian family in Chinatown had bought a house somewhere else and was planning to move their whole family there, and was looking for someone to rent the entire building. He went to see the house and thought it was big enough and had never been rented out before, so it was very clean. There were also many rooms that could be rented out in the building (for example, the room where the old Wei couple lived was the one he asked the Indian landlord to separate from the kitchen and the living room), so he boldly rented it. He signed a contract with the old Indian gentleman, paid a month's deposit, and then started looking for someone.

I was the third call he received for renting a house, but the first person to come and see the house. Zhang Lai was lucky. All the houses were rented out after a week. It can only be said that there were too many Chinese people who wanted to rent houses in " Chinatown " . At this time, he had nearly a thousand pounds left after paying the deposit to the Indian landlord (which was also equivalent to the interim income he would get from this house every month in the future), so he soon rented another house nearby, and his business grew like a snowball.

However, the food in any industry is not so delicious, and soon one thing made Zhang Lai suffer. At that time, he had already

223

rented four or five houses in this area. He did nothing every day but run around to collect rent. Because each tenant moved in at a different time, everyone paid rent on a different day. Zhang Lai not only had to remember who should pay the rent on which day, but also the different prices between them. There were more than a dozen people in one house, and four houses meant forty or fifty people, not to mention some temporary tenants. Tenants moved in and out all day long, looking at houses and checking out, so Zhang Lai was really busy and had a lot of troubles.

One day, a tenant who rented a house from him called him and said that the light in his room was broken, the water tank in the toilet could not pump water, and the sewer was blocked. He asked him when he could come over to take a look or find someone to fix it. The call came early in the morning. At that time, Zhang Lai readily agreed, but when he was busy with other things in the afternoon, he completely forgot about this matter. The man waited from morning to night, and he couldn't wait any longer, so he called him again at seven or eight o'clock in the evening, saying, Zhang Lai, when are you going to come over to fix the light? I can't spend the whole night in the dark in my room, can I? And I live next to the toilet. Now the toilet is blocked and the feces and urine are overflowing. The stench is so bad that it has spread to my room!

When Zhang Lai heard this, he thought to himself, how can this guy be so annoying that he asked me to come over to fix his toilet in the middle of the night? But even though he was furious, he didn't say anything. He just perfunctorily said, " Okay, okay, I get it. I'll get someone over right away. "

The problem was that it was already dark, and it was not convenient for him to find someone at the moment. He made several phone calls but could not find anyone. Zhang was getting upset when the tenant called again to urge him:

" Come on, brother, come here quickly, I've been waiting for you all day! "

" I know, I know, " Zhang said, " Give me a few more minutes and I'll get someone over here. "

After hanging up the phone, he angrily cursed: " What a fucking idiot! "

Unfortunately, Zhang Lai pressed the wrong button when he was hanging up the phone, so the call was not hung up at all, and the last sentence he said was heard by the other party immediately. He deserved his bad luck. Although the boy was not very old, about 18 or 19 years old, he looked like a student and no one would dare to cause him any trouble. But do you know who that boy is? He is the nephew of the deputy leader of the Fuqing Gang, a well-known Chinese gang in London! Zhang Lai is in big trouble now. The child immediately called his uncle and told him this and that. When the uncle heard on the phone that someone dared to bully his nephew like this, he immediately asked Zhang Lai's address and said:

" Don't worry about it. I guarantee that this grandson will come to you and kowtow to you early tomorrow morning! "

That night, at one or two o'clock in the middle of the night, Zhang Lai was sleeping in his room when he was suddenly awakened by a shocking noise downstairs. " Who is it? " He just sat up to see what happened, and before he could turn on the light, he suddenly felt something cold against his neck. Someone grabbed his hair and pulled him out of the quilt like a chicken and threw him to the ground. He was so scared that he was about to scream when the light came on.

" Are you Zhang Lai? " There were already five or six people standing in the room, one of whom was a middle-aged man with a fat face and smoking a half-smoked cigarette.

" Brother, brother, what are you talking about? " Zhang Lai was so frightened that he knelt on the ground and begged for mercy. " Brother, I didn't offend you. If you want something, just ask me. Don't do this, don't do this ..."

While they were talking in the room, Zhang Lai heard that there was chaos in other rooms of the building outside. The residents were all screaming and in chaos, but no one said anything after a while. Then there were only the sounds of cursing, banging, tables being smashed and legs being broken all over the floor. Judging from the situation, there were at least 10 to 20 people who came.

" Xiao Lin is my nephew, did you know that? " The middle-aged man slowly smoked the cigarette in his hand, glanced at him sideways and said.

" Ah? Ah, it's Uncle Lin! " Zhang Lai reacted quickly and immediately smiled flatteringly, " I'm sorry, I'm sorry, I really spent the whole day looking for someone for him today. I found someone in the evening and was about to go over, but who knew ..."

" Stop your bullshit, " Uncle Lin interrupted him. " Do you think I'm an idiot? Or do you think my nephew is an idiot? Huh? Who is the idiot? And now you want to pretend to be my grandson? Boy, you are still too young. "

" I'm an idiot, I'm an idiot! " Upon hearing this, Zhang Lai finally understood where the trouble was. He was so scared that his face turned pale. " Uncle Lin, Uncle Lin, I'm the biggest idiot.

Uncle Lin, please forgive me this time. I won't dare to do it again. I will be filial to my elder brother in the future! "

" Who is your eldest brother? " Uncle Lin pinched his cigarette coldly: " Beat him to death! This kid is lucky - just don't break his arms and legs, and keep his legs to kowtow to my nephew. "

As soon as he gave the order, Zhang Lai started crying like a pig being slaughtered.

* * *

No one dares to live in Zhang Lai's house anymore.

Mingming, who ran out of Zhang Lai's apartment, said: " Oh my god, it was so scary, it was exactly like what was shown in the movies! Those guys all had knives, they smashed and robbed anything they saw, and smashed everything that couldn't be moved. Not only did they take out all the cash, they also unplugged all the laptops and took them away, and even my MP3 player was not spared! - Fortunately, they came for Zhang Lai that day, so they didn't touch us at all, and they didn't ask for our bank card passwords. - Thank God, that's a blessing. "

There was a period of time when gangsters committed robberies in London. They would force people to tell them their bank card passwords at knifepoint. Then another person would immediately go to an ATM outside to withdraw money. If the password was correct, they would let the person go. If it was wrong, they would immediately bleed him until they forced him to tell them the correct password.

This is just a side dish. The Chinese underworld in London is quite powerful. 14K and Fuqing Gang are the two largest gangs.

In addition, there are other gangs such as Bamboo Union and Chaoshan Gang, which should not be underestimated. All the restaurant owners in Chinatown know about these gangs. Every year, no matter who it is, they will obediently give them money as tribute. Otherwise, no matter how capable he is, he will not be able to do business peacefully this year. It's just that no one talks about these things, and no one pretends to know. No place is peaceful and prosperous.

The next day, Zhang Lai ran to Xiaolin's place early in the morning, closed the door, kowtowed to him and apologized, then he personally fixed the lights in the room and the toilet drain pipes, and put on gloves and dug out feces and urine to clear the pipes, then he ran to our house to find Lao Zhu without stopping.

" Brother Zhu, you have to save me this time no matter what, " Zhang Lai said straight to the point, " because you have lived in my house for such a long time. You know what kind of person I am. "

Old Zhu was still half-lying on the bed, fanning himself with a palm-leaf fan, swinging his crossed legs and saying, " Zhang Lai, it's not that I don't want to help you, but the hornet's nest you've stirred up this time is too big. Who is Uncle Lin? I can't help you even if I want to. "

Zhang Lai said with half of his face bruised and swollen: " Brother Zhu, even if I beg you, please find someone to help me settle this matter. In fact, I am doing this for the tenants in my building. You know, not only was their money taken away, but even their notebooks were taken away. - Some of them are still students, and their unfinished term papers are still in their computers. I have to be worthy of the brothers in the building, right? Otherwise, I can't survive in London anymore.

228

Brother, I don't want all the money, but can you help me find someone to talk to them, do them a favor, and redeem the things they took away? How much is it, you decide. "

Old Zhu laughed from the bottom of his heart, stood up from the bed, patted Zhang Lai's shoulder with his fan and said: " Zhang Lai, I'm not saying anything bad about you, but you are still too young. Such a simple matter has caused such a big mess. - But since you think so highly of me, Old Zhu, I will try to help you. But I dare not make this guarantee. Whether others will loosen their lips or not, it depends on your luck. "

" Yes, yes, thank you, brother. Thank you, brother. " Zhang Lai was sweating profusely. " Don't worry, you have done me a big favor this time. I will never forget this kindness, brother. "

" Don't be polite, don't be polite, " Lao Zhu said with a smile, " You are being too polite. We are all brothers, right? It's not easy for anyone to be out there. Everyone needs to ask for help sometimes. Go back. I'll think of a solution for you and give you an answer in a few days. "

Zhang Lai left with many thanks.

Old Zhu was indeed very capable. A few days later, he called Zhang Lai and said, " Zhang Lai, I have everything you want. Come and get it anytime you want. "

I heard that in addition to the ransom, Zhang Lai would not ask Lao Zhu to pay any more rent in the future. Lao Zhu said that he could not live in this house anymore. After much persuasion, Zhang Lai reluctantly agreed to continue collecting rent from him, but the rent was half cheaper than before.

* * *

The last time I saw Zhang Lai was half a year after I moved out of Chinatown . One day, I suddenly received a call from Zhang Lai, saying, "Sister, the Mid-Autumn Festival is coming soon. Do you have any activities?" I said, "What? Mid-Autumn Festival?" At that time, I had already left Chinatown and shared a house with two British people, so I had completely lost the concept of Chinese festivals. I said, "Oh my God, if you hadn't told me, I would have almost forgotten about it. So, what day is it?"

Zhang Lai laughed and said, " Tomorrow is the Mid-Autumn Festival. Come over tonight and have dinner with us. I'm throwing a party at home , and Abao, Achang and the others will be here. "

I immediately agreed happily. I thought, it's been so long, it's amazing that he still thinks of me during the holidays. I think he is really a kind and loyal sub-landlord.

That night we had hot pot in Zhang Lai's house. Because Zhang Lai didn't have a knife to cut mutton in his kitchen, he specifically asked me to bring the kitchen knife I bought from China. As soon as I arrived at his house, Achang said happily:

" Okay, okay, here comes the meat-cutting knife! "

So I wondered suspiciously, did they invite me to this party just because they remembered the sharp kitchen knife I used when I lived with them?

Another friend of Zhang Lai quickly used my knife to cut up a whole frozen leg of lamb, and brought up two large plates filled with lamb and beef slices. Upstairs in Zhang Lai's room, Abao and I had already hurriedly plugged in the power socket of the rice cooker, poured in the prepared spicy soup and put it on the dining table. The table was filled with various vegetables they had prepared in advance. Chinese cabbage leaves, cut potato slices, tofu and vermicelli bought in Chinatown, lettuce, rapeseed, and broccoli, one plate after another on a large table, accompanied by the hot and fragrant hot pot soup, it really looked like a festive atmosphere.

Everyone sat down at the table in a lively atmosphere. The men began to drink beer by the dozen and eat food, while Abao and I, a few other women, gathered together to serve rice, hot pot and chat.

" Your jacket is so beautiful, " I asked, looking at the new clothes on Abao, " where did you buy it? "

While Ah Bao was putting the mutton slices that she had prepared for Achang into his bowl, she said, " Oh, now that you ask me, I really don't know. Achang just bought it for me last week, and I don't know where he bought it. "

" Look how good your Achang is to you, " I said enviously, " I wonder when I will be able to meet a man who treats me well like you. "

" Sister, why are you in such a hurry? " Although Abao is several years younger than me, she is used to calling me sister. " You are so good, are you worried about not finding a man? I think you are too picky and no one likes you. "

Although Abao is young, his words are very sharp and to the point. He also gave me enough face.

As we were talking, Zhang Lai seemed to be discussing what business to do with Achang.

" You know, my company is already established, and the company account in the bank is also available. You can use it anytime you want. " Zhang Lai lit a cigarette and said while smoking at the dinner table.

I then remembered that Chang was an illegal immigrant and could not open a company or a bank account in the UK, so it was no wonder that these two people got together to discuss business. A long time ago, Abao told me that Chang had always planned to open his own brothel.

Achang said: " Let me think about it. I'll call you tomorrow. "

I know he was concerned that there were too many people at the dinner table today and some things were difficult to talk about.

" Come on, come on, eat some food and drink some wine, " Ah Bao said without missing a beat. " Today is the Mid-Autumn Festival. Come on, we, the homeless people, let's drink a toast to the Mid-Autumn Festival reunion! "

Her proposal was really well received. Everyone cheered and immediately raised their glasses to the lively atmosphere of Chinese songs playing in Zhang Lai's room:

" Come on, come on, for the Mid-Autumn Festival, for the beautiful full moon in London, England, cheers! "

I raised my glass with a smile.

——The End——

20 March 2005
Written in London, at the age of 28

[postscript]

People with Stories

Yilin Zhong

In March this year, a friend from China [1] came to London on a business trip from Beijing. I asked him to bring me some books over on the phone. I had lived in London for three years and had almost no books to read. Original English novels were everywhere, but they were difficult to read and I couldn't find the sense of Chinese language no matter how hard I read them. Living overseas, material difficulties are secondary; the most important problem is the difficulties in spiritual life. So when this friend was coming from Beijing, I took the opportunity to call him and asked him to bring some Chinese books for me to read.

Before this, another kind-hearted friend understood my difficulties and sent me a travelogue of India written by Naipaul, a British writer he liked, at a postage costing more than buying a book. After reading that book, I wrote a long novel. It was the previous book, London Love Story. Maybe because I told this friend about this on the phone, he went to the bookstore before leaving Beijing and bought me three more books by Naipaul that were not available online.

I saw the half-full suitcase of books he brought for me at my friend's hotel, and I was so happy. I was definitely "reading poetry and books with great joy", and then "singing and drinking in the daytime", so I took him to a bar in London's SOHO district.

It was already past ten o'clock in the evening when we finished drinking at the bar. When he saw that I paid the bill, my friend seemed a little apologetic and said, " Let me treat you to dinner. Are there any western restaurants nearby? " - My friend asked this only because when we came just now, I specifically took him to visit Chinatown in the center of SOHO district. Seeing that the streets were full of Chinese restaurants that were doing very good business, he began to worry whether there were any western restaurants nearby that could survive.

I took him to a western restaurant near Leicester Square. At first I found two cheap restaurants for him, but he was not satisfied with any of them. He said, " I came to the UK just to eat the most authentic and good steak. Find me a good one, don't save money for me. "

This friend had lived in the United States for nearly ten years, completing his master's and doctoral degrees. When I left China, he had just returned to Beijing a few years ago, so he missed the Western-style steaks in American restaurants.

We ordered steak and red wine, and the waiter came over with a plate with wine glasses.

" How have you been doing in the UK over the past few years? " My friend asked me casually while cutting the steak on the plate. Then he cut a small piece from the side, put it into his

234

mouth with a fork, and said happily as soon as he took a bite: " Well, I haven't eaten such a good steak in a long time. " It was as if his whole body suddenly relaxed.

I looked at him with sympathy, even though I was the one who deserved more sympathy.

" It's OK, " I said. " Just live like this. "

" How long have you not been back home? " My friend asked, chewing beef.

I blinked, as if thinking for a moment: " Three years. "

" Oh, " my friend smiled, picked up the wine glass beside him and took a sip, as if he was still savoring the delicious taste of the steak he had just taken, " So you haven't been back since you left? "

" Yes, " I answered sadly, lowering my head.

" When are you going back? " He asked, continuing to cut and eat. " Don't you miss home? "

" I don't know. I call home every week. " I reported truthfully.

My friend continued to eat heartily, saying, " What are you doing? I've been in the United States for so many years, and life there is so hard. Why don't you go back? "

And then he said, " Everyone misses you. "

I nodded: " I miss everyone too, especially my friends in Beijing. - It's because of you that I haven't been able to find a real friend to chat with in the UK in the past few years. "

He gave me a sympathetic look and continued to eat his steak.

" Don't you have many Chinese friends here? " He asked. He knew what I meant was to talk about deep things in Chinese. I don't have many such friends even in Beijing.

When he said that, I remembered something and suddenly laughed: " Yes, there are many. "

Then I told him a story about a Chinese friend of mine in the UK. The protagonist of this story is A-Bao.

Although I only gave a brief account, he had already finished eating by the time I finished speaking. He was drinking red wine and wiping the corners of his mouth with a golden-red napkin.

I noticed that the steak on my plate was cold. Fortunately, I wasn't very hungry at the time.

After listening to my story, my friend smiled and said, " They won't be able to sell for many years. Who would want them when they get older? "

" They didn't intend to sell like this forever, " I suddenly realized that he didn't understand them. I wanted to say something else, but this topic has been talked about for too long and the restaurant is about to close, so I had to change the subject: " What time is it? "

The friend looked at the gold watch on his wrist: " It's a quarter to twelve. "

" Let's pay the bill quickly, " I said, " the subway will run out soon. " Only then did I realize that we were the last table of customers in the restaurant.

" Okay, " my friend waved to the waiter who was standing in the distance and was getting impatient, made a sign gesture and said, "Bill please."

* * *

That night I went home and started reading the book my friend brought me. It was like a camel that had been thirsty for half a month in the desert and found an oasis. The past few years in the UK really made me thirsty. When I was in school, I read original theoretical books in English. After graduation, I could only read newspapers every day. Where could I read literary books, let alone Chinese books? In fact, in this respect, I am not much different from other Chinese people in the UK. When I was still living in " Chinatown ", Alun once returned to China for vacation and brought back a copy of the Beijing Youth Daily on the day he boarded the plane. He threw it to me. As a result, the people on the first floor of our building read it from top to bottom, from beginning to end, and from end to beginning for several months. In the end, the newspaper was dirty and torn, and it was rotten beyond recognition. In the kitchen, I often saw someone sitting at the plastic dining table they picked up, burying their heads in the newspaper that they had read countless times.

I guess they can recite all the sentences in it.

People talk about sexual hunger, but I think spiritual hunger is the most important. This applies to both educated and uneducated people.

But the current cultural situation in China is not much better than ours. I often go online to read Chinese websites in China, and I often browse the excerpts of the latest best-selling books introduced online. My God. I won't say anything here.

So, these world-class modern literary classics brought to me by my friends really helped me a lot. It was even revolutionary. On the night I got home, I took those dozen books and read them one by one like treasures, and then picked out one or two of them to read some excerpts. Oh my God, at that time, my heart was filled with infinite sighs: Great! This is a really good book! This is a real literary work, this is a real master!

Among this limited spiritual food, I still could not hide my preference for Naipaul. At three o'clock in the morning, I realized that I only had time to finish reading one of the books in the remaining time, so I decided to read a thinner work in the time when I could only read one book, and I chose Naipaul's short story collection, "Miguel Street".

When I read one-third of the content, I already knew how the master was born.

It was already six in the morning. I jumped over and finished reading the last chapter of the book in the last ten minutes before going to bed. Although I knew that he would be sentimental in this last chapter and had prepared myself mentally, and I am also a novelist, I still cried when I saw the last line. And I couldn't help crying loudly. This fucking bastard, how could he make me cry when I knew he was going to be sentimental? And in 1959 ?

It's already 2005 .

I cried for a long time in grief. Then I closed my eyes and fell asleep. I slept until noon that day.

I opened my eyes in bed at noon and saw a bright sunny day outside the window. The sun was shining brightly on my bed. It was a very good day. It was bright and clear.

Then I thought, I'm going to start writing novels again.

* * *

Two days later, the friend from Beijing invited me to dinner again. This time we had lunch in Oxford. I accompanied him there, and we were both hungry at noon. We couldn't find any decent restaurants, so we just ordered some bread and English tea at a small shop on the street.

I talked to him about the books I was reading and the novel I was planning to write.

" I have all the stories, but I haven't figured out how to string them together. " I told him, " I've been thinking about this problem these days. "

He said, " Have you written it? "

I frowned: " Not yet. I haven't figured out how to write it yet. "

He was eating a snack, a kind of stuffed bread from the UK, similar to the Jingdong meat pie in Beijing. At first I joked with him that a Jingdong meat pie would cost 50 yuan in the UK. My friend just smiled and said nothing.

" Then you can try to write a little bit first, " the friend suggested, " maybe the story will come out as you write. " He used to be a writer in China, but he stopped writing for many years and started a business.

" No, no, that won't work. " I shook my head. " I can't help it. I'm just like that. I have to think of everything before I start writing. Otherwise, what I write will be rubbish. "

I said, " In fact, all the stories and characters are already there, and we just need a main line to connect them all. " He lowered his head and thought for a while, then said, " But sometimes, after planning everything, I suddenly can't write anything. "

" So inspiration is the most important thing, " I said to myself, " at least that's the case for me. " As I thought about it,

My friend nodded, drank his tea, and said nothing.

I stared at the street view of Oxford's central street outside the floor-to-ceiling glass window of the small restaurant, and wondered blankly: " What on earth is that string of strings? "

* * *

Until one day, it suddenly occurred to me.

239

Chinatown.

I immediately rushed to my desk in excitement and began writing frantically. Suddenly I was back to writing for 17 or 18 hours straight, sleeping only 5 or 6 hours a day.

The novel was being written very smoothly, almost at a rapid pace. When my friend left, I didn't even have time to see him off at the airport.

" Why, have you found the feeling? " he asked me on the phone.

" Yes, yes, I'm so sorry, I didn't go to bed until six o'clock. " I said on the phone while lying in bed. It was nine o'clock in the morning and I had just slept for three hours. I wrote all night. Now I couldn't get up no matter what. I had to rush to Heathrow Airport before eleven o'clock to see off this friend who sent me coal in the snow.

" It's okay, just keep writing and we'll see you when you return to Beijing, " said my friend.

" Thank you, thank you, " I kept saying, " Thank you so much. "

At this time, I had almost written half of my novel.

* * *

After about four or five days, the novel was completely finished. Only two endings were left to be written in two chapters. For the detailed writing process, you can read my "Creation Notes". At this point, my task of writing this postscript has been completely completed. When this novel was almost finished, I had already thought of the content of the next novel. But it is not yet fully mature, and I need some time to think about it.

Finally, I have to say one more thing. I have never been sure whether this book should be considered a collection of short stories or a novel . [2] As I said at the beginning, I was largely inspired by Naipaul's Miguel Street, which is a collection of short stories. However, when I was writing my own book, I found it difficult to really define its genre. Because as you can see, each story can stand alone, but each story can also be regarded as a chapter in the book, and all the stories and characters are also connected to each other. Therefore, I am still not sure what literary genre this book should be considered. However, perhaps in the end this question is not important at all. What is important is what you see and what you think in these stories.

Finally, let me say one more thing. To put it bluntly, who doesn't have a story? Whose story can be written down into a book? So being able to tell a story is not a skill, and writing down your own story or life in a self-loving and self-pitying way is not a skill either. What is the true standard of a good writer? Perhaps any reader knows better than the writer himself. Speaking of this, in fact, compared to the title of writer, I would rather be just an ordinary storyteller. In other words, a person with a story. Only in such a humble identity can I feel safe and feel my true existence in this world.

18 March 2005
In London

Writing Notes

Yilin Zhong

March 13: Completed chapters 0, 1, and 2. It was written until the early morning of the 14th.

March 14: I finished writing Chapter 3 in the early morning, got up at noon, finished writing the first half of Chapter 4, went shopping and went home in the evening to finish writing 4, and then wrote the beginning of 5.

Overall, the speed is significantly slower than "London Love Story". It's not because of other reasons. I actually have enough energy and time to write quickly, but the problem is that I feel sad for a long time after I finish writing a story. I couldn't get back to it for a long time, so I couldn't continue writing. I had to stop for a while. Let's continue writing when your mood recovers.

But there are times when you are happy. For example, today I wrote about the refugee couple finding the supply channel upstairs, which is really happy for them. After writing that paragraph, I went for lunch and was in a very good mood all afternoon. I am happy for the characters in my novel. Unfortunately, I am so happy that I am too few times and I am still sad. Writing itself is a painful profession. Fortunately, I have learned how to adjust myself now. I wouldn't have been trapped in my entire relationship for writing like I did many years ago, and I almost died.

no way. Because what I wrote is a tragedy.

March 15: I finished writing 5 last night, but I didn't feel very ideal. I woke up at noon today and lay on the bed and finished writing Chapter 6. After writing this chapter, I was suddenly happy for some reason, and I felt a sense of psychological happiness. It's like finding the character's feeling. I thought it would be very smooth to write later, so I went to the library in the afternoon. I didn't expect that when I came back, I planned to continue writing Chapter 7, I realized that my thinking was interrupted.

It seems that it is the point in the middle of each novel I said. Although this is a long story composed of short stories, it is still a whole after all, so it also encountered such trouble. But I comforted myself that I just finished writing a long piece last month, which is very interesting. It doesn't matter if you break it. If you can't finish it, you can't finish it. It's better than writing out scraps. But I still plan to continue to write hard. At least try again. Now writing, I feel that it is somewhat contrary to the original intention of the earliest writing. I mean the formality. I originally planned to write the whole article into a novel like Chapter 2 and Chapter 3, but later I still didn't stop it and started writing it again. However, the content and spirit are closer to the original intention due to the deviation of form. I don't know if it's good or bad for the time being, from the perspective of the novel.

No matter that much, it is important to write it out first. Let's talk about it if it's good.

Also: When I was writing this novel today, I only found the feeling I had when I described love in the novel ten years ago. There is no love throughout this novel, but this is what I really like. Finally back to the past. It took me ten years.

It's not happiness, but relief. A feeling of finding home. Extremely relieved.

March 16: Yesterday I had insomnia all night. I turned on the lights and got up to write Chapter 10 at 3 a.m., which is also the chapter I have always wanted to write the most. I finally couldn't help writing today. After writing for a long time, I found that a chapter of the story could not be finished. After writing one chapter, I only started the story. If I continue to write it in one chapter, this article would be too long, so I simply divided the story into three chapters, which probably should be similar. I finished the first part of this story at 6 a.m., and I was so tired. It's not sleepy, it's mental fatigue, so I stopped to rest for a while, listened to music, and played computer cards.

Anyway, I couldn't sleep today, so I decided to hold on until night before going to bed. It doesn't matter whether you write it or not.

Evening: After finishing the second chapter of this story, it was already six in the morning. I didn't sleep all night.

I always felt very uncomfortable when I wrote this story. Maybe because the protagonist of the story is also a young woman.

March 17: This story by Abao is too tiring, and the key is that it is too mentally tormenting. So after writing the second part, I really don't have the courage or the strength to continue writing the subsequent story. Since I only slept for three hours a day yesterday, I drank a large cup of coffee yesterday afternoon to prevent myself from going to bed early. Unexpectedly, it was this cup of coffee, which made me fall asleep at five o'clock this morning again. From 1:00 to 5:00 in the morning, I wrote novels again. Because I was afraid that I would go crazy if I continued to write, so I chose a relaxed person to write. This passage in the early morning was about Lao Zhu's story. However, because Lao Zhu is also an important figure here, although he writes it very easily, he does not dare to relax at all. I was afraid of writing such a good character badly, but it was a pity for the material.

As a result, Lao Zhu had too many stories, and it seemed that there were still too many chapters. So I was really tired and sleepy at five o'clock in the morning. I went to bed after I was halfway through it.

I got up at noon and made a few phone calls, then ran out to go to the Internet and sent a few emails. When I came back, I finished writing the third chapter of the prostitute Abao, which is also the last chapter of the character. Although her story

I haven't finished telling it yet, but the content behind the plan is put into Achang's story. Because the story of the character Abao has been completed.

245

Chinatown

Strangely, I wrote about several places in the afternoon and cried. I haven't had such an experience for a long time. I mean, when writing the story I made, I was so sad that the fate of the characters I designed was so sad that they shed tears. It's really been a long time since this happened. The last time was about ten years ago when I wrote "Romance".

Today I have already thought about the content of the next novel, but I am not sure whether it can be written yet. This novel will end in two days. I have always wanted to take a good rest before continuing to write it, but I have never had time to rest. It has been more than a month since mid-February until now.

Evening: I wrote the first half of Achang's story one night. Now I found that there is a problem, that is, the story is too long, far beyond the original plan. It seems that just writing a long story for the two of them was enough. Now they have written tens of thousands of words. They have just met and have not yet fallen in love. It seems that the story behind them cannot be told in this book, so keep it and then talk about it slowly. I'll just explain the ending to them later. I really didn't expect to write so many things.

Now that I know I'm about to finish writing, my speed is gradually slowing down. It seems a bit reluctant to let it go. Hehe..

March 18: After finishing Achang at 1:30 am, it is also the second to last chapter of the book. After hesitating for a long time, he still gave them a happy ending. Even if the author is not cruel enough. Just such a little happiness can actually touch myself. — —I hope they can be really happy.

Noon: I want to finish writing a chapter of the landlord Zhang Lai. After thinking for a long time, I found a problem, which is that the more familiar the life I am, the more difficult it is to write and the harder it is to write. Now the last two stories left in the book, namely the story of Lao Zhu and the landlord. The landlord may be a little better to write. Lao Zhu is the most troublesome thing for me now. There are too many things to write.

Afternoon: Change your mind and write the postscript.

Night: I watched the 007 movie on TV and finally got a full rest. I came back and finished writing a chapter of Lao Zhu.

March 19: I feel that I can definitely finish all the work today. Now there is only one landlord Zhang. For some reason, I suddenly remembered the 108 futures of "Water Margin". That is a really good novel, I only wrote a few people here.

I finished writing the middle part of the landlord Zhang Lai in the early morning, then went to bed, went out during the day, and came back in the afternoon to finish the end. I plan to revise the full text tonight and I can get rid of the manuscript.

I feel that this time I'm not that tired and my writing is very loose. Maybe because the main writing is someone else. "I" just plays a role in a series of scenes in the novel.

At night: No single word was written.

Chinatown

March 20: I have been coughing these days (it was shown when the novel was written in Chapter 9 "Xiao Chen"), but I coughed too hard in the middle of the night. I woke up in the morning and just opened my eyes, I coughed violently again. I quickly took a tissue and spit out the phlegm in my throat. When I coughed out, I saw a piece of blood on the tissue.

It's over, and now I even coughed up blood. The previous novel just cut my fingers, but my fingernails have not yet grown well, and this one is coughing up bleeding. I don't know what the next novel will be like. I am only twenty-eight years old now, so I coughed up blood. If I continue writing like this, it will take my life.

I think so, I wrote a long work a week, and the labor intensity is so high, and I know that this is not a job that humans do. And no one forced me, I voluntarily. Living in a dilapidated apartment in London, I don't even need to work anymore, so I just keep writing novels like crazy. (If it were you, would you rather have a job with an annual salary of tens of thousands of pounds or write a novel?) Write every day when you open your eyes, and go to bed if you can't open your eyes. This is not the life that people live.

Noon: I got up and took some medicine (it was a Chinese medicine powder, as if I suddenly took the wrong medicine. I felt so disgusting that I almost vomited it out), and lay in bed and felt dizzy and finished the whole novel in a paragraph that Lao Zhu needed to write. While writing, I kept coughing, so my entire internal organs almost coughed out of my throat. I really don't want to live anymore. After writing, I roughly edited the whole novel. I was dizzy after I got it, and I felt so uncomfortable.

Fortunately, I finally made it to the end. This is already thankful. Now I have to force myself to take a good rest. Treat my illness first and let my parents worry.

All work is now completed.

Writing notes attachments:

1. List of candidate characters (shortlisted but not selected)

No.011 Cousin (A friend came from afar)
No.012 Lily (33 -year-old virgin)
No.013 Xiaoying (Troublesome love)
No.014 Grocery Store Owner (Ten months of pregnancy)
No.015 Landlord Chen Liang (Chinese accountant)
No.016 Zhou Lanlan (a student who works three jobs a day)
No.017 Luo Qing (Transnational marriage)
No.018 Nurse Nina (Spaghetti pasta)
No.019 The Great Jerry (London Student Union)
No.020 Xiao D (Stowaway teenage boy)

2. Deleted Paragraphs from the novel

（1）

One day Xiao D praised me at upstairs: "Oh, sister, who else is as good as you? Beautiful, has a degree, and speaks foreign languages well, oh my, I really don't know which man will be so lucky to marry you in the future."

I said, "You little bastard, are you here to make fun of your sister for fun? Shut up and keep your mouth shut."

Xiao D at once changed his tone and said, " Sis, if you want to know why you can't get married, it's because of this bad thing. You are always so mean to men. Not only your elder brother, but even I dare not marry you. "

I was so angry that my chest was about to explode, so I ran over and grabbed his ears, but he was smart, he got up and ran away. Before leaving, he said:

"Sis, I'm going downstairs to cook for you! You'll have to be nicer to me in the future. "

I was so angry that I didn't know whether to laugh or cry. I stood in their room and shouted to Chunsheng: " Look at how naughty he is, and you guys don't do anything about it?!"

Chunsheng smiled faintly and continued playing his computer game without saying a word. While Lao Zhu was asleep on the sofa chair and smiled.

（2）

All the men in Chinatown drink , but I have never seen anyone drunk. This may only mean that they live too soberly. Or, in other words, they have to live too soberly.

（3）

"Lao Zhu old pig,
　Always sleeping,

Talking nonsense,
A big pirate!'

That day I made up a ballad for Lao Zhu. I was very proud of myself and excitedly ran to the next room to sing it to him, hoping to disturb his sleep.

When Lao Zhu heard my new song, he half opened his eyes from the bed, looked at me, snorted and said:

"Little sis, I see you are the big pirate who talks nonsense all day long."

---

[1] Note1: The friend who brought me the book was Mr. Shi Tao, later the Vice President of Amazon China. However, because I had been abroad for many years, I did not know that he had gone to Amazon at the time. I would like to express my gratitude to him for sending me the book over a long distance.

[2] Note2: This problem had already been solved when Chinatown was published in Harvest magazine: the editorial department of Harvest published the novel "Special Issue on Novels". Therefore, after being classified by China's most professional literary journal, the genre classification of the novel has undoubtedly been fully answered.

[Postscript]

Chinatown,
An Imagined Community

Yilin Zhong

Let me briefly introduce the background of the creation of this novel.

Years ago, when I wrote Chinatown, I was a 28-year-old international student who had just graduated from a prestigious university in the UK. I was sending out resumes everyday to find a job, and I had been looking for nearly a year, but there was still no progress. At that time, I had less than 500 pounds in my bank account, which was about 5,000 yuan in savings, and I had to pay 250 pounds in rent every month, which was half of this money. I can't say that I was penniless at that time, because after all, I still had 500quid, but the word "poor and destitute" can definitely be used to describe my situation at that time.

At that time, there was no internet in the house I rented, so I could only spend one pound every day to go to a nearby internet cafe to surf the internet for an hour, search for the latest job advertisements, and then screen the jobs that seemed to have a little possibility, and then write emails and send resumes one by one, or fill out online application forms as required. I would never even think about doing these things in China. Before going abroad, I ran an advertising company with my friends in Beijing, lived in an export-oriented apartment of over 1400 square foots next to the World Trade Plaza in CBD, and drove a Honda to the cinema alone on weekends to watch movies. However, here, overseas, in the UK, in a foreign country, I am nothing, I have nothing, no one knows me, and I know no one. Like thousands of foreign students, I am just the most ordinary one among them, and even the one who is least likely to find a job here, because I am not from an EU country (they do not need a work visa), but from China.

In the famous British university where I was studying, there were three Chinese students who were studying for an MBA in the business school living in the same dormitory building as me . Before going abroad, they all had extremely strong work experience in the management of Fortune 500 companies, so they were able to be admitted to this world-class business school among thousands of applications and became one of the 30 students in the class. Students like me who study liberal arts are simply on vacation in their eyes: I only have two days of classes a week, and the rest of the time I read books and do homework by myself, while they, these poor business elites, need to complete seven courses in a semester, and on average, they have to complete one subject a week, and they also have to take exams and pass them once. When I heard them talk about this, I, an ignorant liberal arts student, opened my eyes wide in disbelief, blinked and exclaimed: " Oh my God, how can you live like that? "

" So, we can only sleep for four or five hours a day, otherwise we can't even finish reading the books on the list, and we will definitely fail the exam. " A, a Chinese elite from the business school , said to me. Before coming to the UK to study this terrible degree, he worked in a multinational bank in Singapore. For him, studying this MBA is a necessity for promotion.

" Just reading is not that tiring, " Chinese elite B told me, " the key is that we have to do group discussions and group debates every day, which are all compulsory courses for us. " Before going abroad, this absolutely beautiful elite B worked at the Shanghai Coca-Cola Company and held a senior position. Her English eloquence was already brilliant in my opinion, but she would even have a headache over winning or losing a debate with other European business elites in the same group on a topic. For example, the topic of their debate was: Which economy has more advantages in the next five years, the Asian economy or the European economy, and so on.

Speaking of debate, Elite A once told me a joke about Elite C , a finance graduate student from the Department of Economics at Peking University who worked at the Bank of China for several years after graduation. " Yesterday, our whole class had an economic analysis class. After the teacher finished, he asked everyone to discuss in groups and analyze the economy of their own countries, " Elite A said with a teasing smile, " A German student in the same group talked about the high risk of Chinese bank lending, which might cause a bubble in China's economic development. Elite C immediately went crazy. He stood up out

255

of control and gave an indignant and impassioned English speech in front of the whole class. "

" Hahaha ..." I was already laughing so hard that I fainted. " He has such a heavy accent and he's giving a speech to the whole class? "

" Yes, he is from Peking University, " said Elite A. " He is so patriotic. "

I laughed out loud: " So what did he say in his speech? "

" They are all very irrational rhetoric, " Elite A said with a smile, " For example, China's economic level is now among the best in the world, and in the next few decades, China will definitely become the world 's number one economic power, and so on. "

Elite C is truly a typical patriotic Peking University student.

" And then? What did your teacher say? " I couldn't stop laughing.

Elite A, who graduated from Fudan University, said : " You know, the teaching method of the British is very equal. You can say whatever you want and the teacher won't care. However, his remarks made us all feel so ashamed. I don't know how to explain it to other students. These can only represent his own thoughts. "

Elite A said: " Because our course is about calm and objective economic research and data analysis, not this kind of hot-headed, wishful and irrational patriotic speech. "

" He was talking to himself, " I said, nodding.

" Many Chinese people are like this. They don't care what is happening in the world and are only willing to believe what they want to believe. " Elite A, who has worked in Singapore for many years , said, " I'm used to this. "

Let's get back to the point. These three Chinese elites' professional background are so strong and they now have MBA degrees from the best business schools in Europe: the wise and rational A , the beautiful and domineering B, and the scholarly and bold C, when we were about to move out of the student dormitory building after graduation, I asked them, do you plan to stay in the UK to work after graduation?

These three Chinese people, who are all top-notch in IQ, told me: " No (foreign) person in our class plans to stay in the UK after graduation. "

" Why? " I was a little surprised. " London has all the big companies in the world. "

" The investment cost is not in line with the return rate. " Elite A, who is good at data analysis, answered, " Our tuition and living expenses have cost nearly one million (RMB), so we must find a job that can recover this investment within three years, and the jobs that can offer us this salary are not in the UK. "

Elite Beauty B gently told me: " Besides this, the weather in the UK is not good either. It always rains and I am not used to it. Also, the company had already reserved a promotion position for me before I came to study abroad, so I will definitely go back. Unless the company sends me to the UK in the future, I will come here. "

Elite C 's reason is even more unquestionable: " I am Chinese, of course I have to go back to China! "

But I know that out of face, no one told me the real reason why they didn't stay in the UK, which is: they simply couldn't find a job in the UK.

Of course, it is not a job like sweeping the streets as a cleaner, nor is it a job for an ordinary employee of a foreign company. Rather, it is a high-paying, high-level, senior management job at their level.

Although they are all absolutely excellent, compared with their European and American classmates, firstly, their English is not their native language after all, and secondly, even if they find a job with great difficulty, the company still needs to apply for a work visa for them to work in the UK.

Elite executives like them, with MBAs from top business schools around the world, absolutely cannot compromise themselves and stay in a second-rate company doing a low-paying job just for a work visa. As Elite A said, the return on investment is too low and not worth it.

So, in the end, there are only two kinds of people who stay in the UK: one is the literary youth like me who doesn't care about anything and doesn't care about the return on investment or the salary as long as he can have a job (please allow me to be humble and not call myself a writer), or those who are willing to reduce their salary and do a tiring job in order to have an identity; and the other kind of people are the people I described in the novel "Chinatown".

They have nothing, no identity, no passport, no job, and can't even speak the most basic English. But they are the largest Chinese group living in the UK.

Black person.

In their own words, they are all " blacks ", so they are called black people. In official terms, they are illegal residents or illegal immigrants. There are two sources of these illegal residents: one is to enter the country with a legal visa, then overstay and stay here illegally, becoming illegal immigrants. The other is to enter the country directly by smuggling through various means. Most of them come from Fujian, China, and a few come from Guangdong and Northeast China. For these Chinese who have smuggled into the UK, as long as they enter the UK, it is basically a paradise for smugglers: no one will ever catch them here, and the police will never come to find them. They can live freely in the UK for the rest of their lives without being discovered. There is only one situation in which they will be arrested and deported, that is, they are really unlucky and are caught when they are doing something illegal. Or, more tragically, like the shellfish picking tragedy that happened in northern England that year. From the large-scale news reports, we know that those smuggled Chinese who pick shells on the beach for a living sometimes only get one pound per person per day from the snakehead.

When I was a graduate student at the university, I took a course called "Postcolonial Literary Studies". There was a very interesting concept in the course called "Subaltern Studies" , which can be translated as " poorest studies " or " untouchable studies ". Subaltern refers to a very low social class, a class excluded from the mainstream of society. In the words of Marx and Lenin, Subaltern belongs to the oppressed and exploited proletariat. In the words of Mao, Subaltern is the red five categories of poor and lower-middle peasants with a red root. In the academic field of literary research, Subaltern represents the lowest working group without any social status, political status or voice, and their counterparts are the so-called "elites" in the upper class of society .

Illegal immigrants, a large social group, have always been a group missing from all literary works, not only in Chinese literary works, but also rarely seen in world literature. There are many reasons for this. First of all, writers generally rarely have access to this group and this level, and have no way of understanding their lives. Without life experience and understanding of them, of course, it is impossible to write good novels. Lin Yutang's "Chinatown Family" written in English is an example. Xia Zhiqing, who is also in the United States, criticized him and said: "... He has no life experience and lacks understanding of the history of Chinese laundry workers. In his writing, the details are not real - he makes the laundry workers recite the "Tao Te Ching" and "The Analects" all day to express their cultural baggage. If the details are not real, the work will be superficial. Lin Yutang wrote about laundry workers he was not familiar with, but what we read in his novels is not the life and feelings of the laundry workers, but Lin Yutang's high-handed pity for them."

In addition to the lack of understanding of this group among writers, there is another strange phenomenon. I found that almost all Chinese writers living overseas often write about things that happen in China, rather than the foreign country where they live. For example, the novels of American writer Ha Jin, from the earliest "Waiting" to the recent "Nanjing Requiem", are all about China. The same is true for another Chinese American writer, Li Yiyun, whose novels are all about stories that happen in China in English. It is true that every writer has their own preferences when writing novels, but this is a strange preference of most overseas Chinese writers that I cannot understand: they obviously live abroad, but they write in non-native English in their imaginary China in an attempt to move foreigners, while they turn a blind eye to the real overseas Chinese life that happens around them every day. And it is precisely because of the collective aphasia of overseas Chinese writers in this subject and field that such a major theme as overseas illegal immigration has never appeared in any contemporary literary work, so that a strange blank has been formed in the history of contemporary Chinese literature.

Therefore, not only in the boundaries of history and law, but also in the world of literature, the faces and living conditions of these illegal immigrants who have no voice and are called Subalterns have also become a veritable blank. It is as if they are an invisible society. Although in real society, this is such a large group. It is estimated that there are about 40 million illegal immigrants in the world. However, in our world, in law, and in literature, they have never existed.

"Chinatown" is about such a "non-existent" group of people.

There is an important topic in Subaltern Studies , that is, the subaltern groups have no voice, they will not and cannot express their own voices (because most of them are uneducated and have no channels to express their ideas), so they can only speak for them through the elites . I strongly refuted this view in my term paper at the time. I said that on the contrary, the subaltern groups not only have their own voices, but they also have very vivid and rich language. Their voices even far exceed those of the so-called elite groups. However, these voices of the subalterns have never been valued and discovered by society and the elites.

If I were to explain the above passage in more popular terms that every Chinese could easily understand, I might as well

261

borrow a passage from Mr. Mao's "Speech at the Yan'an Forum on Literature and Art". He said: " In the people's lives there exists a mine of raw materials for literature and art. These are things in their natural form, crude things, but also the most vivid, richest and most basic things. In this respect, they make all literature and art pale in comparison. They are the only inexhaustible source of all literature and art." He also called on all party members to "learn language from the people" because "the people's vocabulary is rich, vivid and reflects real life." I think what he said here makes sense.

Of course, according to his class classification of literature, my works such as "London Single Diary" and "London Love Story" must be classified as decadent literary genres such as "bourgeoisie" and "petty bourgeoisie". However, sometimes literary young women like me occasionally might forget the petty bourgeoisie sentiment, reform my thoughts, pursue progress, and write some proletarian literary works such as "Chinatown" that describe the working-class people at the bottom of society. So from this point of view, "Chinatown" could have represented the highest achievement of my literary works in a sense. - However, this is definitely not because of the education I received in China, but on the contrary, it is the result of my Western education in Britain, the evil old capitalist empire.

When I was preparing for my master's thesis at university, I told my English tutor: "The research topic I want to write for my thesis is: [Chinatown, an imagined community]." My tutor was very surprised and praised me highly, and asked me to start writing immediately. However, I spent a whole month looking up all the information about Chinatown in Chinese and English in the university library in the UK, but I still couldn't perceive

262

this mysterious social image of Chinatown in my mind. In these materials, I can see the historical origins of the formation of Chinatowns overseas, and I can also see pictures and descriptions of various Chinatowns and Chinese settlements in various countries around the world. I can also see the past, present and future of Chinatown, as well as everything about it. But in this complex and vivid picture of Chinatown, which is like a floating world painting, but I can't see the real core of this unique social form: human.

The real individuals living in Chinatown and in this small piece of land the size of a palm all over the world.

In the overwhelming historical materials, social studies, news reports, and the few literary works written by overseas Chinese writers, I can't see them. I can't see the Chinese who live in the present and live in the reality around us every day. In the piles of texts and books, I can't see their existence at all. I can't see the chefs who cook in the Chinese restaurants on the street, nor can I see the illegal refugees who wander around London's Chinatown every day without money but still smile, and the various Chinese people who can be seen in every foreign city and even town. Although they live in a foreign country thousands of miles away from China, they still speak Chinese, write Chinese characters, eat Chinese food every day, celebrate every Chinese festival every year, and live the same life abroad as countless people in China. Chinatown is like an oasis in the desert. It exists like a mirage in their overseas where they have no relatives. This is a Chinese society they imagine. Only in this small world can they find their true sense of belonging.

However, I cannot see all of this, at least not in the library. In the world of words, in Chinatown, a street described in the same

263

way by countless experts and scholars, these people, they, do not exist at all. Or at most, they exist as a punctuation mark like a small wax figure, frozen in the social picture drawn by the intellectuals of the upper class. Similarly, this is also a Chinese society that exists entirely in imagination, but the difference is that it exists in the imagination of them, the "elites" . This is a condensed picture of overseas Chinese society that is perfectly fictionalized. It is as if the countless Chinatowns in various countries and regions around the world were created by China, not by them, the overseas Chinese who have been passed down from generation to generation on the land of Chinatown, but have been forgotten by literature and history.

In the vague and empty maze of texts about Chinatown constructed by cultural elites, I only saw cold history, solid buildings, various fragmented Chinese symbols that existed like rituals, and a nihilistic social picture. Like a photo taken by a long lens that has lost its focus, I can only see its vague and nihilistic shape, but I can never see the vivid characters in the photo, their smiles, words and deeds. In the long river of history, they are so small and insignificant; in this huge picture called "Chinatown", their figures are so grey and blurred, as small as a mustard bean, or even less than a spot on the wall. Although they have existed so tenaciously from generation to generation, in the vast amount of text materials, I can't perceive the truest inner thoughts and daily faces of these Chinese living in Chinatown, this overseas island-like land, and their deepest souls.

So, after nearly a month of preparation, I finally had to decide to give up this topic (which really disappointed my tutor, unfortunately), and instead wrote my graduation dissertation with another subject, which I successfully passed later: "Postmodernism and the Third World."

Then, as described at the beginning of this novel, when I moved out of my university dormitory and returned to London to begin preparing to write this graduation dissertation on postmodernism, purely by chance, I suddenly came into contact with this real group of overseas Chinese people in the lowest class in society: the Subaltern.

Then, about two years later, I wrote the novel you are reading now: Chinatown.

London,
20 September 2014

[Interview 1]

Dialogue

The value of contemporary Chinese literature from the perspective of the various lives in "Chinatown"

Dang (Dang Xiaoyu, the same below): (A weblink of an analytical report on the history of Chinatown in the United States) Is the observation of Chinatown in this report objective? In addition, will your work "Chinatown" be helpful to the living conditions of overseas Chinese?

Zhong (Yilin Zhong, the same below): Haha, this kind of political commentary has nothing to do with literature.

Dang: It would be great if Western media could report on Chinatown. I feel that although the readership of serious literature is not that many, it's good to have some coverage so that more potential readers can see it.

Zhong: It doesn't matter; serious literature is inherently a niche genre.

Dang: Yes, serious literature doesn't have many readers, but I just feel it's a pity if there aren't many readers. After all, if you ask me to live in Chinatown, I don't dare to go, and I may not be able to make friends with all kinds of people.

Zhong: I think the reason why you have this idea - you think you would not dare to do the things that the protagonist " I " in "Chinatown" does, is because first, you have contact with the author of the novel himself. But if you read a novel and have no idea who the author is, you will not have this idea.

Secondly, even if you have come into contact with the author, the reason you would have this feeling of worry or fear, as you said, worrying about the protagonist of the novel, means that subconsciously you still believe that all this is true.

I am not saying that these stories are not true, but when you read a novel, if you strictly follow the boundaries of fictional novels, first of all, you should not believe that everything written in the novel is true, because the label of the novel itself is fiction. And even if I, the author, only say that this is a work of fiction based on some of my personal experiences, it is not a non-fiction report or news report. If it is a news report by an undercover reporter, you may worry about the safety of the reporter; but as a fictional literary work, strictly speaking, you should not worry about the characters and have such thoughts.

Of course, as I mentioned in the first point, maybe because you have had contact with the author, you may subconsciously care about her as a friend and worry about her safety. But as a person who studies literary works, from the perspective of literary criticism, the author and the work should be completely separated.

There is a problem with traditional Western literary theory, which is that it always studies the author's writing motivation, personal experience, writing psychology, etc. I know that in Western literary theory, this research method has occupied a large proportion of the theory in the past, so later a new theory came out, saying " the author is dead. " In fact, this is to against this kind of literary theory that analyzes the author. Because in fact, when you read a literary work, the author does not exist. It's like what Nietzsche said in philosophy: " God is dead. " In literature, it's what Roland Barthes said: " The author is dead. " What it actually wants to deny is this feeling in your subconscious.

Of course, the theory of " the author is dead " belongs to the early postmodernism and the late modernist literary theory, so this concept may not be very popular in China. Of course, there is a certain amount of research in the professional field of literary theory, but it may not be very popular in the mass media or mainstream literary criticism. Because Chinese literary criticism mainly focuses on ideology, revolution, class, etc., so we must study the author's origin, analyze the theme of literary works, etc. Many Chinese literary theories are still limited to these concepts, so you may still be more or less influenced by these theories.

But in fact, the theory of " the author is dead " has long existed in ancient China. For example, "Jin Ping Mei" was written by Lanling Xiaoxiaosheng. Once he used this pen name, the author immediately became invisible. You can't find any trace of this author at all. You don't even know the author's date of birth or who he is. So you can only focus on analyzing his literary works, that is, the text itself. This is the best example of the theory of " the author is dead " .

Of course, this is just one of the analytical methods and a genre of literary research. But personally, I am in favor of completely separating the author from the literary work. Because in this way, at least you can solve your unnecessary worries about the character in the novel, the protagonist " I " .

Dang: The mainstream literary research method in the United States and Britain may be the New Criticism. The New Criticism proposed a method called " intentional fallacy " , which means that the author's intention should never be linked to the work itself, but should be based on the text. I quite agree with this view. Because only by looking between the lines can we see the true intention of the work, rather than looking for the author's meaning behind it.

I would also like to explain why I have such worries. It is because the novel itself gives people a very real feeling. And I think some details may come from life, such as the details of " I " and Mrs. Qing, and her washing dishes in the kitchen. I think if such details are not taken from life, it is difficult to write them into the novel. So when I don't interpret literary works, when I come into contact with the author, I start to worry. Because although the novel may be fictional, the scenes that appear in the novel and the things that the author sees, I think they may be true.

Zhong: I know a little about the New Criticism. From the perspective of the New Criticism you mentioned, I agree with or understand its critical approach. Because in literary criticism, the author's point of view is actually irrelevant.

Then you mentioned this worry about the author. Well, let's assume: suppose this is a news report, suppose " I " am a reporter, suppose everything written in this novel is true, and then you still worry about me, then do you feel that in your subconscious, in fact, you still have a judgmental mentality towards them (the many characters in the novel)? In other words, in fact, you still have a judgment or critical consciousness towards their values and their lifestyle. Do you have this consciousness? This consciousness is actually wrong, or anti-literary, and this is an attitude that a literary critic should not have. As a social critic, you can criticize these people and their lifestyle, but as a literary critic, this is precisely the taboo of literary criticism. Many domestic literary critics confuse these two criticisms, confusing social phenomena with literary works. In fact, these two are exactly opposite, and should even be two kinds of criticism that are incompatible with each other.

The most basic reason is that if I were to look at these people and their lives through such tinted glasses, I would never be able to write the novel Chinatown, and I would never be able to write a truly good work. For a truly good work, you can say that the author is dead, or invisible, or does not exist at all. Of course, this is also a novel writing technique. If you can write about the " I " who observes all this until it is invisible and does not exist at all, then this is a truly good novel, at least according to my standards. If this " I " has a judgment, or looks at these characters through tinted glasses and with preconceived views, then this novel would not exist at all and could not be written at all.

One very important point is that the value of literature is far greater than its social value.

Dang: I want to talk about my feelings when reading literary works. No one is born with a perfect soul. I admit that I do have tinted glasses for these people in the novel, but after reading the novel "Chinatown", my previous feelings have greatly faded, or even disappeared. I think this may also be a great significance of this work. That is to say, if there is no such work, our understanding of the world will be particularly narrow, but with such literary works, our understanding of the world has then been changed. We are influenced by this work and have a deeper understanding of these non-mainstream characters and their lives.

Zhong: I know what you mean. In fact, the real meaning and value of literary works lies here. This is the important dividing line that distinguishes literary works from social reports, news reports, and other media that give the public a sense of pleasure.
This is the meaning of literature.

Dang: I think everyone is an independent individual, and the world that everyone sees is always very limited, but by reading literary works, we can see all kinds of different worlds. A person only has one life, but if we read a lot of literary works and experience many different lives, it is equivalent to living many different lives. This may also be one of the values of literary works.

Zhong: Finally, I would like to add one more thing. I have read the article you just sent me about the history of the

271

development of Chinatown in the United States. That article is an analysis of Chinatown written by an American sociologist. So, the difference between sociology and literature lies here. Sociology will analyze from a political and ideological perspective. No matter whether it is Western politics or Eastern politics, it is a subconscious political social analysis. But from the perspective of literature, this kind of thing is meaningless. As I said in the postscript of "Chinatown", I have read a lot of this kind of social analysis, but I can't see the people. You can tell me about the historical origins, racial discrimination, political background, etc. of Chinatown, but it's useless. Where is the human? Where are the individuals? In political science and sociology, individual people do not exist. This is the biggest difference between sociology and literature.

Yilin Zhong,
complied based on voice chat records

[Book Review 1]

Oversea Chinese Living in The Post-industrial Imagination

Yao Peipei
Department of Chinese Language and Literature,
Nanjing University

Chinatown exists in the alleys occupied by Chinese in major countries. There are music halls, restaurants, Xinhua Bookstores, massage parlors, gangsters, prostitutes, stowaways, and migrant workers of all kinds. Everyone has their own story, whether happy or sad, love or hate. Everything has its roots, and every root is closely related to Chinatown . They live at the bottom, the bottom of society, and they have moved from China to London, Britain. They can and can only live in the same houses as in China, eat the same food, and make friends with the same people. They are still living in the old times, while London has entered the postmodern era.

Chinatown

The London in the book "Chinatown" is a gathering place for
the old-time Chinese in the postmodern society. When society
enters post-industrialization, or when British society enters post-
industrialization, the people's civilization quality is greatly
improved. For example, people don't eat in the subway, don't spit,
and immediately turn the other cheek with a smile when someone
slaps them. I am noble, you are great. But over time, these
Chinese living in the UK found that their spirits began to be
confused, because they are Chinese after all, and the China they
come from has not really entered the post-industrial era, so they
are still people of the old era. As long as they are native Chinese,
they are still people of the old era. We live in high-rise buildings,
drive luxury cars, and participate in various entertainment
activities, but we can never erase our rusticity. They also want to
erase it, but no matter how they fly into the clouds, dive into the
sea, or run on the grassland, they still can't get rid of the thick
rusticity. They are rustic, from the spiritual soil. Although China
is moving very fast, even if it has not yet reached post-
industrialization, in fact, everything that the Chinese natives own,
use, see and touch is exactly the same as that of Londoners in the
post-industrial society. Perhaps it is just because the Chinese are
too busy and read too few books, so it is inevitable that their
spirits are empty, and therefore it is inevitable that their spirits
are rustic. Just like those undocumented people in London's
Chinatown and the narrator of the novel , a British student, living
together in the same house, one room for each or two people,
peaceful, chaotic, simple, and dirty. Because they are busy
making a living, they not only have no time to read any book,
but they can't even slow down to kiss and touch. This is how the
lower-class people are, for a living, fast, fast, fast! Work hard!

Work hard to make money! Even in the UK, they still live in the old days of China.

Apple, the tenant downstairs , lived there for two weeks and moved out soon. Like all the tenants, she was nervous and nervous with intermittent happiness. Alang, who worked in a Chinese restaurant, was very busy, leaving early and returning late, washing dishes. He and Apple were in love and living very fast, as if he was a fast person, so fast that he had no sense of existence. Just as Luc Besson once said, borrowing the words of the beauty Scarlett in the new film "Lucy": "Time determines existence." When I saw this, I was confused, but I finally understood it when I read this book. Only those who have time have a sense of existence, and in modern society, busy Chinese people have no time to feel their own existence. Although Apple broke up with Alang soon afterwards, maybe she became a lesbian and was together with Mingming, a tenant who had moved in before, or maybe not. A year later, when " I " met Apple, I remembered the memories of these people. Apple got off the car and left, her earrings shining in the sun, but she was still living in the old times. If " I " never see Apple again , after a long time, then love will no longer be love, memory will no longer be memory, and existence will no longer exist.

In the novel, Abao is a prostitute with a good life. When she was a teenager, her parents from a well-off family sent her abroad to bring honor to the family. " She took the special car of Uncle Li, an official in the municipal government, and carried dozens of kilograms of luggage . " With her parents sobbing reluctantly, Abao happily rushed to the plane and traveled directly from the old era to post-industrial London. This was faster than any imagined time-travel novel. When she arrived in

Chinatown

the new London, she was eager to get rid of her rusticity. She mixed with the rich and handsome men who bought Ferraris as soon as they arrived in London, compared with the rich and beautiful women who were covered in luxury goods, and went to nightclubs with the governor's son who swiped his credit card without blinking. She seemed to be no longer rustic, as if she had instantly walked from a small rural town in China to the upper class of Britain. In less than a year, the hundreds of thousands of RMB she brought with her were about to evaporate, and her boyfriend, who was really in love with her, also spent all his money. He had no choice but to give up his love and ask his family for money. He broke up with Abao like a mama's boy. Ah Bao was desperate and illiterate. I guess she couldn't even tell the difference between those words: 'men', 'women' and 'children'. Later, she became a prostitute by chance. Later, she met Achang who loved her and they got together. It should be a happy ending, although it's not a perfect match between a prince and a princess, but a pimp and a prostitute eloping and living together. Although it's also love, it's sad because happy endings mostly only exist in fiction. Ah Bao was originally called Tingting, a very ordinary Chinese girl's name. Since she became a prostitute, the girl named Tingting no longer existed. From then on, she became a fictional person, a prostitute named Ah Bao.

Brother Qing and his wife Mrs. Qing should be the most ordinary couple in the world. They worry about food and clothing, and are hurt by the cost of cooking and salt. They quarrel, swear, and fights, curses the Fujian dialect of his hometown in London, a city of orthodox English. He overturns tables, kicks chairs, smashes bed boards, and breaks TVs or radios, destroying the tranquility of the midnight. Sister Qing is

276

not to be outdone. She opens her throat, pulls her throat, howls and cries, she swears, and beats her chest and stamps her feet. Unlike ordinary couples, they may be a couple who got married halfway, so they quarrel and fight more. They often dislike each other, but they love each other deeply. Their love is simple and rough. Their feelings are the feelings of millions of families, love and annoyance. They are both my tenants and I am their tenants.

As for the narrator of the novel, the study abroad life of "I" in the UK is lonely. I can revel, be lonely, or be silent. Although I have mastered some knowledge and moved from the old era to the post-industrial era, "I" from China is still rustic, empty, and crazy. Although she can speak English, she is incompatible with the brave new world outside called Britain, just like these Chinese who can't speak English. "I" can only sit in the rented house and watch the daily life of the tenants. Apart from watching Hollywood movies on pirated discs, there is no entertainment that can enrich her heart. Is this the case for everyone? In the novel, "I" did not tell many of my own stories, because when it involves myself, I often can't help but cover up something when I express it in the first person, but all these stories in the novel have the shadow of "I". "I" is a person, a highly educated graduate student, but "I" is also a life, a life from China, so I am not much better than those so-called black people. I cannot write Miguel Street like Naipaul, even though I am from outside the UK like him, and both of us are Asian. So I just want to write something for myself and for you to see, to see how we, overseas people, live in a real Chinatown in a foreign country.

The day I finished reading this book, I suddenly heard Yanni's music, The End of August. I was riding my bike uphill at the time.

277

Chinatown

When I turned my head up and entered the road, I saw a cloud floating in the sky. A cloud from my hometown. It must be free, except that its direction is controlled by the wind. It should be able to see all living things in the world, see people of all kinds walking, eating, sleeping, fighting, taking drugs, visiting prostitutes, see the farewells at the airport, the tears of kisses, see the hurried footsteps, see the aging young people, and see the stories by the bedside. It may just laugh it off, and then follow the wind to another place and see another era, just like getting rid of the heat at the end of August, going to a new season and seeing the Chinese outside the post-industrial society.

[Book Review 2]

The Day does not Understand the Darkness of the Night

——The differences in values in the novel Chinatown

Dang Xiaoyu

Department of Chinese Language and Literature,

East China Normal University

In the novel Chinatown, the narrator, as an overseas student, goes deep into the community of illegal immigrants and interacts with overseas Chinese from all walks of life. The characters in the novel are of all kinds, including gangsters, chefs, small vendors, prostitutes, pimps, and so on. As the author said in the postscript, the novel itself is mostly based on her personal experience, so sometimes readers can't help but worry about her safety while reading. But what I think is more interesting is that although the narrator is alone, she has walked out of her own safety zone in Chinatown, a small society with chaotic values, and has gone deep into this tropical rainforest that hides all kinds of human nature. Although in the eyes of readers, there is a huge difference between the narrator and these people, but in the whole process of the novel, there is no collision of values between them. This is a very interesting phenomenon. In "Chinatown", various values seem to react with each other like colorful chemical reagents in the story, but the narrator is neither an element nor a catalyst; the " I " in the novel is like a test paper, which makes the various values of the various characters in the novel appear vividly through the medium of " I " , and jump off the paper.

When I was reading Chinatown, I kept wondering why the author wrote about Aguang first. You know, the first person mentioned in the book is not him, but Apple , a female foreign student. However, after the author inserted the experience of renting a house, the novel did not immediately return to the character of Apple , but first told the story of Aguang, and then talked about Apple . Who is Aguang? Aguang is Lao Zhu's subordinate, a chef in a Chinese restaurant, and has visited prostitutes. From the first two characteristics of Aguang, I can't see why he is qualified to be the first character in the book, but when I think of the third point, I suddenly understand. Except for the first chapter and the penultimate chapter related to renting a house, the story of Aguang and Achang - the client and the pimp - constitutes the second and penultimate chapters of the book, making the two symmetrical and echoing in the structure of the novel, completing the erotic production chain from one end to the other. Aguang, who has visited foreign women, is obviously not a veteran in the world of love. He is more like a child who has eaten candy, and he is complacently showing off how he enjoys himself in the process of visiting prostitutes.

In a small society like Chinatown , where there are all kinds of people, the narrator has to deal with all kinds of people, so how to gain the trust of others becomes a problem. Except for Po's story, the stories of all other characters in the novel are brought out in the process of interacting with the narrator. Therefore, whether these characters can reasonably open their hearts to the narrator is the key to this book. For example, Apple 's trust in " me " is based on identity. When she heard that " I " was also a student, she immediately developed a kind of trust in " me " . But when she learned that " I " and she were not the same kind of students (" I " was a graduate student, and Apple was still in a language school), this trust suddenly turned into panic and fear. In any communication, if you cannot establish a basic trust relationship with the other party, the other party will not tell you his true views and plans on life; conversely, if you unconsciously impose your own views and plans on life on others, you will not be able to establish a trust relationship with others. In this book, only the student girl Apple, whose identity is similar to mine , did not establish a trusting relationship with me. This is because Apple , like most people in real life, completely relies on their identity to judge others .

However, sometimes things go wrong, just like the day does not understand the darkness of the night. Even after establishing a trusting relationship, the illusion of equal values between characters will arise. For example, the old Wei family kindly introduced a boyfriend with a green card to " me " who was single and living abroad , because people with permanent residency stood at the top of their values; while Chunsheng, who was depressed all day, thought that happiness was the best thing, so all he could think of was to share drugs with " me ". Interestingly, whenever this happened, the author's tone became secretly cheerful, with a sense of comedy. For example, the section where Lao Zhu asked " me " to help him smuggle in Malaysia, " me " pretended to hold the worldview of the smuggling group, so even when Lao Zhu refused, there was a sly ridicule between the lines. Obviously, Lao Zhu is also an old man, knowing the importance of the matter, so even though he checked " me '" s passport and knew clearly that " me " was a student, he did not let " me " do it in the end. When I read this, I felt that this kind of contact seemed more like flirting - not flirting in a derogatory sense, but the kind of necessary flirting that men and women test each other in the early stages of their relationship. In this story, it seems that the " I " in the novel is flirting with Lao Zhu's values.

We often say that we should learn to respect other people's values. Because everyone is born different, their views on the world are naturally different. This is not necessarily just a difference in ideas, it can also be manifested as a difference in physical sensations. There are many wonderful details in the novel. We can take the story of the rich second generation Lin Qi as an example to talk about this. As for Qi, the first time the reader came into contact with him was when he just moved in and went to the bathroom when he was chatting with Xiaoli; the second time he came into contact with him was when he met him at the door of the bathroom. Throughout the ages, there are really few literary works that specifically portray characters at the door of the bathroom. But don't underestimate going to the bathroom - eating, drinking, defecating and urinating are all basic forms of material exchange between people and the world. From the moment Qi moved in, the novel explained that " the room downstairs was empty " , which means that Qi lived on the first floor. When writing about going to the toilet, the novel wrote: " Until one day I wanted to go to the toilet, and found that the toilet on the second floor was occupied. There was another toilet on the first floor, but that toilet was too dirty, and Xiaoli, Abao and I and other women didn't like to use it . " Finally, " I " met Qi at the door of the toilet, which was in the toilet on the second floor.

From this very subtle detail, we can see that my pity and sympathy for Qi, a young man who is " poor and precious, but finally falls into the mud ", is not because I am a materialist who thinks that rich young men should live a better life than the lower-class people, but because Qi , even though he gets much less salary than Lao Zhu and his gang, cannot use the toilet in the same environment as them. Such a person who was born in a wealthy family, grew up in a mansion with a net worth of tens of millions in Beijing, and now has fAlun to the point of not being able to afford a bowl of fried rice in the UK, cannot get used to using the toilet on the first floor, so he can only go to the second floor to use the toilet used by these women. Values are not just concepts, but are reflected in all aspects of life. The author just lightly wrote about the naked reality by using the toilet, the most inconspicuous place in life. A good work is like this. You may think it is nothing when you first read it, but when you think about it, you will find that there is a small thorn in your flesh. When you think about it again, you will find that there are countless small thorns like this all over the article. The seemingly plain words, when recalled, become full of thorns and shocking.

Interestingly, although the narrator is surrounded by huge differences in values among all classes, he remains calm and leisurely. When a high-ranking official's son like Alun, who is a spendthrift, invites me to dinner , I go , but I do not envy his life. And for those who are generally considered to have a hard life, the " I " in the novel does not have the slightest sympathy. In fact, forcing others to live a good life is a kind of violence, and is sympathizing with others not also a kind of violence? Behind the saintly attitude of compassion for everything, the essence is actually deep discrimination - I am right, you are wrong, I live well, you live badly, and you will be saved if you obey my opinion. However, there is no saintly attitude or sympathy in "Chinatown" from beginning to end.

The most obvious example is that when the novel is about the story of the prostitute Abao, the original narrative style is suddenly changed to use the third-person omniscient narrative. Objectively speaking, Abao's fate has experienced great twists and turns. If the narrator and Abao were face to face and listened to Abao talk about her experience, the reader's attention would be attracted to the tragic parts. Using the third-person narrative is to avoid the novel from falling into the vulgarity of sensationalism to the greatest extent, distance the reader from Abao, keep all chapters of the novel consistent in style, and avoid readers from sympathizing with the characters.

In the narration of the novel, the author did not sympathize with Abao at all, because as described in the novel, in Abao's own opinion, her life returned to normal after becoming a prostitute. We learned her psychological activities from the absolutely reliable omniscient narrator: " Thank God, I finally live like a human being again . " If Abao married a young man, a rich businessman or a student, the other party would more or less reject such values. However, this is not a vulgar story of a prince charming saving Cinderella. The wonderful part of the novel lies precisely here. Abao is more of a peace of mind about her experience of becoming a prostitute, and she does not feel ashamed of it; on the contrary, anyone who is self-motivated to feel ashamed for her becomes a spiritual rapist to her. Therefore, the reason why the narrator of the novel can let these people who are not tolerated by the mainstream values of society talk to " I " heart to heart, and treat " I " as a friend and one of them equally is because " I " fully respects their values and treats their various " illegal " lives without value judgment or tinted glasses . The fact is, the greatest respect is to have no sympathy or mercy.

At this point, I particularly like the love story of Abao and A Chang in the novel. This is a love story between a prostitute and a pimp, but the author writes it in a unique and tender way. Due to his profession, A Chang has seen many women. When he first met Abao, he didn't even look at her. The author wrote that he " seemed to be trying to lower his head and look for something on the ground . " With just this sentence, we know that in A Chang's mind, Abao looks radiant. When we Chinese in ancient times wrote about beautiful women, we often described her eyebrows, eyes, lips, skin, fingers, and neck. These are actually objectified descriptions of women, which is not a very respectful way of writing. If a pimp sees a new prostitute and focuses on her specific appearance, he will inevitably evaluate her appearance. Therefore, A Chang's looking at Abao without looking at her just reflects the greatest respect for her: subconsciously, he just regards Abao as an ordinary woman, not a prostitute.

285

Chinatown

In the novel, Achang, who is usually not sensitive, did not realize that he had feelings for Ah Bao at first. He could not grasp his own mentality, but only clumsily discovered that Lao Gen's brothel had an inexplicable attraction to him. This shows that although this young man is a pimp, he is actually very simple in terms of feelings. This certainly does not mean that Achang lacks social experience. He did not promise anything to Ah Bao, but took her directly out of Lao Gen's brothel on the pretext of a job invitation. In contrast to this lie to deceive Ah Bao, Achang also lied when renting a house from Zhang Lai: " To be honest, I have encountered some troubles here recently, and I just want to move as soon as possible. " - How much effort is needed to explain beauty and happiness to people who have been deceived by life! In terms of creating happiness, actions are always more powerful than words. Sometimes it is so redundant to explain your views on life to others, and the real happiness is that as long as you feel happy in your heart, everything is fine.

In short, in all social classes, especially in the different values of the lower classes described in this book, how to politely refuse mental violence and how to respect other people's values are fully demonstrated in the narrative between the lines of "Chinatown". Although the author involves all aspects of London's black and white society and grey areas in the novel, what "Chinatown" brings us is not just a curiosity and adventure, but a variety of different characters in this different world, and their different values. A vivid and colorful Ukiyo-e of the " illegal " life of contemporary overseas Chinese.

[Book Review 3]

Chinatown: The Other in the Postcolonial Context

Li Jiaoyang
Department of English Literature,
Goldsmiths, University of London

Wordsworth wrote in " My Sojourn in London " in Book VII of his long poem "Prelude":

In a metropolis like London , with its busy streets ,
I am such an ordinary person / Walking alone in the crowd /
That feeling is / passing through every face of yours /
It's all a mystery

In the bustling London, not only are you facing blond and blue-eyed foreigners, but even seeing countless Asian faces in Chinatown still makes people feel alienated. Yilin Zhong's novel "Chinatown" outlines the life picture of a group of overseas

Chinese who are both familiar and unfamiliar to us. They came to the UK illegally due to different identities and reasons, but they don't know English, and some of them can't even speak Mandarin. Foucault's most powerful dualism points out that knowledge is power. Being abroad, these people don't even have the most basic knowledge - language, which means they have no right to speak at all. Therefore, these illegal immigrants who " stayed " in the UK and survived in the cracks between countries, plus they don't know English, are collectively voiceless in various dimensions and have become the opposite of the cultural elites: the real subaltern class.

In reality, this group of people have become voiceless or even missing people in the cracks of history. They may not even be as lucky as Paddington in the fairy tale "Paddington Bear", who, even though he is a bear from a foreign country, can integrate into a British family. On the one hand, they live in a post-colonial context, willing to be humble and silent, self-identifying as " the other " , a self-internalized Orientalist ideology; on the other hand, due to their common Chinese birth and belonging, and because they all speak Chinese, they have their own unique Chinese cultural imagined community: Chinatown.

In Yilin Zhong's novel, we can truly see the intersection of "the other" and "our own people" , these Chinese illegal immigrants with special identities, their illegal bodies, and their contradictory and unsettled souls. Although all their lives run counter to the people who are eager to squeeze into the mainstream society, they live safely in this " Chinatown " where non-mainstream marginalized people gather . They are in London, but they speak Chinese, eat Chinese food, celebrate Chinese festivals, and interact with Chinese people. Although they do the most ordinary or even humble jobs, they are still full of hope and smile. Their years are hollow, not remembered by anyone, and have never been recorded in history books or literary works, but they have the most real, most human love, struggle, bitterness, and joy. Their lives, under the calm and seemingly relaxed narration of "Chinatown", we see the sparkling waves of an era, so light and so heavy.

The story of the novel is set in " Chinatown ", which is not the real Chinatown full of delicious food in the center of London, but a Chinese settlement in the north of London. Zhang Lai, a Chinese, rented an Indian house in this place where " half of the street is inhabited by Chinese people " and became a sub-landlord, making money from those Chinese who don't speak English. In this small house, twelve or thirteen people were squeezed in. They came from different backgrounds and professions, lived under the same roof, shared kitchens and bathrooms, and formed a miniature overseas Chinese society. And there were tenants moving out and new tenants moving in, which naturally expanded the extension of the story. The author cut into this group from the first-person internal perspective of " I " . As an international student who had just finished her course and moved to London to write her graduation thesis, what she saw with her eyes was not the inertia of the world and the snobbery of the rich and the poor, but a kind of cordial and trusting coexistence. Under the same roof, she witnessed the daily life of these Chinese people who were her neighbors upstairs and downstairs and lived in the same room.

Of course, she may not have thought that her life with these illegal immigrants would be like going deep into the tiger's den and accidentally entering the dragon's pool. The author did not use the traditional grand narrative, but used a postmodern fragmented way to structure this novel; according to the traditional Chinese novel theory, the structure of the novel is "Water Margin" style, seemingly scattered, but actually embracing all rivers. Basically, every little character in the novel is a chapter, in the order in which " I " know them; there is A Guang, a restaurant chef who smuggled in, homosexual couple Lu Ping and Mingming, Chunsheng who sells pirated CDs, A-Qi, a poor young man who dropped out of school to work in a restaurant, Abao, a prostitute, and her husband A Chang, the head of the pimp, and Lao Zhu, a gangster who smuggles and sells drugs ... Each chapter has a narrative focus and other characters involved, just like the spotlight shines on each person's face in turn, but we have already obtained the relationships and secrets in the dark of the crowd in the shadow of the wine, and through the display of each of their own language, we have glimpsed their own and others' true stories and emotions. The amount of information in each story is added little by little in the previous and next chapters, which is very similar to the imitation of our normal cognitive methods in life , rather than the omniscient narrative perspective and preconceived outpouring commonly used in traditional novels. This narrative method not only benefits from the author's mature narrative skills and restrained skills, but also coincides with the writing concept of " showing, not telling " advocated in British and American creative writing. Therefore, after we read the bizarre and wonderful stories of the characters in the novel one by one, just like the Qingming Shanghe Tu, these vivid people automatically projected into a complete " Chinatown " in the reader's mind.

Kevin Lynch, an urban research scholar, once said that a city should not only be something that exists in itself, but should also be understood as a city felt by citizens. The center is people, and people's perception of the city is condensed into a form called city impression. And the superposition of individual impressions becomes a collective impression, which to some extent becomes urban imagination. So it is Chunsheng, Zhang Lai, and A-Qi, this group of people, their lives, that make up the invisible city, the Chinatown in our minds. And it is these stories told by Yilin Zhong, in the form of novel text, that have developed the secret film of these marginalized people in the city into tangible photos, and finally restored them in the minds of readers.

In our daily life, when we go to Chinatown to eat and consume, we may meet great chefs and versatile vendors. We may rarely think about the unknown bitterness of their survival. This bitterness is not just the kind of alienation of the colonized as "the other" as Said said in "Orientalism" as the West, as Eurocentrism,but more of a self-examination, a self-examination of one's own illegal identity and humble status, confrontation, judgment, and bitterness of identification. In his "Cultural Identity and Diaspora", Stuart Hall positioned this kind of thought that caused the colonized to use " the other " to judge themselves due to contradictory desires as a kind of Orientalism's deferral, which is the result of Orientalism taking root in people's hearts, internalized tug-of-war and reaction. The deep analysis of the novel's story is actually the real film behind these colorful characters. In the text, we see that A Guang, who has been smuggled to the UK for 13 years, was once the top chef of a Chinese restaurant in London's Chinatown and cooked delicious dishes. However, because the inspection of illegal workers

291

became more and more stringent, he had to hide further and further away, and finally went to Scotland. This is his helplessness and escape from his illegal identity. Chunsheng, who sells pirated discs, and Lao Zhu and his group fully admit their illegal identities and admit that they are " the other " . Only then can they endure injustice in silence. They see that they cannot buy mobile phones with monthly payments, that the rent is extorted by the second landlord, and that they have to use money to buy relationships everywhere. They can only obey and cannot resist. When the " I " in the novel asked them, (You have such a hard life) then why did you come to the UK? At this time, Chunsheng said a particularly intriguing sentence: " How do you know what it means to come to the UK in our hometown ? Coming to the UK is the ideal of our whole family. All my dreams are here. "

In Chinatown, we can see that the "the other" who were colonized in the past are now going against the tide and rushing back to the colonial master who colonized them. They are willing to be humble and become "the other" . This is the struggle, contradiction, helplessness, and inertia of illegal immigrants in the current social situation where the economy dominates everything. For example, the character of A Guang reminds me of Dunhuang, which also sells pirated CDs in Xu Zechen's Running Through Zhongguancun, but that is the bitterness of Beijing drifters. This bitterness is probably far less than one-tenth of that of " British drifters " , because here, not only what you do is illegal, but also you yourself are illegal. Your existence itself is illegal, and you have always been completely living a miserable life. However, what is even more tragic than this is that this humiliation and compromise is full of the light of dreams, because it represents the ideals of your fathers, folks and family in your hometown, because you are living the most advanced life in their imagination.

If I were to ask what is the most hopeful thing in this world, I think it is children. Then what is the most hurtful thing? It is to kill hope in its infancy. There is a very touching description in the novel, which is about a couple of illegal immigrants who often quarrel and live downstairs from " me " . They are Bro Qing and Mrs. Qing. I don't know what they do, but they may be drug dealers. Mrs. Qing can't even speak Mandarin very well. She even steals other people's plates and pots in the kitchen. She and Bro Qing don't have a harmonious relationship and are often subjected to domestic violence. But when she mentions her son in China, she always reveals a kind of maternal soft light. She once couldn't help showing "me" a photo of her son. It was a boy of eleven or twelve years old, wearing very neat clothes and taking artistic photos in the art photo studio in the town with countless soft lights. But Mrs. Qing said that when he is older, she will " get " him (smuggle) out too. At this time, you can feel the love in their humanity, but this love makes you sad, because we can see that this internalized "other" consciousness is already deeply rooted. I am afraid that some saplings will never have the opportunity to grow up in the sun. They must accept the fact that they were born in a humble way from the moment they are born, and then grow up in a humble manner in the adult world, bending over and twisting, becoming the children of nature, Mrs. Qing, and will only become the next Chunsheng, endlessly. In this cycle, we can't see hope. All hope has been strangled in the cradle.

Of course, through hard work, the identities of these illegal immigrants can also be gradually changed and improved. Stuart Hall said: "The formation of identity is a process of continuous adjustment and positioning." We can clearly see this in the story of the old Wei couple. The two of them were also illegal immigrants, making a living by selling fruits wholesale in the market. But later, because one of their relatives got a British passport, they suddenly became bright. In the words of the author, "One person's success brings success to the whole family." This "promotion" means that from now on they can apply for a family visit visa and no longer be a "black person". Going further, they can apply to become a refugee" and receive government relief and welfare. Even so, after they have "promoted" with the blessing of their ancestors, from illegal to semi-legal refugees, the person they envy the most is still Xiao Chen, who has a legitimate work visa and works as a porter in the supermarket. They even introduced this precious "connection" as a favor and a thank-you gift to me" in the novel, an international student whose visa is about to expire. Most people may find this kindness absurd and funny, but it is the normal logic and behavior under "the other's" thinking.

There is also a story about Abao who squandered her parents' savings and became a prostitute. Her story also contains a huge reversal, a struggle of human nature, and a questioning of the bottom line. People who are not so poor that they have to microwave stolen potatoes are not qualified to talk about life. After all, Abao also relies on her hard work to make money and survive. You can never hate prostitutes who have been disenchanted in such daily life. So, how can you not be afraid of lack of money and hunger and become a good son and daughter of China? Bro Qing in the novel tells you that it is to memorize the menu. This is an absolutely reliable secret. As long as you can recite the Chinese and English menus backwards, you can immediately fill in the gaps. Such stories and details from the life experience of the lower class are like light rolling towards you, as if the light of life is brilliant, but in fact it is a thousand arrows piercing your heart. As you read, you seem to have absorbed all the oxygen and have to hold your breath or even suffocate. The life skills accumulated by these stowaways from the lower class are bubbling up from time to time in this new society. Indeed, through this kind of hard work and effort that is ten thousand times more difficult than that of the " Beijing Drifters " , they do live better than before, or become richer, and obtain and make up for the meaning and value of their existence from other places, but the second half of Stuart Hall's sentence in the previous article is: " Cultural identity is a kind of production that can never be completed. " Admittedly, you may not hate a prostitute because of sympathy, but no matter what, a prostitute who struggles to make money by herself cannot reach the level of respect. The ants who " search up and down " on the shoelaces have struggled all their lives, and even if they climb up from the soles of the shoes, they are still ants on the shoes. The huge gap still exists, that is, the cultural identity that " the other " can never complete. The residents in "Chinatown" can only live in Chinatown forever, the Chinese society they imagine in their minds, rather than the real world outside this street, Britain.

However, whenever you feel so dull that you are almost suffocating, and feel sad and depressed about their lives, you always hear faint and continuous laughter running out of the

295

story, bringing you a light smile in your heavy heart. For example, Xiaoli, the wife of Lao Wei in the novel, is an optimistic and homely person. She noisily invites everyone in the family to watch the Spring Festival Gala, and the sound of hearty laughter is endless. And her favorite words are " soon " , as if life will soon get better, and " eat, eat " , as if all troubles will disappear during the meal. This kind of laughter shuttles through the faces of everyone in the " Chinatown " house without sound insulation. When we read this, we feel relieved. Chinatown is actually their real home and belonging in the UK. Just like the two elements summarized by Benedict Anderson, this group of people were born together with destiny. They all come from China and widely use the common language, Chinese, and the extended culture. For example, they can feel at home by watching the Spring Festival Gala and Zhao Benshan's skits together. This is the community they imagine. Although they may not completely like each other, they are friendly, close, and helpful in their bones. These things are more. In this circle, they can also live out their own sense of achievement, such as being happy that they have the secret to buy cheap tickets, happy that they have prostituted a foreign girl, and happy that they sent back more than one million to their wives and children in their rural hometown to repair the house. They are in common. Only in this " Chinatown " they imagine, the concept of " the other " in a foreign country will dissipate. They share, love, socialize, and play cards. Only here, in Chinatown, are they not others, but their own people. At times like this, we seem to feel that life is light and that there is no ultimate meaning in life. Isn' t happiness just gathering under the same roof and playing poker with friends all night?

Chinatown

Under the undercurrent of all these stories, the narrative of the novel is calm from beginning to end, with a leisurely taste of the urban wanderer as described by Benjamin. And it is precisely because everyone else in Chinatown has complete trust in the narrator " I " that we can feel the high perspective and closeness of the story. And because of the fun and innocence of the character " I " in the novel, the whole narrative becomes light, which makes the best reconciliation between the darkness of the story itself and the heaviness of the theme, and also adds a relatively soft spacing and filter to the focal point of the perspective of this Chinatown picture. Maybe she doesn't know the danger of the drug trade that Lao Zhu is doing, and she doesn't know why the rich kid Alun invited her to eat in an expensive restaurant. She just has a curious, friendly, and just-looking attitude towards everyone around her. So she just keeps walking and walking. She once talked about the English-style kissing Snog with a girl in bed on a foggy night , and later slept with the lesbian back to back for several nights in panic; she also ran into the nobleman Qi, who was so poor that he had no food or clothes but was still like a fairy tale prince, wearing a snow-white shirt and clumsily writing a letter to a girl far away in the back garden; she also ran into the autumn streets of London, where Ping disappeared in the sunlight reflected by her fresh and gorgeous pearl necklace earrings; she also ran into countless couples who quarreled and chased each other without avoiding disturbances, and people who were high after smoking marijuana, as well as those who washed their consciences and the true feelings that were not revealed until dawn. Walking, walking, she has seen and heard too many people, those various characters, and their various stories. In this postmodern metropolis of

Chinatown

London, in the Chinatown that has never "existed" and has been framed by history and law , she and these people played the colorful and bizarre real life.

The whole novel ends with a reunion dinner on Mid-Autumn Festival. At that time, the " I " in the novel had moved out of Chinatown and was called back to join everyone's party. They toasted to their lives and the beautiful full moon in London. Although they were gathered together, they were all parting. This was a farewell party. Everyone knew it tacitly, but no one would reveal it. Everyone just sat around together and enjoyed this pot of strong hot pot soup and strong Chinese friendship in a foreign country. As illegal immigrants, no one knew where their next stop would be. They didn't want to be asked or remembered. They had neither names nor voices. They were just one of the crowds that came and went from the world, and had come to and disappeared in Chinatown. The face of each of them was a mystery.

At this point, I can't help but think of this year's Chinese Film Festival in London, when I watched Lou Ye's "Tuina" in a shabby little cinema in Leicester Square. At the end of the film, the voice-over said softly: Later, Sha Zongqi's massage clinic was sold, and everyone went their separate ways, but the only tacit understanding among everyone was that they would never mention the days in Sha Zongqi's massage clinic. There is no Nanjing, no Xiao Ma, and no Sha Zongqi. Fortunately, we have Yilin Zhong. In her intimate and alienated narrative, we have restored the brilliant and lively Chinatown, and the various people on the street. They are not recognized by the news, history, country and law of the mainstream world, but they will always remain in good novels and literary works. Their stories are so heavy, colorful and thrilling that they make people breathless, but they are also so light that they can never be weighed like the sea.

[Interview 2]

The Paper Interview

The Current Situation of Illegal Chinese Immigrants Overseas from the Perspective of "Chinatown" (Part 1)

Interview: Day 1
Interviewer: Xia Yiping, reporter from The Paper
Interviewee: Yilin Zhong, author of Chinatown
Interview date : April 4 , 2015
Interview location: Chinatown, 13th arrondissement, Paris
(where the author was at the time)

On the Authenticity of the Novel

The Paper: I would like to ask, do the characters in "Chinatown" have real-life prototypes?

Yilin Zhong: Yes, all of them, or most of them.

Chinatown

The Paper: Because the novel writes about Chinese gangs and drug lords, readers were quite surprised when they read it.

Yilin Zhong: When a friend wrote a book review for me before, she also asked a similar question, asking whether these characters were real or had real-life prototypes. Then she said that even if she met these characters described in my novel and lived with them, she would not be able to become friends with them and would not be able to dig out so many stories. Moreover, when she was reading this novel, she was always worried about the protagonist " I " in the book. At that time, I corrected her idea (I communicated with her on WeChat, and later I sorted out my answers to her on WeChat, which became the conversation published on WeChat of "Harvest"). I told her that the reason why she had such an opinion on these characters in the novel was actually due to her own value judgment on these characters, that is, she felt that these characters and lives written in the novel were very dangerous, because they were illegal immigrants themselves, and most of them were doing illegal businesses, just like what you mentioned, such as gangsters, drug lords, etc. I guess all readers will have similar value judgments.

Now let me answer your first question. Most of the characters in the novel have real life prototypes, and many stories are also based on real materials in real life. As I said in the postscript, I happened to have the opportunity to get in touch with this (lowest) class, to get to know their lives, their food, clothing, housing, transportation, their joys and sorrows. This is the original material that any writer needs to experience and collect in the process of experiencing life. Of course, to create a novel with

301

these collected materials is another matter. Now let's talk about the authenticity of these life prototypes.

There are about 20 to 30 characters in the novel "Chinatown", including the main and supporting roles, and these characters all have their own real-life prototypes. The interesting thing is that this novel was written in March 2005 , and it has been exactly ten years since April 2015. Because April is the annual London Book Fair, 10 years ago, the vice president of Amazon China happened to come to London to attend the book fair. He brought me a box of Chinese novels , which made me very happy. Because I couldn't see Chinese books in the UK. Later, when we were having dinner together in London, I accidentally talked to him about the story of Abao. It was purely coincidental that after talking about this, I suddenly had an idea to write this story down. In fact, before that, these characters and stories had been stored in my heart for many years, but I had never found an inspiration, or an opportunity to write them down and write them into a novel. It was not until that day when I was telling the story of Abao that I suddenly found the inspiration to write this story.

Later, when I was writing this novel, there were definitely some fictional elements in it. But the funny thing is, when I was writing the novel, I definitely knew which characters were fictional, but ten years later, when the novel was ready to be published and the publisher asked me to proofread it, I read the novel carefully from beginning to end. Because I hadn't read this novel for many years (who would read their own novels after completed it), I only read it now because I had to proofread it, and as a result, when I reread the novel, I had completely forgotten which characters were fictional.

Chinatown

It's so funny, I actually fooled myself. Because it's been so long, I actually completely forgot which characters are fictional and which ones have real prototypes. I even feel that all the persons in "Chinatown" really existed. As an author or a reader, I already felt this way when I was reading the proofreading manuscript. Later, when a friend wanted to write a book review for me and asked about the authenticity of the characters in my novel, I suddenly remembered: "Oh no, that's not right; I did make up some characters at that time? " But who are the fictional characters? I couldn't remember it at all now. So later I went back to read it, and only then did I pick out one fictional main character. I won't count those fictional supporting characters, but I want to mention that among the dozen or so main characters in this book, there is a protagonist who does not exist at all. He has never existed. Everything about him from beginning to end is 100% fictional.

So, who is this person? I will leave this mystery to the readers to find out. I will never reveal the answer, please guess it yourself. But I don't think anyone can tell which protagonist is fictional, because this "anyone" includes myself, even I almost couldn't tell. Later, the friend who wrote the book review posted a very funny Weibo post saying:

*A dozen main characters sat around a round table, and only one of them drew a different card from the others ... Who is the undercover who infiltrated their group? Please stay tuned: Chinatown version of the murder game. ^_^*

The Paper: Why was Chinatown not published until ten years after it was completed?

Chinatown

Yilin Zhong: This is a long story. To put it simply, Chinatown could not find readers who could understand it, and it was even difficult to find literary editors who could understand it. So even after Chinatown was published in Harvest, the best serious literature magazine in China, no publisher was willing to publish it. This can be said to represent a certain literary situation in China. It is not without sadness that serious literature works no longer have an audience in China. For a long time, I almost thought that only a few editors of Harvest magazine in China could understand this novel and see its literary value (I would like to especially thank Liao Zenghu, my editor of Harvest magazine, who is definitely the mentor of Chinatown, and the chief editor Cheng Yongxin, who has always supported me), because for a full ten years, no publishing house or literary editor of a literary magazine was willing to publish or publish this novel. So when Huang Xiaoyang of Jiangsu Literature and Art Publishing House suddenly found me one day and said he wanted to publish this novel, I felt like I was dreaming. Because this novel had been rejected too many times previously.

However, it is gratifying that after the paperback version of the novel was published, I found that many young readers among the readers born in the 1980s and 1990s wrote many wonderful book reviews. This brought me great surprise and surprise. Previously, "Chinatown" was frequently rejected by the mainstream media and publishers of Chinese literature. Now, it is the younger generation of readers who are still in school who understand my novel and the various social situations, joys and sorrows in it. The comments and impressions they wrote are very talented, which makes me very happy and moved. This also makes me finally relieved that Chinese literature has not been completely destroyed. On the contrary, from the understanding and comments of young readers on my novel, I see full of new life and hope. So sometimes a literary work is not only the work of an author, but also the work of a reader. Because to understand it and appreciate the various inner things in the work, readers also need their own cultivation and understanding. This kind of literary comprehension and communication is actually two-way.

The Paper: Just now you mentioned readers' value judgments on the characters in the novel. Does this include young readers?

Yilin Zhong: I just answered your question about the authenticity of the characters, but I only answered half of it. Later, you mentioned the overseas Chinese gangs and drug lords described in the novel. You want to know whether these things are real or fictional. Now I will answer the second half of your question: I can answer you with certainty that the parts of the novel involving the underworld are 100% real. Not only are they real, but I was in the scenes in the novel, such as the scenes where the drug lords and the snakeheads took drugs together all night, and so on. It is true that they are all criminals and do illegal things, but in life, as private friends, they are all very real and even kind people.

The first sentence and the first scene at the beginning of the novel "Chinatown" are the scenes where Lv Ping, the only female international student with legal residence status in the building, and the " I " in the novel meet in the kitchen. Lv Ping is a female student who is still in school. Her identity in the novel is relatively orthodox, or relatively simple. Unlike other people in the building, there are all kinds of people mixed in, such as smugglers, refugees, illegal businesses, etc. Compared with them, Lv Ping is still a member of the mainstream society, right? Students are also a mainstream identity, so when she looks at other tenants in the building, she naturally wears a tinted glasses of the mainstream society. This is a very normal mainstream value judgment on such a group of illegal immigrants or marginal people living in the non-mainstream society. Just like most readers of the novel "Chinatown", they will unconsciously look at these marginal people who are mixed in the black and white society or the grey area with this perspective, so they think these people are dangerous and unsafe. So in the novel, Lv Ping asked me in the kitchen with some concern, "Don't you think it's a mess here when you live here?" In other words, aren't you afraid and don't you think it's dangerous here?

The question she asked actually represents a very mainstream view of most people in the mainstream society on these non-mainstream marginal characters, illegal immigrants, and disadvantaged groups with nothing described in the novel "Chinatown". Or it is a value judgment of the mainstream society on them. Many readers may not understand why I wrote about Lv Ping in the first sentence of the whole novel, who seems to be the most insignificant little person in the whole book; I directly cut into the encounter between Lv Ping and " I " in the kitchen at the beginning of the novel. Such a seemingly irrelevant and ordinary life scene is actually positioning the theme of this novel in the big coordinates. Or it is a symbol of values. This positioning has nothing to do with the structure of the novel, but it is made clear at the beginning to tell readers the theme of the whole novel. It is to subvert this tradition, or the value judgment of the mainstream world on this non-mainstream group.

Back to the novel, the protagonist " I " answered her: " No, I think they are all very good to me. " Her answer itself is a kind of subversion, or it can be said to be a starting point of the whole novel. Because she does not think that these illegal immigrants who do illegal business are " dangerous " or " very chaotic " . Although they may be gang bosses, illegal immigrants, snakeheads, prostitutes, pimps, and even drug dealers, all kinds of people, all doing illegal things, but in the eyes of this " I " , she does not think they are bad people, but thinks " they are all very good to me " . Because they really showed great kindness to this " I " , a single girl living abroad, no one hurt her, and these illegal immigrants, who are already very lowly, even tried hard to help her, showing her all kinds of care, love and help. For example, they introduced her to potential partners and even introduced her to people they knew who had legal residence, hoping to help her " stay " . Another example is when she was cooking in the kitchen and accidentally mentioned that she was running out of money and wanted to find a job, then A-Qing immediately ran to get her a menu without saying a word and asked her to memorize it quickly so that she could find a job in a Chinese restaurant in the future, fearing that she would run out of money. These are all places where they are very kind and even touching. Just like my editor, Mr. Liao Zenghu, said: " The flow of human emotions is good intentions in every branch and leaf. " The portrayal of these characters in the novel, these places should all be felt by everyone, that is, you may have thought that these people were dangerous before, but in the novel, you will feel that they are actually all very friendly and kind people, and not that scary at all.

Therefore, although the " I " in this novel comes completely from mainstream society, and even from the " elite " class that Lü Ping, who is still studying languages, dares not even look up to, and is already writing a " master's " thesis , she does not have the tinted glasses that most people have towards these illegal people living at the bottom. This is why she can become good friends with these people, get along with them, eat seafood noodles and barbecued pork buns together, even though in the eyes of outsiders like Lü Ping, these people's identities are very different from " I " , but " I " is completely unaware of it, because she does not have any preconceived value judgments of mainstream society towards them.

This is just like the Hong Kong gangster movies we usually see, such as "God of Gamblers", "The Saint of Gamblers", "Young and Dangerous", "Infernal Affairs", and the American "Gangs of New York", "The Godfather", etc. Although the protagonists of these movies are doing illegal things, they are all underworld mafia and even drug lords, and they fight wits and courage with the police in the movies, but we don't think they are hateful. On the contrary, we think they are all affectionate, flesh-and-blood people, and sometimes even think they are heroes who are loyal and good friends. Although in real life, if these people encounter the police, they will all be arrested and imprisoned; but when we watch these movies or read these literary works, we don't look at these characters like a policeman, thinking only about how to catch them, bring them to justice, and reform their education, right? So in the world of literature and art, the traditional mainstream social values do not exist, and are even ridiculous. Because literature or art, it itself is a kind of existence that transcends the mainstream social values. Moreover, the role and value of literature are often reflected in its subversion and rebellion against mainstream social values.

About illegal immigration in the UK

The Paper: Are there many Chinese communities in London like the one in the novel? Have the British authorities noticed this? After all, the novel mentions that Britain sometimes takes the initiative to crack down on illegal immigrants.

Yilin Zhong: There are many Chinese communities like this. Because the exchange rate in the UK used to be very high, before the financial crisis, the exchange rate of the pound to the RMB was always between 1:12 and 1:15 , and the highest was 1:16 . Such a high exchange rate makes Chinese people feel that it is easy to make money in the UK, because it seems that one dollar earned here can be equivalent to more than ten yuan earned in China, so this temptation is huge for the lower-class people. Especially in the small mountain villages like those in Fujian, those farmers may not earn more than 2,000 or 3,000 yuan in a year, so they would rather bear a huge debt of hundreds of thousands of RMB to smuggle overseas to make a living. These people usually rely on usury to pay for the smuggling expenses, and then after the smuggling is successful, they make money abroad to slowly exchange the debt.

However, this phenomenon does not only exist in the UK. In the US and Europe, there are illegal immigrants sneaking in from China everywhere. It is the same everywhere in the world. Wherever there is money, there are Chinese people and illegal immigrants from China. This is a natural reaction of the immigration tide. This is human instinct. Wherever there is money to be made, I will go there to make money.

As for the British authorities, they must be aware of the phenomenon of illegal immigrants sneaking in. And not only the British, but also the French government, the German government, the American government, and all governments must be very aware of it. And the customs are also very strict, but as the saying goes, the devil is one foot high and the road is ten feet higher. No matter how strict you check, they will always have a way, just like the snakehead Lao Zhu in the novel said: " As long as you spend money, you can buy anything. " Money can make the devil work, as long as you spend money, you can do anything. They will always have a way to sneak people in.

The UK does crack down on illegal immigration, but generally speaking, they are still relatively humane, and their methods of crackdown are very humane. Basically, in the UK, if you are an illegal immigrant, as long as you have not committed any illegal acts and are caught by the police, you will be fine. For example, if you are just walking on the street and are caught by the police, and then you say that you have no identity, they will not make things difficult for you and will let you go. I know a smuggler who said that he went to the police station several times and was released every time. So under what circumstances will you be arrested or forcibly deported? That is, if you do something illegal and are caught by the police, such as if you kill someone, or if you rob or are caught for drug trafficking, only in this case will they arrest you, sentence you to prison, or deport you back to your country. But if you have been an honest citizen after smuggling here, even if you are just stealing, the British police will not care about you. They are actually quite humane, and it cannot be said that they do not enforce the law strictly. It is just like the urban management in China. If there is an old lady selling vegetables on the side of the road, this is also illegal in China. If the urban management is kinder, he will turn a blind eye. If he enforces the law more strictly, he will go over and overturn the old lady's vegetable basket, right? The same is true for British police.

And why do I say that the UK's crackdown on illegal immigrants is very humane? A friend once told me such an example: the couple came here illegally, got married here, and then had a child. Although they both have no identity and are both black, when his wife gave birth, she gave birth in a local hospital, just like the British. Because all hospitals in the UK are free, his wife didn't spend a penny when she gave birth, and the hospital even provided meals. And as long as you go to the hospital for emergency delivery, British doctors will not ask you if you have British residency status, because for them, saving the lives of adults and children is the most important thing, no matter what your identity is. This is the humanitarianism of British hospitals.

Later, the child grew up and had to go to school. If it were in China, this would be a big problem. Because I have seen many news reports saying that in Beijing, Shanghai and Guangzhou, there are many migrant workers from other places working here, but it is difficult for the children of migrant workers to go to school here; because their children do not have a household registration, they cannot go to school and can only be separated from their parents and go back to their local area to go to school, or they can only drop out of school. So in the UK, do you think it will be difficult for these children of illegal immigrants who do not even have an identity to go to school? The answer is exactly: No.

Why? Because the British government has a policy. I believe it is not just the British government, but also the American government and the governments of European countries. They all have this humanitarian policy, that is, if the parents of a child are illegal immigrants, when the child grows up, you can send the child to school to go to school normally. From schoolmates to teachers to principals, no one will ask you or your child what your identity is, whether you have legal residence, whether you are an illegal immigrant, and no one will check your identity or the identity of your child. Why do they never check or even allow to ask about the identity of the child? Because they have legal provisions, just to avoid the parents of the child worrying about being discovered their illegal identity because of sending their children to school, so all schools are strictly prohibited from asking or checking the identity of the children sent to school, and what their parents do. Why do they do this? Because they think that every child has the right to receive education, and the right to receive education cannot be deprived of the child because of the identity of the child's parents. In their view, this is part of human rights.

Therefore, the children of the illegal immigrant couple not only go to school happily like other British children, but also receive completely free education like other British children, without paying a penny. Because they don't know which child's parents are legal and which child's parents are illegal. They never ask, never check, and don't even know what these children's parents do. They just want to protect these children whose parents are illegal immigrants or even criminals, so that they can receive normal education, not be discriminated against, and grow up quietly and healthily in school like all other British children. This is the humanitarianism of the government.

The Paper: What do these illegal immigrants think of their illegal status? To outsiders, it seems quite shameful, especially since some of them work in shabby jobs.

Yilin Zhong: Their identities are definitely dishonorable, and the jobs they are engaged in are not decent at all, and are even illegal, but I feel that they have long been accustomed to it. Just like the underworld in Hong Kong movies, those young and dangerous gangsters in the gang, they all know that they are doing illegal things, but none of them will feel that they are dishonorable and inferior. They may even think that they are very capable, heroes, and good brothers and big brothers who are loyal. Perhaps only those outside the underworld, such as the urban poor and laid-off workers like the old Wei couple, may sometimes feel a little self-pitying and inferior, but even so, they feel that they are already very lucky. Because like Lao Wei, compared with his former factory colleagues who are also still in China, as laid-off workers, they may still be in a city in Jiangsu, picking cabbage leaves on the street. They are middle-aged people in their forties or fifties, and are still struggling to find a job, trying to find a job to make a living and support a large family. Compared with them, Lao Wei may feel that he is already very lucky, because no matter what, he is now in the UK. Because as he himself said, " Maybe I can even get a status? " That would be a great honor to the family.

I think people's inferiority complex comes from comparison. So if he compares himself with people of the same kind, he will feel very lucky and even have a sense of superiority. After all, he is in the UK. Even if he lives a life of picking up rags in the UK, he still feels that he is much better than those people in China who don't have the opportunity to go abroad. This kind of thing sounds a bit ridiculous, but they really think so. So I think most of them not only have no inferiority complex, but also live very happily.

For example, the character A Guang who stowed away from the rural Fujian province at the beginning of the novel was very proud. He was very proud! He earned more than one million yuan and sent it back home, because in their village, who could earn more than one million yuan to build a villa in the village? So he was really very proud. The local farmers were very proud of earning a few thousand yuan a year from farming. Who could earn more than one million yuan to build such a big house? He had to compare himself with his peers. If he compared himself with the British, of course he lived a very miserable and unfortunate life, but he would not compare himself with the British. He only compared himself with the people in his village. Compared with them, he was already very, very lucky.

For example, if A Guang is now in China, working at a construction site, he might be asking for his salary with a receipt, right? He might work for a developer, working as a migrant worker, working himself to death, earning one or two thousand yuan a month, and still not getting paid at the end of the year. In the cold winter, he still has to set up a tent at the construction site and burn firewood to keep warm, waiting for his salary, and can't go home for the New Year. If Abao is now in China, working as a prostitute, for example, she is in Dongguan. I have read relevant reports that a prostitute only earns five or six hundred yuan for a two-hour full set, which is not much money. Then, when the anti-pornography and anti-illegal publication campaign comes, she is caught by the police in a surprise attack, and has to be sent to labor camp or even jailed, right? In fact, I think those prostitutes in Dongguan will envy Abao. I am just giving an example, so they will only compare themselves with their own kind. If they think they are doing well among their own kind, then they will feel very lucky and even have a sense of superiority. At this time, whether or not he has legal residence, whether he is an illegal immigrant, whether his job is respectable or not, these issues are not important, because he feels that he is living a better life than people of the same kind. This is why there are still so many people who borrow money at high interest rates and risk their lives to sneak out, stay in foreign countries illegally as illegal immigrants, and live an illegal life.

The Paper Interview
The Current Situation of Illegal Chinese Immigrants Overseas from the Perspective of "Chinatown" (Part 2)

Interview: Day 2
Interviewer: Xia Yiping, reporter from The Paper
Interviewee: Yilin Zhong, author of Chinatown
Interview time : April 5 , 2015
Interview location: Café on the Left Bank, Paris (where the
author was at the time)

The Paper: It's been exactly ten years since the creation of Chinatown. During these ten years, has the overall situation of the lower-class Chinese in London changed?

Yilin Zhong: I think that not only in the past ten years, but also in the past few decades or even half a century, the overall situation of the Chinese at the bottom of British society has not changed much. This is because the British government's policy on overseas immigration has remained relatively unchanged, especially for illegal immigrants, who have always been managed by relevant laws and immigration laws. So it is actually the changes within China that are affecting the immigration of Chinese smugglers. At this point, I will briefly review the history of Chinese immigration to the UK.

Before the 1970s, there were very few people illegally crossing the border from China, because at that time, on the one hand, China had very strict control, and on the other hand, most of those who illegally crossed the border went to nearby Hong Kong, or to the United States, and very few went to Europe or the United Kingdom. So in the 1950s and 1960s, most of the Chinese who immigrated to the United Kingdom were from Hong Kong. Because it was a colony, most of them came here legally, and very few came here illegally.

China began to produce a large number of illegal immigrants in the late 1970s and early 1980s, because the political situation was relatively relaxed at that time, China began to reform and open up, and going abroad became relatively easy and relaxed. However, during that period, most of the Chinese who went abroad legally and illegally went to the United States, and there were still not many people who went to Europe illegally.

As for the UK, the real influx of Chinese immigrants began in the mid-to-late 1990s, which is only about 20 years ago. Why did a large number of Chinese immigrants come to the UK in the past 20 years? Let me talk about legal immigration first. First of all, one of the main reasons is that China had been reforming and opening up for more than ten years at that time, and had accumulated a certain economic foundation, and the Chinese people began to have money. Unlike the early 1980s, the group of immigrants who went abroad all went to the United States

317

with 30 or 40 US dollars. For example, Wendi Deng and others belong to this generation. In the 1990s, the Chinese began to have money and could afford tuition fees and go abroad or study abroad at their own expense, instead of relying on overseas connections or government-sponsored programs. Therefore, a large number of overseas students and immigrants have formed a trend. In the past, if Chinese people wanted to study abroad, they had no money, so they could only take the GRE and apply for scholarships from American universities. It was very difficult. The GRE required a vocabulary of 20,000 words. I attended a short-term training course at New Oriental before going abroad, so I knew how hard it was. Memorizing words was like going to hell (they called the vocabulary book with tens of thousands of words the " Little Red Book "). It was shocking. But it was also very understandable, because at that time it was the only way for them to change their fate, that is, to go to the United States by memorizing words and taking the GRE , and realize their American dream. It was a very cruel and difficult way to go abroad legally.

But after the 1990s, Chinese people could pay for their own tuition and no longer needed scholarships, so the language requirements were greatly reduced. Basically, as long as college students have passed the CET-4 or CET-6, they can apply to study in Europe or the United States. For example, I went to the UK to study in the early 21st century, and I did not take the GRE , because you do not need to take the GRE to study for a master's degree in the UK , you only need to take the IELTS.

After the 1990s, the legal immigration wave from China to the UK, in addition to a large number of students who came to the UK to study at their own expense, also had a major channel of

Chinese medicine practitioners. Although Chinese medicine seems to be almost extinct in China, it is very popular in European and American countries, especially in the UK and the US, and only rich people will see Chinese medicine practitioners. Why do you say that? Because as we all know, the UK implements a policy of free medical care for all, that is, from small colds and fevers to major surgeries and hospitalizations, even bone marrow transplants or cancer chemotherapy, all are free, and the British do not have to spend a penny. So since seeing a doctor and taking medicine does not cost money, who is willing to pay for seeing a Chinese medicine practitioner out of their own pocket? That is, the rich who have too much money and have nowhere to spend it.

For example, in an episode of the American TV series Sex and the City , Charlotte went to a Chinese medicine clinic in a skyscraper in New York for acupuncture to treat her infertility. This is an example. There are some difficult and complicated diseases, such as skin diseases and infertility, which cannot be cured by Western medicine. Rich people would rather spend money to treat them, so they go to see Chinese medicine. And we all know that it rains frequently in the UK, the weather is damp and cold, and many elderly people suffer from arthritis. Western medicine cannot cure this disease, but acupuncture in Chinese medicine is particularly effective. So all these factors together have resulted in no one seeing Chinese medicine in China, but in the UK and the US, there are Chinese medicine clinics everywhere, and they are all making a lot of money.

As soon as Chinese medicine became popular in the UK, the clinic owners here constantly looked for experienced Chinese medicine practitioners from China to make money for them, so a large number of Chinese medicine practitioners from major domestic hospitals, such as herbalists and acupuncturists, came here. At the same time, there were more cultural exchanges between China and the UK during this period, such as the Chevening Scholarship, etc., and a large number of Chinese government-sponsored students came here, such as Long Yongtu and others. Some students who studied popular majors such as accounting and IT found jobs here after graduation and stayed here. Therefore, since the mid-to-late 1990s, the two largest groups of legal immigrants to the UK are students and Chinese medicine practitioners.

Illegal immigration has also increased during this period. Since it is easy for Chinese people to come here through legal channels, it is easier to come here through illegal channels. Because it was easy to forge passports at that time, and the anti-counterfeiting technology of passports was not as perfect as it is now. Moreover, human traffickers did not make fake passports at all, they used real ones. Do you know how they smuggled people here in the earliest times? They just brought a passport, changed the photo, attached a photo, and flew over directly. But that was 20 years ago, there were not so many high-tech technologies as there are now. Now, let alone passports, we even have biometric chip cards, so it is impossible to forge them. But even so, I guess human traffickers still have ways to smuggle people over.

Why do I know these methods of smuggling? Because when I lived next door to the human trafficker " Lao Zhu " in the novel , he told me that he wanted to buy my passport. Then I understood why they bought passports. Of course I refused to sell it, but many international students were willing to sell it because it cost them nothing at all. They just had to report the loss of their passports at the embassy and spend a few dozen pounds to get a new passport. But the price of this transaction was several thousand pounds, which was 30,000 to 50,000 RMB, which was not a small amount for them. So 20 years ago, it cost them almost nothing to smuggle a person. It was very simple. It was a huge profit.

So when did the British government begin to discover that there were a large number of illegal immigrants pouring into the UK? Because these Chinese, and not only Chinese, but also Indians, Africans, Middle Easterners, etc., people from all over the world who illegally smuggled into the UK, as soon as they got off the plane and entered the UK, they would immediately apply for refugee status or political asylum. Because this is the only way for them to change from illegal to legal status.

When I was a student looking for a job, a friend recommended me to be an interpreter for a British lawyer. I was surprised at the time, saying why do British lawyers need Chinese interpreters? Later I learned that these Chinese immigrants who illegally smuggled in often declared refugees at the London airport. Once he claimed that he was a refugee and needed asylum, the British government must assign him a lawyer according to the law to help him handle the legal procedures for applying for asylum. So at this time, the lawyer needs a Chinese interpreter. By the way, the fees for these lawyers and interpreters are all paid by the British government. The reason is very simple. They are refugees who have fled here. Where can they get the money to hire a lawyer? So out of humanitarianism, the British government has to pay for it.

Then, as these illegal immigrants continued to come to the UK to apply for refugees and political asylum, the British Immigration Bureau saw that the number of cases was increasing, and it was getting higher and higher. They couldn't finish approving them even if they died. Then the British people felt strange, where did so many international refugees come from? Where did these people come from? Why can't they even see the entry and exit records? So they knew that these people came to the UK through smuggling or illegal means.

(The four audio clips from 60' to 1:01 are omitted here, which are about the tragedy of stowaways on a ship in the United States)

But once these illegal immigrants set foot on this new continent, whether it is the United States, the United Kingdom, or Europe, their lives will change from then on. They can live the life they want from then on, and they can realize their life dreams. Just like Chunsheng in the novel "Chinatown", the " I " in the novel asked Chunsheng, why did you come to the UK, you look at the life you are living here now, what's the point, why do you still want to stay here? Then Chunsheng answered her: " How do you know, coming to the UK is the dream of my whole family. All my dreams are here. "

We really can't understand this kind of thing. We really can't understand it. We may never understand that they used to work in the lowest, hardest and most menial jobs on Chinese soil for generations, and then suddenly one day, they can study abroad, one day they can suddenly come to the United States or the United Kingdom, this legendary brave new world, and then sit on an equal footing with all the Chinese and foreigners here, without any difference in status. Abroad, no one knows your past, no one knows who you are. Here, you are the same as everyone else, and everyone is equal. They can finally walk on the street like everyone else, without being discriminated against, or being regarded as inferior. In the UK, no one will discriminate or bully them. Perhaps only here can they feel a kind of equality and dignity as human beings.

So in addition to the material motivation of going abroad to make money, I guess this spiritual equality is another reason they dream of. And they can finally be envied by others. By their relatives and friends in their hometown. For example, when his relatives and friends in the village meet on the road, they will say with an envious tone, so-and-so's son is in the UK, so-and-so's daughter is in the US. No matter what kind of life they live in the UK or the US, they don't care. They just imagine that these people in the UK and the US must be making a lot of money and must be living a happy life that they can't even dream of.

It is not just the relatives and friends of the lower-class people who have illegally smuggled out who have this idea, but also the residents of small and medium-sized cities or small counties who have come abroad through legal channels. Europe and the United States have become a myth in their imagination. For example, the prostitute Abao in the novel originally went to study in the UK with a legal student visa, and then stayed illegally after her visa expired. The novel describes that she once returned to China. She originally wanted to go home, but her relatives and friends in China thought she was still studying in the UK. They thought she was a female student in the UK, and she was surrounded by a halo, shining like gold. So when she wanted to return to her hometown, she wanted to admit the reality of her failure and go back to being the innocent 17- year-old girl, but she couldn't go back. Because she had no way out, she couldn't face these relatives and friends anymore. This way out was not cut off by herself, but by her relatives and friends in China. The cruelty of Abao's tragedy lies here. She was not forced to become a prostitute by Britain, but by China, by those who loved her the most.

So she could only go back to England. She would rather be a prostitute in England than go back to her hometown and be the innocent, happy and carefree high school girl. She could never go back to that 17-year-old girl. She had no way to tell them the truth, which made her parents and relatives and the whole family unable to raise their heads in the small town. They were looked down upon and gossiped about by others for the rest of their lives. So she could only choose to go back to England, even if she had to stay in the dark and become an illegal immigrant, or even do the lowest profession of prostitution. Because only in this way could she keep the beautiful imagination of her fellow countrymen in her hometown. In the imagination of her relatives and friends in her hometown, she was not Abao. She was still the carefree, happy and lucky Tingting, a British female student they imagined, living in a Britain they imagined. In their imagination, everything was still as beautiful as a fairy tale.

Finally, back to your question, over the past few decades, the British government's policies have not changed much. They have been cracking down on illegal immigrants. The overall situation of illegal Chinese in the UK has not changed much. On the contrary, China's rapid economic development has brought a sense of longing for home to these illegal immigrants who work illegally overseas to make money. The most significant change in immigration policy was after the global financial crisis

Chinatown

in 2007. The British economy was in recession. In order to ensure the labor and employment rate of its own people and prevent foreigners from taking away their jobs, the government tightened its immigration policy significantly. This has had a great impact on both legal and illegal immigrants overseas. So now, whether you are working or studying in the UK, these legal visas are already difficult to obtain. In order to crack down on illegal visa fraud, the government has even closed down many language schools in the UK, and the visa approval procedures have become increasingly strict. Illegal immigration is even more difficult, because the anti-counterfeiting technology of passports is becoming more and more high-tech. It is almost impossible to just change the photo like ten years ago, so it is becoming more and more difficult to smuggle. However, these phenomena are not only in the UK, but also in the United States, France and all over the world.

The Paper: With the development of the Internet and the popularity of smartphones in recent years, have the lives of these " black people " changed in some way? I wonder if these high-tech developments have been reflected in their community?

Yilin Zhong: When Chinatown was written, the Internet was already very popular, and it was not much different from now. I have a special chapter in the novel about Alun downloading movies, songs, online novels, etc. in an Internet cafe. Smart phones have become popular in recent years, and some of them have started using them, but as I mentioned in the novel, Chunsheng spent a lot of money to buy a new mobile phone at that time. The " I " in the novel asked him, why don't you sign a

325

monthly subscription for a mobile phone? In this way, the mobile phone can be free and you don't have to pay for it. Then Chunsheng said, can you sign for me? - In other words, because these blacks came here illegally, they have completely disappeared in the entire legal world. Without an identity, they can't even use their ID cards to buy a monthly subscription mobile phone from a mobile phone company.

So, they can only use prepaid mobile phone cards and then spend money to buy mobile phones. It is very expensive to use such prepaid mobile phone cards to surf the Internet. Moreover, smart phones are quite expensive, which is also a luxury for them. It is not easy for them to make money. For example, the old Wei couple in the novel only buy ribs when they entertain guests, and usually eat radishes and vegetables. Therefore, in order to save money, few of them spend money to buy smart phones to surf the Internet. Although smart phones have not brought much impact on their lives, some emerging high-tech software, such as WeChat, Weibo, QQ video, online video, etc., have a great impact on their lives. Because although they may rarely use mobile phones to surf the Internet, there is generally broadband in the places where they live, so they only need to use their mobile phones or computers to connect to WIFI , and they can use those softwares to call their family members without spending money.

Before those new software appeared, overseas Chinese mainly relied on buying phone cards to contact their families in China. Although the phone charges were not expensive, the maximum length of a call was ten minutes. Now with free calling software such as online phone and video, they can chat with their families as much as they want. For example, a boy from Jiangsu who used to live next door to me would use QQ video to talk to his parents for several hours every weekend, and the chat would last for a whole afternoon. But because they spoke in dialect, I couldn't understand a word.

Subaltern Studies

The Paper: Although you said in the postscript of Chinatown that " the lower classes have their own voices, and they have very vivid and rich language " , now people have almost no chance to hear their voices except in your novel. And this novel itself is actually a retelling. As far as you know, is this because they are unwilling to tell the story, or because no one is listening and recording? Is it possible that this situation will change in the future?

Yilin Zhong: This is actually a very important topic. As I said in the postscript, when I was a graduate student, I took a post-colonial literary theory course. This course was not my major, and I did not get any credits. I took it purely out of interest. Subaltern Studies is a very important research topic in post-colonial theory. If you search for this English phrase on the Internet, you can see that there are many theoretical monographs that specifically study this issue. Among the more famous theorists are Edward Said (author of Orientalism) from the US, Stuart Hall from the UK, etc. In fact, this is still a relatively new literary concept. In Europe and the United States, many scholars and university professors are studying this issue.

So I will try to answer your question from the perspective of subaltern studies, because this question is too big and I may not be able to explain it clearly in one or two sentences. Let me first briefly explain the concept of subaltern studies. The concept of Subaltern was actually first proposed by an Italian Marxist Antonio Gramsci , but this concept was not widely used in literary theory until the beginning of the 21st century. The objects of study and attention of subaltern studies are the common people living at the bottom of society, but they study these subaltern people from the framework of European and American postcolonial literary theory. In other words, they mainly use this word to describe and study the residents of their colonies and their descendants, because compared with Europe and the United States, these poor people in the third world are Subaltern , the bottom group.

Because it is well known that in developed Western countries, due to the relatively mature and perfect development of their capitalist system, this so-called bottom group does not exist or even can be seen in developed countries such as Europe and the United States. Because they impose heavy taxes on the rich, killing the rich to help the poor, for example, the UK imposes heavy taxes of 40% to 50% on high-income people , that is to say, if you are a rich man with an annual income of one million, then the 500,000 must be taxed according to the law, and in the end you will only get 500,000. But if you are a poor person, then you only need to pay very little tax, or even no tax, and the government will subsidize you. For example, if you are unemployed or a low-income person below the poverty line, then

328

you can not only get free housing, but also unemployment benefits and government subsidies every week, which are basically enough to maintain food and clothing, and you will definitely not be hungry or homeless. Of course, these are benefits for their own residents, which foreign immigrants cannot enjoy.

Thus, solving the problem of food and clothing for the lower classes, the gap between the rich and the poor in developed Western countries is not that big. Because no matter how poor or rich you are, you can be guaranteed a house, clothes and food in this country. For example, the UK and many EU countries have free medical care, and you can go to the hospital for treatment and take medicine for free. I think these are the areas that China needs to learn now. In this case, the gap between the rich and the poor in society will not cause social problems, and the contradictions between different social classes will not exist. Because everyone has their own duties and does their own things. If you have money, it's fine. Anyway, you have to pay half of the tax to feed us poor people. So no matter how rich you are, I won't be jealous of you. I won't be jealous of you being a nouveau riche. Moreover, if I am willing to work hard to start a business, I can also become a nouveau riche. In this society, everyone has equal opportunities. Everyone is competing fairly, and no one has privileges, because the government is changed every four years. For example, the former British Prime Minister Tony Blair is also unemployed and lives on his old capital. So the mentality of the poor is also very peaceful. Just as Confucius said, a country's problem is not scarcity but inequality. If there is equality, there will be no poverty; if there is harmony, there will be no scarcity; if there is peace, there will be no instability.

So in terms of material, the gap between the rich and the poor in European and American countries has become more even, and the poor can live well with government welfare without worrying about food, clothing, housing and transportation. Now let's talk about political rights. I recently watched the movie " Selma " ("Selma Parade"), which was nominated for many Oscars. It tells the story of Martin Luther King, a black political leader in the United States, who led the black people in the United States who did not have the right to vote or be elected at that time, to fight for their political rights in the 1960s. In fact, this is a good example, because black people in the United States at that time were subalterns . In the movie, US President Kennedy persuaded Martin Luther King, saying that you are living a good life now, aren't you? You are not slaves now, and you have food and clothes, everything is equal, why do you still want this useless right to vote? Do you want to go into politics?

Then Martin Luther King answered him, because this is a world you don't know. You know nothing in the White House. You don't know that at this moment, outside the White House, there is a black world, in which our children are not guaranteed to go to school, the police can beat us at any time, and shoot and kill an innocent black person on the road at will, just because he suspects that the black person may be suspected of committing a crime. Do you know why all this is? It is because we don't have the votes. Because we have no way to elect our own government leaders, they(white people) bully black people unscrupulously. Whereas you don't have the votes anwaya, you can't do anything to me. Then he said, so we must fight for this vote and fight for our political rights.

Of course, this is the history of the United States in the 1960s .
Now, black people in the United States not only have the right to
vote, but also have the first black president of the United States
(Obama). So in Europe and the United States, these lower-class
groups in society are not only equal to others in terms of material,
with food and clothing, but also have the same political rights as
the rich, one person one vote, and are equal. So now, what are
they still lacking? That is: the right to speak, at the spiritual
level.

Now the voice we are talking about, the subaltern 's voice, is
actually what Foucault called: the power of discourse . Because
now their food, clothing, housing, transportation, and political
rights are no different from other social classes, so what is
missing now? It is this. In the mainstream society, their voices
are missing and disappear. In mainstream newspapers,
magazines, television, radio and other media, you can't hear their
voices, nor can you see their existence. So the question now is,
where are the voices of these subaltern groups? Where is their
power of discourse?

I mentioned in the postscript of the novel that when I wrote
Chinatown, I was inspired to a great extent by Naipaul's novel,
Miguel Street, which was Naipaul's debut novel published in the
UK when he was 28 years old. This book was one of the books
that a friend brought to me in his suitcase when he came to
London to attend the book fair. The inspiration that this novel
brought to me at that time, or the places that I felt I could learn
and draw lessons from, can actually be used to answer your
question. It is the individuals written in Miguel Street, the
inconspicuous residents living on this ordinary street, ordinary
people, who may not have any outstanding aspects in their lives,

no dramatic events, and no glorious deeds that can be reported in the news. They are just ordinary civilians. Just like you and I can see Zhang San, Li Si, and Wang Mazi every day when we walk on a street.

If there was no novel like "Miguel Street" to write down and record their daily lives, those ordinary people in the streets and alleys may be forever submerged in the long river of history and will never be remembered. But Naipaul wrote down their stories and recorded these people in words, so their stories will always exist in books and in our memories in the form of words. And not only in novels, but also in words, they will always exist in the memory of our future people and become the eternal spiritual wealth of mankind. These people will also be remembered and thought of by us because of this way of literary works. This is an expression of their voices. Otherwise, you will never hear their voices. This is one of the reasons why I wrote the novel "Chinatown" at that time, and it is also the biggest inspiration I got from him.

And it includes anyone in real life right now, such as the people sitting around me in this cafe, each of them has their own story. No matter where you are now, on the busy streets, in high-rise buildings, office buildings, residential buildings, or park squares, in your streets and alleys, your neighbors, every family, every person, has their own story. But you can't hear their voices, right? This voice cannot be heard, because it is all behind closed doors. You will never know what kind of person is behind this closed door, what kind of story he has, what kind of life he lives, and what kind of life he has.

They are neither wealthy celebrities nor celebrities, nor are they successful people admired by this society. They will never appear in mainstream media reports, newspapers, magazines, or TV programs. Those media will only interview social elites and successful people, but what about those other people? In addition to those mainstream successful people, don't we come into contact with so many ordinary people in our daily lives, on the streets and alleys? You can call them the bottom group, or you can call them the disadvantaged group, or ordinary people. They may be a sanitation worker cleaning the road, or an old man looking for rags and Coke bottles along the street, or an old lady selling mobile phone cases and insoles on the overpass, or a homeless child begging passers-by at the entrance of a shopping mall ... These non-mainstream bottom groups excluded from mainstream society are encountered in our daily lives every day, but do you think they have a voice? And even if they say something, will anyone listen? Will their voices be heard by mainstream society and mass media?

If you are just an ordinary citizen living at the bottom of society, then you have no news value for the media, right? Because you are too unimportant. Your story, your voice, all your life, old age, sickness and death, joys and sorrows, are not important. Their stories and lives are meaningless in the eyes of the mainstream society's values. This is definitely not the kind of lament of intellectuals and elites, that there are few people who understand you, and no one will listen when the strings break, but for the whole society, your existence is non-existent. Your voice is no different from drinking pesticides or crying to death, and no one will listen. These people are completely speechless in the mainstream media. They are even speechless in our entire social system, and they are collectively speechless.

There is only one situation in which we can hear the voices of these grassroots people, that is: something happened. For example, someone died, someone jumped off a building, someone was killed or killed someone, an old man who collected scraps was cheated of his life savings, a farmer who had more children than allowed killed a cadre of the Family Planning Commission, and someone committed suicide by drinking pesticide in front of the newspaper office after failing to petition, and so on and so forth. Only in such abnormal situations will they receive attention, and you will interview them, and you will listen to their voices, listen to what they want to say, what they are saying: Why did this person kill people? Why did he rob? Why did he commit suicide, why did she become a prostitute, why did he jump off a building?... Only in such extremely extreme situations will you hear their voices. Journalists will interview them, and they will suddenly have the news value that the media needs.

This is the voice of the subalterns. Their tragedy or pity is that their voices are completely drowned out in the mainstream society. No one pays attention to them, and no one listens to them. If he is just an ordinary person, you will never think of listening to his voice. They often even have to pay the price of their lives to make the world pay attention to them and hear their voices. For example, the illegal Chinese immigrants in the UK last appeared in the Chinese and British media because of the shellfish picking tragedy (in 2004, dozens of Chinese illegal immigrants were picking shells on the beach when the tide suddenly rose, and 23 people died). Those illegal immigrants have been in the UK for more than ten years or even decades, but it was only because of this tragedy that they were widely noticed and known by those news reports in the UK. Why? Because 20 or 30 Chinese stowaways died. Only when they died did they have news value, and only then did people pay attention to them, and only then did the British and Chinese governments pay attention to this issue and the miserable living conditions of these illegal immigrants.

This is probably not just their sorrow, right? It is also the sorrow of our entire human society. But what is good about it? Fortunately, we still have novels. We still have literature. What sociologists, political scientists, journalists, and social elites cannot do, there is literature to compensate. There are also novelists to record. This is the value of literary works, the significance of literary works. What literature does, what it wants to dig out, what it wants to record, are these things that are submerged and covered, ignored and forgotten by society, history, law, politics, news, elites, mainstream, and everything else. These grassroots people, ordinary people, their normal living conditions, their ordinary lives, the voices and faces of each of them, their insignificant joys and sorrows, their tears, their laughter, these are what literature wants to record.

The Paper Interview

The Current Situation of Illegal Chinese Immigrants Overseas from the Perspective of "Chinatown" (Part 3)

Interview: Day 2
Interviewer: Xia Yiping, reporter from The Paper
Interviewee: Yilin Zhong, author of Chinatown
Interview time : April 5 , 2015
Interview location: Café on the Left Bank, Paris (where the
author was at the time)

Chinatown, the Imagined Community

The Paper: In the postscript of Chinatown, you mentioned that Chinatown is an "imagined Chinese society." Do you mean that the Chinatown in literature and historical materials was constructed by the imagination of the "elites"? Or do you mean that the actual Chinatown as a "Chinese society" is the imagination of the residents of Chinatown?

Yilin Zhong: Both situations exist. In fact, when I was writing this postscript, which was a few months ago, I wrote the postscript for the single volume of this novel to be published. The first draft only wrote that I could not see any real people about Chinatown in the university library, so I gave up the research on this topic and turned to writing postmodernism. Then after I moved from the student dormitory on the university campus to London, I came into contact with this lower-class group of overseas Chinese in " Chinatown " . My postscript ended here. Later, my editor-in-charge Mr. Huang Xiaoyang at the publishing house asked me, why don't you continue writing? I said, isn't this the postscript to my novel? If I write more, it will be a theoretical article, that is, the graduate thesis that I didn't write. I said that readers buy books to read novels. Who would read such boring pure theoretical articles for no reason?

Then the editor told me, it's ok, just keep writing. He said we want to see more of this kind of content. At that time, I felt it was incredible. I said this is a completely theoretical article. You are the literary editor of the publishing house. Of course you like to read this kind of literary research paper, but most readers can't understand it. If this problem is written further, it will be a master's thesis. For ordinary readers, this kind of thing is too profound and they can't accept it. If readers can't understand the postscript, they will think that the whole novel is the same. If they can't understand it, they won't buy the book. I said that the whole novel uses very colloquial and non-literary language, which is very easy to understand and popular. It's because I'm afraid that using literary language or writing these too profound theoretical things will scare away ordinary readers. Because this novel is about the lives of these people at the bottom of society, the readers of my novel are also this group. Most of them are not well-educated. They may have sneaked out before graduating from junior high school. My novel is written for them. So I use the most lifelike and simple language in the whole novel, just to make everyone understand this novel.

If I use the highbrow language of intellectuals, it will become Lin Yutang's "Chinatown Family", which is neither fish nor fowl. Just like what Xia Zhiqing said in criticizing his novel, it is completely the Chinatown imagined by Lin Yutang himself, a Chinatown society imagined by an intellectual, so even the laundry workers in the novel are reciting "The Analects" and "Tao Te Ching", but in fact the real Chinatown is not like that at all. Why is it like this? Because Lin Yutang lacks life, he has no such life as the laundry workers in the lower class of Chinatown. He can't get in touch with this group, nor can he really understand the joys and sorrows of these working people, so of course he doesn't know what these people think. Xia Zhiqing said that once the details are not real, the whole work is superficial. I think his criticism is particularly accurate.

Therefore, works like this that depict the lives of the lower classes must use their own language to tell their own stories, and must never be written in the language of intellectuals or literary language. Otherwise, the entire novel will be fake, and it will not be the characters in the novel who are speaking, but you who are speaking for them.

Back to your question, in the whole novel, you can't see any literary language at all, it's all colloquial language, the language of the lowest class of people. When I wrote the postscript, I also tried my best to continue this style. I didn't want the novel to be read by only intellectuals, but to be understood by all ordinary readers. So even in the postscript at the end of the book, I didn't want to write those boring and difficult master's thesis things, for fear of scaring away readers. I told the editor about my concerns at the time, and the editor said, it doesn't matter, just keep writing, it doesn't matter if you write the whole postscript as a thesis, people will be willing to read it.

So I had no choice but to write the outline of the graduation thesis that I wanted to write but didn't finish ten years ago. This is the last paragraph of the postscript you see now. Thanks to his encouragement, I was able to write these things more than ten years later. The question you are asking now is the content that the editor asked me to write at that time. Because all these things are literary theories, and if I really want to write this paper, it will take at least 50,000 or 60,000 words to write it clearly, so I will try to explain this issue in the simplest language below, and I hope you don't find it boring.

(1) What is an Imagined Community ?

First of all, in the modern Western literary theory, there is a very important point of view, saying that human society is an imaginary community . Why do we say that? For example, you are a Chinese, and we think we are Chinese, so where does the concept of China come from? What is China? What is Britain? What is the United States? What is the concept of a country?

What is a country? Is there any difference between me being born in China, America, and Britain? What is the difference? Am I still myself? When I was born, I was a person, myself, right? So why do I have different nationalities just because I was born in different places? What does this nationality mean? What is the concept of a country? Or, are all these concepts actually our own imaginations?

You were born in the United States, so you imagine you are an American. I was born in China, so I imagine I am Chinese. There was once a baby who was born on a flight from the UK to the US, so he automatically had the nationality of both the UK and the US. This is the most interesting example. There are many such examples in real life. For example, you were born in France, and then your parents took you to the US when you were just one month old. Are you French or American? For you, a baby who is just one month old, is there any difference between these two countries? Because you are just one month old, you don't have the ability to think yet. Then when you grow up, you have the nationality of both France and the US. Now for you, what do these two countries mean to you? Now that you can think, do you think you are from France, where you were born, or from the US where you grew up? As a person, is there any difference?

America is just a country in your imagination. You grew up there. France is also just a country in your imagination. You were born there. It is very likely that after graduating from college, you went to Africa, worked and lived in Africa, and then acquired African citizenship and became an African, right? Are all these countries and regions different to him? In the same way, China has experienced so many dynasties over thousands of years. If a centenarian was born in the late Qing Dynasty, and then he experienced the Qing Dynasty, the Taiping Heavenly Kingdom, the Republic of China, and the current People's Republic of China, do you think he is a Qing Dynasty person, a Tianguo person, a Republic of China person, or a current Chinese?

Are all of this just human imagination? What kind of person do you imagine yourself to be? What country do you imagine yourself to be from? Where do you imagine yourself to be from and where do you imagine yourself to be going?

The entire human society, the entire country, and the world, all these concepts, in the final analysis, are actually our own imagination. The so-called community , such as the country. The country is an imaginary concept. Two hundred years ago, the United States had not yet been founded. Were there Americans at that time? No, they created an imaginary America by themselves and imagined themselves to be Americans. The same is true for China. Were there Chinese three thousand years ago? No, there were only primitive people. The Chinese created such a concept, and we imagined ourselves to be Chinese. All concepts are our imagination, and they are all created by humans themselves. The same is true for society. So we call the country an Imaginary community — A country is an imagined community. It is a big community, the same as those small communities. Such as, every village, every tribe, and even every street is also an imagined community. For example, you are from Hunan, I am from Shanxi, he is from Northeast China, and I am from Guangdong. Aren't these regions also communities imagined by us?

Therefore, if we use this concept to describe Chinatown , it is absolutely accurate. Because Chinatown itself is a non-existent place, it is completely our own imagination. Why do we say that? Well, what is Chinatown? Chinatown is overseas, outside of China, in any non-Chinese country in the world, in any corner where Chinese people live. There are Chinese restaurants, Chinese residents, Chinese supermarkets, shopping malls, etc. If you have been to Chinatown in the UK or the US, you will see Chinese buildings, Chinese archways, and red lanterns hanging high. There are temple fairs and markets during festivals, as well as various traditional Chinese celebrations, such as lion dancing, stilt walking, firecrackers, and worshiping the God of Wealth. There are also vendors selling all kinds of snacks, such as candied haws, big bowls of tea, pancakes, fried squid, fried stinky tofu, soy milk and tofu pudding, kebabs, popcorn, freshly made sugar figurines, blown cotton candy, lanterns, rattles, colorful paper toys, face painting for children, balloons, New Year paintings, couplets, and Chinese characters for good fortune, etc. Walking on this street, you will feel that you are completely in China. But, is this China?

No way.

However, for the Chinese living on this street that is not in China, these residents from China, is there any difference between their lives here and their lives in the real China far away? Is there really a difference? Think about it again. They are here, eating Chinese food every day, wearing Chinese clothes, speaking Chinese with their relatives and friends, writing Chinese characters, reading the local Chinese newspapers everywhere in Chinatown, reading domestic news on Chinese websites on the Internet, and watching Chinese TV programs. In this era of almost completely synchronized global information, their lives abroad are no different from their lives in China.

The only difference is that if they leave this small street and walk to the next street a few meters away, they will come to a completely different world. A world called Britain. Here, they see British people, they all wear British clothes, speak English, read English newspapers, walk on British streets, and live a British life that is the same or different from theirs. This is Britain.

If you are in these two time and space at the same time, if you are somewhere other than London's Chinatown an hour ago, visiting Tejafara Square and the Queen's Buckingham Palace, and then you go to Chinatown to eat Chinese food the next hour, will you suddenly feel a sense of time and space confusion? Just like in a time-travel novel, you suddenly travel from Britain to China, and now you are sitting in a Chinese restaurant next to your home eating familiar rice and stir-fried vegetables. At this time, where are you? Whether it is Britain or China, are these concepts of countries or regions completely derived from your own imagination of this place in your brain? Are all these concepts of countries and geography actually generated by our own imagination?

OK, now I have explained this topic, what is Imaginary community , what is the concept of imagined community. If I were writing my master's thesis, then the explanation of the first chapter would be completed (although I haven't started to discuss it yet, I am just explaining this theory). Next, I will try to use the shortest language to explain this issue from two aspects, one is from the perspective of the elite , and the other is from the perspective of the subaltern . Explain why Chinatown is an imagined Chinese society, and the elites and intellectuals from the upper class and the common people from the lower class have completely different dual imaginations of Chinatown. And when it comes to writing, why, in the existing written records, I can't see the real Chinatown, I can't see the real Chinese people in Chinatown.

(2) Chinatown from the Imagination of the Elite

If you type the word " Chinatown " on the Internet now , what will you search for?

If you search for images, it's going to come up with a bunch of archways, right? Archways in Chinatowns all over the world. Old-style Chinese archways.

If you search for news, you will find various activities in Chinatown, such as Chinese New Year celebrations in Chinatowns in various countries, visits by mayors or government officials, etc.

If you search for events, you will find all kinds of major cases and incidents that happened in Chinatown, such as robbery, murder, illegal workers, restaurant owners being arrested, or racial discrimination, anti-Chinese riots, and so on.

If you think that the above contents are of no value and want to see something more in-depth, then you search for books, papers, articles, and descriptions about Chinatown. Then what will you see? You will see various social analysis reports of Chinatown, or a review of major events in Chinatown in history, etc., right? If you find a better book or monograph, you can see slightly deeper content, such as how Chinatown was formed, what is the origin, what is the current situation, and the political background of Chinatown in different periods; what restaurants and Chinese supermarkets are there in Chinatown now, and what they used to be like; what gangs were there in the 1950s, what gangs evolved in the 1960s, what is happening now, and what major fights have occurred. And so on. And even these contents are actually very difficult to find, because these can only be written by insiders, and it is definitely not possible for any journalist or sociologist to find these original materials. Why? Because many of these things are illegal in themselves. Who would come out to tell you these things when they have nothing to do? Isn't he afraid of being destroyed? Right.

Then, among all the text materials you see, I could also find them in the university library at that time, and the text materials found in the library must be much more comprehensive and detailed than those found on the Internet, right? For example, I can find all the news reports about Chinatown in British newspapers over the past 100 years, and I can also find theoretical monographs on the history or social analysis of Chinatown published in English or Chinese in countries around the world. Of course, I can also see all the literary works related to Chinatown, such as Lin Yutang's "Chinatown Family" written in English , and the domestic translated version is called "Chinatown", etc., etc., but - I can't write this paper, why? Because I can't see the " people ".

I can't see " people ".

Where are the people? I want to see the people in Chinatown, but where are the people? In all these texts, I can't see any real, living people. Why are you describing an empty Chinatown to me? What are the people doing here? Where are the people? What's the use of this empty shell you describe as "Chinatown"?

Chinatown

What I want to see is not this street you imagined, but the living people who live on this street. Where are the thousands of people who walk on this street every day? Why can't I see these people in the text? Why can't I see them in the news reports of various newspapers and magazines, and in these mountains of historical materials and social analysis? Why can't I see anything in this world of text created by elites and intellectuals?

Where are they? Don't they live here? They are here every day. We pass by them every day and can see them. They are on this street, passing by us every day. Don't they exist in this real world that we can touch every day? Why do they disappear and completely do not exist in the world of words? Why doesn't anyone write about them?

So, why do I say that all the written records and materials about Chinatown in the past are all from the imagination of the elites, not the real world. Because they don't understand at all, and there is no way to go deep into the hearts of the grassroots people in Chinatown to understand their true inner world and what they think. They (elite) don't know what they (subaltern) are thinking. They only see the outside, the flashy surface of Chinatown, these superficial Chinese buildings, and these hurried passers-by. They can't see the spirit of the grassroots people living here, can't see their souls, and can't see what they are thinking in their hearts. So of course they can't write about the lives of these people. Because they can never imagine, imagine the life of this illegal group that exists completely outside of their imagination and experience. They can't imagine it, they only live in their own world. An intellectual can only live in the cognitive space of an intellectual, to imagine the world outside, the Chinatown imagined in his mind. Just like Lin

346

Yutang, his "Chinatown Family" is completely a world called Chinatown that he imagined. That was a Chinatown imagined by the intellectual elite, not the real world in reality.

So in the past, Mao Zedong criticized intellectuals for being out of touch with reality, out of touch with the working people, and not knowing the suffering of the people. Then he used a particularly simple and crude method to directly send young intellectuals from the city to the countryside to experience the life of the lower-class people in China's rural areas. In fact, from a certain perspective, it can be seen that he had such a similar understanding in his thoughts. But whether his way of doing things is correct or not is another matter.

Although we say that novels are an art of imagination and fiction, this kind of fiction and imagination has a premise, that is, it must be based on reality. Otherwise, it is not fiction, but falsehood. There is a difference between fiction and falsehood. Fiction may be true, but falsehood must always be false. If there is no truth as a basis, all your imaginations are empty. Just like those online novels and time-travel novels now, they are completely unrestrained and fabricated. Such things have no value in literature. In Western literary theory, they gave this kind of work a very interesting name, called "quasi- literature " . That is to say, it is a work that belongs to " similar to literature " , but it is not a real literary work. In fact, the best-selling things in China now are this kind of " quasi-literature " , because this kind of thing is easy to write and can be copied in batches without limit, just like playing computer games. But real literary works can never be copied, let alone mass-produced in a fixed time and quantity like the Hollywood industry. Of course, this is another topic, and I will not go into details here.

Then someone will definitely ask, what is the difference between fiction and falsehood? In fact, I have already said before that the basis of fiction is reality. Fiction is the imagination and continuation of reality, not the opposite of reality, that is, falsehood. If this is still a bit nihilistic and difficult to understand, then I will take "Chinatown" as an example. Many readers do not believe my novels when they read them, even though I have told them many times that my novels are fictional. For example, the first question you ask me is whether the people in "Chinatown" have real life prototypes, because you think these people are real. In fact, many things in the novel are fictional, but you can't see it. So why do you feel that my fictional novels are so real? It is because the fictional framework and foundation of my novels are very real and solid.

Hemingway has a famous writing theory, saying that in a work, a writer should only write the tip of the iceberg above the sea. I would like to borrow his metaphor. I think that a novel is the tip of the iceberg above the sea, that is, the part that readers can see. Then what is the part below the sea that readers cannot see? That is the huge and solid real world:

The reality.

For me, when it comes to the question of truth and fiction in a novel, truth is the huge iceberg hidden under the sea, and fiction is the one-tenth, or even less than one-percent, part of the iceberg above the sea. That is the final novel you see. This is how I understand the relationship and proportion between truth and fiction in a novel. Just like the novel "Chinatown" has only a few hundred thousand words in total, but you see, I have said so much just to answer a few questions of yours, probably tens of thousands of words. These are the invisible iceberg under the sea of the novel "Chinatown". In fact, there is an old saying in China, " The skill lies outside the poem" , which is about the same principle.

Now back to your question, why in the world of the elites, in our existing written records, these illegal immigrants in Chinatown have completely disappeared, do not exist, are completely invisible and intangible, and even have a huge blank in the text? Because in the world imagined by the elites, they do not exist. It's like if you ask a university professor, an American university professor who studies Chinese Oriental literature, to write about Chinatown, what would he write? He might go to Chinatown, have a meal, walk around, and then go back to the library to read the books and papers written by the elite intellectuals in the past about Chinatown, and then he compiles these text materials together and writes a paper on Chinatown. Then do you think the article he wrote will be the real Chinatown? Or is it the Chinatown imagined by him, the literature professor?

This is the first level of the problem we are talking about. In the existing written records, what is recorded is only a Chinatown imagined by the elites, or in other words, a fictitious and imaginary Chinatown constructed by the cultural elites through their own imagination of Chinatown. In this Chinatown imagined by the elites and suspended in mid-air, there are only cold buildings and scattered Chinese archways, but real people do not exist.

(3) Chinatown from the Imagination of the Subaltern

At this level, now, we are finally down to earth, back to the ground, and back to the real world of real life. We are finally no longer floating in the text materials, no longer stuck in the piles of old papers in the library, looking for those false imaginations about Chinatown. Now we are back to the ground, back to this down-to-earth land. We finally came to the real streets of Chinatown and saw the vivid reality happening in front of us. We saw all of this, the Chinese restaurants lined up, various street shops opened by Chinese people, Hong Kong cake shops, Taiwanese milk tea houses, Xinhua Bookstores, lanterns, firecrackers, cheongsam jewelry, lucky cats, jade, all kinds of roast duck and cured meat hanging in the restaurant windows, and during the New Year and other festivals, the streets are also full of strings of big red lanterns, and there are Chinese people walking among them, and so on. With just a few lenses, you can capture the vivid street scenes of Chinatown.

Now we have finally come to the Chinatown in the real society, not the empty and false imagination of the cultural elites in the past textual materials. Now, in front of you, all the Chinese scenes of Chinatown are so real and vivid, but, is all this in front of you China? It is not China. It is in Britain, it is in London, even the houses are British-style buildings, but the decoration and furnishings in the houses are Chinese. It is not in China, it is still in Britain, on this British road in London.

So why do we all call it Chinatown? Because there are all Chinese restaurants here, all supermarkets and shops run by

Chinese, and all the people coming and going on this street are Chinese. All these people, whether they are illegal immigrants or legal immigrants, will run to this street intentionally or unintentionally whenever they are hungry or miss home. Even if they may not buy anything or do nothing, they just walk around here, stroll around, and see that there are Chinese people all around, instead of the British people they see every day outside this street, speaking a language they don't understand. Everyone meets or chats on this street, speaking various dialects from all over the country. You may hear Northeastern dialect, someone over there is speaking Fujian dialect, someone else is speaking Wenzhou dialect, and a few steps ahead, there are several people speaking Sichuan dialect, Shanghai dialect, Cantonese, and so on. Although these dialects are like listening to British people speaking English to you, and you can't understand a word, you still feel inexplicably familiar. Here, you will feel that this place is similar to China. The people and streets here, everything here, seem to be the China in your memory. Walking here, you feel like you have returned to China and are walking on the streets of your hometown. The Chinese language you can understand is spoken around you, and the food sold on the streets is the food you have loved since childhood. Although you know very clearly in your mind that you are now in the UK, a foreign country thousands of miles away from your motherland, there is a trance moment when you seem to feel that this is the same as being in China, and it seems that there is not much difference between here and China. You can see the food, clothes, drinks, there are Wanglaoji, Jiaduobao, iced black tea, pearl milk tea, and food, there are also steamed dumplings, meat dumplings, Tianjin pancakes, Sichuan spicy hot pot, soy milk and fried dough sticks...

However, even if you can find all your memories of China in this palm-sized street, from the actual geographical location, this place is still not China, and is even 10,800 miles away from China. So why do all of us call it Chinatown? Because it is based on our own imagination of this place and this street. It comes from all these Chinese who are drifting overseas, whether they are illegal immigrants or legal immigrants, cultural elites and professors in the upper class of society, poor people struggling on the poverty line, wealthy businessmen with a lot of money, or homeless vagrants who are in danger of losing their jobs every day, all of them imagine this street as China, as a microcosm of Chinese society. All of these people, without the gap between the rich and the poor, without the hierarchy, at this moment, when walking on this ordinary street, their imagination of this Chinatown is the same as their imagination of China.

It's like this is China. We live here as if we have never left our hometown or our motherland. When you are struggling alone overseas, feeling lonely and helpless, and missing your family, your mother's bowl of steaming hand-rolled noodles, and your grandmother's candy, you walk and look on this street, and you will feel that you have not left your motherland or your home. Everything seems to be very close and within reach, and the distance between Britain and China is only the distance of a subway station. You enter the subway from the previous subway station, and two minutes later, you walk out from another subway station, and once you come out, you are in China.

The next stop is Chinatown, and the next stop is the motherland. This is a microcosm of Chinese society imagined by all overseas Chinese in their minds. Chinatown is the street in their imagination, the China in their imagination. This is an imaginary Chinese society, which comes from the imagination of all overseas Chinese. This is the Chinatown we are talking about.

This is a very warm imagination, a helpless imagination. It is a very sweet imagination, and also a tear-jerking imagination of the homesick wanderers. They imagine this street as their motherland, their hometown, their Chinatown, and the Chinese society in their minds; this is a kind of imagination that they clearly know is a Chinatown they made up out of thin air, but they would rather continue to live in this false imagination, in this Chinatown that clearly only exists in their imagination.

This is the second level of the imagined community of Chinatown, that is, the imagination of the lower classes in real life. This imagination is essentially the same as the imagination of the elites mentioned above, because they are both false, or in other words, they are purely imaginary imaginations of this street. All overseas Chinese imagine this small street in a foreign country as China in their minds. For them, Chinatown is an imagined Chinese society. Chinatown, is China.

This is the real theme and purpose of the postscript in my book, and my master's thesis that I failed to finish ten years ago. But this is not the theme of my novel Chinatown. The theme of Chinatown is much bigger and broader than this. Because the value of literature is always the broadest; it covers all of this, but it is far more than that.

Chinatown

———The End———

April 25 - May 3 , 2014
Yilin Zhong, compiled based on
the original interview recordings

Appendix

Chronological List of Works

By Yilin Zhong

Novel	Publication Year	Writing Age
Embrace the Sun	2025	14
Sunshine and the Monsoon	1995	16
Say Love	1998	19
A Love Fiction	2001	21
The Postmodern You	2025	22
Personal Statement	2013	23
London Single Girl's Diary	2009	26
London Love Story	2010	28
Chinatown	2015	28
In London	2018	28

Chinatown

London Single Lady series (Season 1-5)